Prospect of Death

Prospect of Death

Margaret Duffy

PIATKUS
CRIME

First published in Great Britain in 1995 by
Judy Piatkus (Publishers) Ltd of
5 Windmill Street, London W1P 1HF

**The moral right of the author
has been asserted**

*A catalogue record for this book is available
from the British Library*

ISBN 0-7499-0327-9

Phototypeset in 11/12pt Times by
Computerset, Harmondsworth, Middlesex
Printed and bound in Great Britain by
Bookcraft (Bath) Ltd

Burns Night 11.48 pm

The car had crashed right through the hedge and come to rest at an angle, the front bumper and part of the radiator jammed into the heavy clay soil of the ploughed field. It was a miracle it had not turned right over, thought the man who had leaned over the gate farther down the lane to check that he was not imagining things in the bright moonlight. He toiled up the hill, his breath steaming as he panted in the frosty air, walking as quickly as he could. Harry Fuller was not a young man.

Stopping for a moment to catch his breath, he heard the unmistakable sound of the ticking of cooling metal. And although Harry was in his eighties there was nothing wrong with his sense of smell. There was a strong reek of petrol.

It was a bad road, of course, always had been, with its deceptive bends and gradients. Vehicles had been leaving it with almost monotonous regularity since the days when Harry was a boy and Wood Lane, as it was called, was just a cart track linking the village of Little Nashby with the high main road that ran along the ridge above, Lansdown Hill. Harry could remember a time during the war when a steam ploughing engine had toppled into the field, killing the driver, its sheer weight causing the edge of the road to collapse. It had happened on almost the exact spot where the car had gone through the hedge. But these days most mishaps occurred farther down the hill at the next bend where water ran off the pastureland on the right-hand side of the road, causing a notorious icy patch in winter. Harry had lost count of the number of distraught people who'd turned up on his

1

doorstep late at night, asking to use the phone. His cottage was the only habitation for about half a mile. Most of the accidents were caused, in his view, by young idiots driving as though the Devil himself were after them, and all to impress the silly little tarts they were hoping to tempt into a quick, furtive coupling in Bryant's Copse at the bottom of the hill just before the village. Some of them ended up in hospital, a few on mortuary slabs.

Quite out of breath, Harry stopped right by the gap in the hedge and bent to look through the rear window of the car. He could see nothing. The interior of the vehicle was in deepest shadow. He glanced the other way, up the hill, expecting to see wheel tracks where emergency vehicles had parked – they would have to pull right over onto the verge here where the lane was narrow – but there were only long skid marks, obviously made by this car. The driver had tried to brake then.

Feeling really alarmed now, Harry pushed his way between the vehicle and the shattered hedge (which young Steven Dando had made such a lovely job of trimming early in the New Year) and, holding onto the rear door handle for support, tried to open the driver's door. There was no doubt about it; the engine was still hot and one of the headlights was still on. The accident had only just happened.

The smell of spilt fuel was very strong here.

The door would not yield; it was jammed somehow. Slithering on the mud, Harry made his way around the front, holding onto the car for support.

'Dear God,' he muttered as he beheld what looked like an outflung arm and a blond head, partially obscured by a long smear of blood on the inside of the windscreen.

The front passenger door opened easily, the powerful yank that Harry had given it proving quite unnecessary and almost causing him to fall over backwards. Floundering in the furrows, he regained his balance and looked in.

The interior light had come on and for several long moments Harry thought that the driver was a girl wearing a tartan skirt and that she was dead. He soon discovered that he was wrong on all three counts.

2

Chapter One

On its journey towards the city of Bath the river Avon
meanders in the company of the Kennet and Avon Canal, the
Warminster Road and the railway line. Before all four reach
Claverton the canal crosses both the railway and river on the
Dundas aqueduct – this structure enhancing rather than being
detrimental to the serene beauty of the valley – and at
Batheaston the quartet is joined by the London Road. The
river's creation of the valley has made the construction of the
man-made arteries possible but before it reaches the city it
seems as if it shrugs these off in order to travel alone. This it
does in several generous curves which commence just before
Pulteney Bridge and a weir. From Grand Parade above there
is a fine view of the bridge – the only one in England with
shops on both sides – and in summer this is a favourite
vantage point for tourists. On this particular late January
morning, with the rain pouring down in grey curtains that
obscured the playing fields downstream on the other side of
the river, there were no visitors in sight, only a few people
going to church huddled beneath umbrellas. No one paused
to look over the stone balustrade at the river below and there
was no reason to – the muddied torrent was hardly an
attractive sight. A dead tree had jammed against the weir, its
branches festooned with long strands of dead grass and
lengths of the black plastic that farmers use to wrap large
round bales of silage.

Detective Sergeant Bob Ingrams of Bath CID hardly
noticed the rain. It had been raining on and off since the New
Year anyway and he was not an outdoor sort of person, his

3

interest in the weather being limited to whether or not he needed to use the windscreen wipers. And right now he had something particularly diverting on his mind, an occurrence that had made working over the weekend almost a pleasure.

Humming tunelessly, he parked behind the Manvers Street police station and made his way across the car park towards the rear entrance. He was of rather short stature although powerfully built – a fact that stood him in good stead with the rougher element – and had a sailor's rolling gait. He actually hurried this morning, eager to learn if there were any more developments in the fascinating scandal of his boss, Detective Inspector James Carrick, having been found very drunk in charge of a car, having driven it right through a hedge.

Sergeant Woods, at the desk, was glumly checking a duty roster.

'This could be the end of him,' was Ingrams' opening remark.

Woods, frowning, glanced up. He had an air of neat efficiency about him that irritated Ingrams. 'Who, Carrick?' he said, looking surprised. 'He's not that badly hurt.'

'No, I mean his *career*,' said Ingrams, playing catch with his car keys.

Woods shook his head. 'I very much doubt it. Besides, they've discovered he wasn't that drunk. It was concussion. Over the limit though.'

Ingrams quickly shoved his keys into a pocket as Detective Chief Inspector Haine erupted from his office and strode into the reception area. The habitual frown that he wore was deeper than usual but otherwise all was as normal, like a bald scarecrow in a gale.

'I've been to the hospital,' he said. 'He can't remember what happened. Not that he feels like talking yet. Told him he needn't look to me for sympathy. That's the trouble with Scots. Drink. The malt and all that. He'd been to a Burns Night do at that country house hotel.' Haine sighed. 'Can't think what got into him.'

Crisply, Woods said, 'Inspector Carrick was on leave, sir.'

'I'm fully aware of that,' Haine snapped. 'That's no

excuse.'

'No, what I mean, sir, is that he'd planned to stay at the Crawford Hotel for a couple of days afterwards for a short holiday. What was he doing driving away on Friday night?'

'You tell me,' Haine retorted. He jerked his head in the direction of his office. 'I'd like a word, Ingrams.' Once they were in his office and he'd slammed the door behind them, he continued, 'God knows, he's good at his job so I suppose I ought to support him through this, but it doesn't do, Ingrams. We arrest the public left, right and centre for drunk driving so we can't be lenient with our own.' He fixed the sergeant with his dark unwavering gaze. 'Have you known him do this before? Drink and drive, I mean?'

Ingrams thought very carefully. 'No, sir,' he had to admit, then added, 'not that I've worked with him all that long. Where was he found?'

'Halfway down that hellishly steep lane off Lansdown. Does he still live up there?'

'Yes, but he wouldn't have to go down that way to get home. It leads to Little Nashby. He has a flat in one of those big houses on the main road.'

Haine was irritably rearranging the papers on his desk. 'I simply can't imagine what the man was up to. All I know is that his car left the road and a blood test confirmed that he was over the limit. I don't know why he wasn't killed – he hadn't fastened his seat belt, either. What I want you to do is go out to this hotel and make a few enquiries. Find out how many people – guests or staff – saw him leave and get behind the wheel of his car. If I'm to try to hush this up I first need to know my chances of success. Perhaps we can put it about that he was taken ill or something. And be *discreet*.'

'Are we sure there were no other vehicles involved, sir?'

'It seems not. There's no bodywork damage to the car other than that caused by it going through the hedge – no traces of another car's paintwork to suggest a collision. The old codger who found him said the road's a real danger to those who don't know it. You could talk to him too. Perhaps you ought to get him in to make a statement in case the Chief Super decides to make an example of Carrick. I need all the facts.'

'Someone said the car was burnt out, though.'

'No. A lot of smoke was coming from under the bonnet but the fire brigade got to it before it really went up. Someone said something about the chassis being twisted, so it might be a write-off. Now don't make a song and dance over this, Ingrams. I've enough to do without having to waste time on something that could have so easily been avoided. It's just as well there's nothing really big on at the moment what with everyone going down with the flu.'

It was all right for Haine, Ingrams thought resentfully on his way out. Ingrams himself had plenty to do to keep him occupied, the deadly boring run-of-the-mill jobs that people like Haine never became involved with: the stolen cars, and the petty theft and shop-lifting cases that sometimes made him wonder if he was a social worker instead of a policeman.

'You never did like Carrick, did you?' Woods growled at him as he went by.

Ingrams didn't respond. No, was the answer to that.

He had often driven past the Crawford Hotel, for it was situated just off the main road to Chipping Sodbury. The actual house was set well back and only glimpses of it could be seen through the trees. The gardens were extensive, with woodland walks, a lake and a golf course as well as large formal gardens famous in the district for shrub roses. In summer there were special Sunday afternoon 'Rose Teas'. Set within walled gardens near the house were an indoor swimming pool and a gymnasium.

A noticeboard at the side of the road indicated that the main entrance was situated two hundred yards up a lane to the left and that the restaurant was open to non-residents. A smaller notice beneath it conferred the information that the Avon and Somerset Caledonian Society held its meetings on the premises.

Trust Carrick, Ingrams thought sourly.

All the same, it was rather pleasant to progress slowly up the drive – there was a fifteen-mile-an-hour speed limit – and pretend for a moment that he had the kind of money to frequent such a place. But he had to admit to himself that he would feel uncomfortable in these surroundings, suddenly aware that his suit was somewhat creased and shiny and that his shoes were in need of repair.

The sumptuous entrance lobby did nothing to allay his discomfort. There seemed to be acres of pale blue carpet to cross in order to reach the reception desk. In one corner, near a huge stone fireplace with a roaring log fire, a group of people laughed and talked loudly. They were wearing the kind of designer tracksuits that never saw mud.

The young woman behind the desk – upon which there was a magnificent arrangement of fresh flowers – gave him a very friendly smile. Ingrams, fumbling for his warrant card, introduced himself and explained that one of the guests at the previous Friday night's celebrations had had an accident in his car and that he, Ingrams, was making a few enquiries. That was as discreet as he could make it.

'Was that the Burns Night Supper or the Horticultural Society dinner dance?'

'The former,' Ingrams replied.

She reached for one of the three phones on the desk. 'I'll ask Mr Grayson to have a word with you. He's our Functions Manager.' She gave Ingrams another dazzling smile. 'Do step into the lounge, sergeant, and help yourself to coffee. Mr Grayson won't be long.'

The coffee was in large silver pots standing on a special hotplate, the crockery thin bone china. Arranged on small trays were fancy chocolate biscuits of a kind Ingrams had never seen before and also very small ones that his wife had once told him were called *petits fours*. A sudden burst of laughter caused him to start violently, spilling some coffee on the immaculate white cloth covering the table. But the woman who had laughed was quite oblivious of his presence, riveted by the photographs her male companion had handed to her.

'That *hat*!' she shrieked. 'I mean, I know just about anything goes at Ascot, but if you plonked something like that on a house you'd need planning permission.'

The pair, seated in a window alcove, continued to chuckle.

A few minutes later, the Functions Manager arrived. He was in his twenties, of broomstick leanness. He approached the corner where Ingrams had seated himself close to a large potted palm.

7

'Did I hear correctly?' he asked when he had introduced himself. 'Someone mentioned an accident involving a guest.'

'On Friday night, sir,' Ingrams replied. 'Mr Carrick's car left the road.' He cleared his throat. 'Inspector Carrick, actually. No other vehicles seem to have been involved and we're trying to piece together what happened.'

Grayson looked horrified. 'But I *spoke* to the man. Is he badly hurt?'

'Minor head injuries and cracked ribs, I understand,' Ingrams replied, having had this officially confirmed over his car radio on the way to the hotel.

'But he was staying here, sergeant. What on earth was he doing driving away?'

'That's what I'm trying to find out, sir. What time did you speak to him?'

'After dinner. As a matter of fact I congratulated him on his rendition of "Tam O'Shanter", all the more remarkable I felt because he doesn't normally speak with much of a Scottish accent, yet he delivered the poem in Burns' broadest Ayrshire. He mentioned that he was looking forward to a couple of days off and that a lady friend who was away on business would be joining him on Saturday night for dinner.'

'Did you see him later on in the evening?'

'No, but as you know I had another function to supervise. Oh, dear, I can imagine there'll be trouble for him. No doubt ...' He broke off, frowning. 'But I can assure you, he wasn't drunk.'

'Over the limit, though – there was a blood test.'

Grayson spoke quietly. 'I'll speak frankly. I take it that the Avon and Somerset Police would prefer that this matter did not become public knowledge.'

'It rather depends on how many people saw him leave and get into his car.'

'But no, surely. As I said, he wasn't obviously drunk. That would only have been of concern if he had been. No one here would have thought anything of him leaving and driving away – unless it was a member of staff who knew that he had booked a room. Besides, he doesn't live all that far away, does he? There was every possibility that he went home for something.'

'Or that he'd forgotten he was staying here.'

Grayson shook his head emphatically. 'No, sergeant. Sorry to keep on disagreeing, but someone who has recited a long poem like "Tam O'Shanter" is hardly likely to forget where he's staying the night.'

'But surely there would have been time for him to have a few whiskies after you spoke to him and before he left the hotel.'

'I suppose so, but there was every indication that he intended to take part in the dancing.'

Ingrams decided to swallow his pride. 'Perhaps you could explain to me what exactly goes on at these, er, suppers.'

If Grayson thought him ignorant he gave no sign of it. He began, 'Robert Burns was born on the twenty-fifth of January, 1759 and he's regarded as the foremost Scottish poet. It's his birthday that is celebrated by Scots all over the world. Here at the Crawford Hotel we have a tradition of Scottish connections from the days when it was a private house and was known as Crawford Grange. The Crawford family came from Lanarkshire originally but made their money in coal locally, in the Midsomer Norton area. Their parties at New Year and on Burns Night were famous all over the district. There was Highland Dancing and, more recently, ceilidhs – gatherings with storytelling round the fire – and I gather that anyone in this area with even remote Scottish ancestry was made welcome. It was natural that when the house was sold – the last of the daughters of the family having passed away – it should retain its Scottish connections. We are pleased that the local Caledonian Society holds its meetings and social events here. But you're asking about last Friday ... Well, sergeant, haggis is the traditional fare and it's piped in. Mr Bruce Campbell did the honours for us.'

'Bagpipes, you mean, sir?'

'Oh, yes. It's a bit loud for my ears indoors, but doesn't go on for very long. Someone, usually the chairman I believe, then addresses the haggis, so to speak, with another of Burns' poems and then it is ceremonially slashed open with a dirk. It is then removed to the kitchen where it is served onto plates. We make our dinners rather special, with the haggis as a starter and then a main course of Tayside salmon. Cheese

9

and a blueberry sorbet followed.'

'What time did it end?'

'The dancing stopped at eleven. You really can't continue after that because of the other guests wanting to get some sleep. People tend to drink coffee and chat and then drift away if they're not staying – it wasn't late when it finished.'

Ingrams, very reluctantly, had abandoned a mental picture of a riotous clannish knees-up, everyone swilled to the ears with whisky. Carrick had been found at about midnight – not a lot of time, then, for him to have done *anything*.

'I can give you a list of staff who were on duty,' Grayson was saying. He gave Ingrams a searching look. 'Sergeant, Inspector Carrick is a very *respected* member of the society. If he got into his car and drove off that night there must have been extenuating circumstances.'

'Was there any trouble?' Ingrams enquired.

'*Trouble*?' Grayson echoed, sounding quite affronted. 'No, of course not. We never have trouble here.'

'I was just following your train of thought, sir,' Ingrams said humbly. 'Perhaps something happened that the Inspector felt he had no option but to deal with.'

'No. Nothing like that. The only small problem we sometimes have is when someone has had a little too much to drink. We organise a taxi to take them home and I must add that the staff here are very discreet at managing that kind of thing. No, as I said, everything went off very smoothly.'

Grayson gave Ingrams a list of names, informing him that all these members of staff would not be on duty again until six that evening, so if he wanted to interview them he would have to return.

Ingrams left, having already decided that he would return only if he had nothing more important to do. He had a good idea that the lady friend who was to have joined Carrick for dinner was Joanna Mackenzie, his one-time sergeant, now in business as a private investigator with an office over a herbalists' shop in Milsom Street. It occurred to him that no one had mentioned the woman checking on Carrick's where-abouts at the nick and she might not know what had happened to him.

He realised that he had stopped in the act of unlocking his

car. No, he did not like Carrick, and liked Mackenzie even less. He thought she had got what she deserved for having an affair with her boss, who had been married at the time. She had been dismissed – or as good as, moved to a dead-end job, which effectively forced her to resign – and Carrick had received a severe reprimand. The Super of the day had especially hated women on the job.

That this had been monumentally unfair had not occurred to Ingrams before. Perhaps, really, it was something that he had not wanted to admit to himself, no more than he could accept the uncomfortable thought that the two still swapped ideas and that Carrick missed her intellect.

'To hell with it,' he said out loud, getting into the car and slamming the door. 'Why should I care?'

He shoved in the ignition key but did not turn it. You never used to be that sort of bastard, an inner voice seemed to say . . .

No, Carrick could sort out his own personal problems.

At a little before noon council workmen arrived to remove the dead tree from the weir. For one thing, no one wanted it to be an attraction to children who might then fall into the river and drown; for another, large items of flotsam could remain jammed against the weir for months and in Bath, one of the finest cities in Europe, such unsightliness is not permitted.

It had stopped raining but the river was quite high, not high enough for the flood gate on the opposite bank to come into operation but flowing over the top of the weir in brown, glassy curves. Standing upon it, although the water was only a few inches deep, was an extremely hazardous undertaking. After a while, when efforts to manhandle the tree in the direction of some riverside steps had failed, someone fetched a chainsaw and began to cut it up into manageable lengths. A branch that had snared what looked like a bundle of clothing was pulled beneath the surface by the weight of it and was left until last.

The sodden bundle turned out to be extremely heavy and it took all the men's efforts to draw the slimy wood it was attached to towards them. It came, at last, in a rush and they

11

stared in horror as the current slapped a dead hand onto the stonework they were standing on. Then the river gave up the rest of the corpse and it bobbed, white and oozing, the black hair of the head given snaky life by the movement of the water.

Chapter Two

'Fair, fa' your honest, sonsie face,' James Carrick said sleepily.

'I beg your pardon?' said Joanna.

He opened his eyes and frowned in puzzlement. 'I thought you were somewhere else.'

'No, I'm here,' she replied with a grin.

He gingerly felt the bandage that swathed his head. He hurt all over, but his head and particularly the side of his neck were flaring agony.

'James, what the hell have you been up to?'

'That's the trouble, I don't remember.'

'But you were found in Wood Lane. That leads to Little Nashby. There was no reason for you to drive that way even if you'd decided to go home.'

He had tried to think it through in the hours since he had recovered consciousness. The entire evening was intact in his memory until the moment when he had gone up the stairs to his room with every intention of going to bed so that he could rise comparatively early and enjoy a swim before the pool got busy. He had seen the Campbells in a small lounge and they had invited him to have a drink with them. He had made an excuse; they had a whole bottle of whisky that had just been opened and appeared to have every intention of getting seriously drunk.

What had happened then?

'*Was* there any reason for you to leave?' Joanna said. 'I mean, had anything happened during the evening that made you change your mind about staying for a couple of days?'

'No.'

'You're quite sure about that then?'

'Yes. The complete blank starts after I decided to go to bed. Joanna . . .?'

She took his hand. 'Yes?'

'What the bloody hell have I done to myself?'

'They haven't told you?'

'Someone in a white coat came and spoke reproachfully when I first woke up. I didn't really listen.'

'You've three stitches in a cut on your head and a couple of cracked ribs. Concussion's the watchword, though. They're not quite sure why you didn't go through the windscreen.'

'I heard the bit about no other vehicle being involved and my being over the limit. Of course I was over the limit – I had no intention of driving. Haine said I deserved it if traffic threw the book at me.'

'That's a bit cruel when no one knows what happened.'

'If you're behind the wheel of a car and found to have too much alcohol in your blood . . .'

'I know, I know. James, do you want me to go and talk to the old chap who found you?'

'I can't afford a private detective.'

She was about to explode furiously when she saw that there was a hint of a smile on his lips. 'You might need one, boyo. A body was found in the river this morning, and your brother officers are all running round in small circles.'

'Have they identified it?' Carrick asked eagerly, wide awake now.

'Not yet. All I know is that it was a man in his fifties. There's no wallet or any means of identification and no one's been reported missing.'

'How did he die?'

'That's a bit iffy at the moment until the PM's been done. Drowned, probably, so it *might* have been an accident. But the fact that there's no wallet does make it suspicious.'

There was a short silence and then Carrick said, 'We had a date last night.'

'We can have it here if you like – I'll trot along with a bowl of calf's-foot jelly and two spoons.'

14

In the days when Joanna had been his sergeant, she had looked at him like this when she thought he had really screwed something up. Carrick met the look urbanely. The latter part of Friday night was a mystery to him but he was sure of one thing: he had not joined the group at the bar. He could remember leaving them. If the car had gone out of control it was not because of his inability to drive it due to an excess of drink.

'Where is the car now?' he asked.

'I can find out for you.'

'I'd be most grateful if you'd get the AA to have a look over it for me. I want to know why it crashed.'

'James . . .'

'Look, I *wasn't* drunk.' All of a sudden Carrick felt rather desperate. 'Please, Jo,' he whispered. He loved her so much, he realised with a jolt, and here she was looking at him with those wonderful green eyes as though . . . Well, as though he was something the cat had sicked up.

'You gave me an awful fright,' she said softly. 'Someone actually said that you were dead. It was only a drunk in casualty, but for a few moments . . .'

'Sorry.'

She gave his hand another squeeze. 'Of course I'll check up for you. I'll talk to the hotel staff too and see what I can find out.'

'Please thank the old man who hauled me out of the car. The whole thing could have gone up in flames.'

She stood up to leave. 'No problem. Every operative of Tyler and Mackenzie will be pressed into service.'

'You and who else?' he retorted. Lance Tyler, Joanna's business partner, had been killed in a car accident some months previously.

'Oh, I've hired a chap called Greg Perivale to do the donkey work. He's ex-Bristol CID.'

'I see.'

'We get on okay and he's not too keen on getting involved with anything challenging as he was smashed up falling through a roof arresting someone. It finished his career. I felt that in view of Lance dying the way he did it was right to give him the job. But it's not charity on my part; he's very thorough.'

'Can't you exert some charm and get me out of here?' Carrick asked, postponing worrying about possible rivals.

'You have to stay until the concussion is *quite* better. I'll come back tomorrow when I'm sure you'll feel more like yourself and might have remembered some more.'

He groaned in frustration.

'Get some rest,' Joanna ordered, kissing him quickly.

He watched her walk away down the ward. How could he rest with his head feeling fit to burst and the pain at the side of his neck like a red-hot sword slowly carving him into rashers?

A nurse approached carrying a small dish that he suspected contained a syringe filled with his total oblivion. He eyed her warily.

'Just something to help you to sleep,' she said soothingly. She was rather pretty and looked about fifteen years old.

'I'd really like to make a phone call first,' Carrick said.

'Staff Nurse said . . .'

'It's rather important,' he said when she faltered and managed a smile that he hoped was sufficiently winning. 'I want to call someone and ask them to come in and see me.'

As it happened the Staff Nurse was talking to a consultant just then, so the junior nurse entered into the spirit of complicity Carrick seemed to have conjured up and drew the curtains around his bed. She was somewhat taken with this patient. Even though he was looking rather battered, there was something undeniably attractive about that thick blond hair and those blue eyes. She fetched the telephone trolley.

When Carrick had made his call he submitted to the needle, having time afterwards to wonder if he was the first man ever to book his own post-mortem. Then he was wafted away into a deepening twilight.

By midday on Monday the body had been identified and only then because the landlord of the Crossbow, a public house on the banks of the Kennet and Avon canal near the Dundas aqueduct, had contacted the police about a car that had been left in his car park since Saturday evening. About an hour before closing time he had advised a customer, a man whom

16

he was used to seeing most weekends and who was always alone, that for him to drive himself home would be most unwise. The man had insisted that he only had a short distance to travel and a real problem might have evolved if someone who had just arrived had not volunteered to take him to his cottage. No one had been to collect the car, a new Jaguar, and the publican, Tim Brockenhurst, was worried that it might be stolen if it stayed where it was.

The vehicle was registered in the name of Marvin Gilcrist, a name not unknown to Chief Inspector Haine. By now Haine knew that he was conducting a murder inquiry: this had been confirmed when a preliminary examination of the body revealed a serious head injury and bruising around the neck consistent with attempted strangulation. He contacted Special Branch and very shortly afterwards a photograph of Gilcrist had been faxed to him. There was not the slightest doubt that the body in the mortuary belonged to Gilcrist, a film producer who had specialised of late in television documentaries exposing police corruption and miscarriages of justice. Haine had not needed the phone call from headquarters in Bristol – from which his ears were still burning – to be made aware that this case had to be solved immediately.

The aggressive manner in which Gilcrist had tackled his subjects, coupled with a ready willingness to take the word of people very closely connected with the criminal underworld whilst doubting statements put out by the police, had earned him the enmity of just about every Chief Constable in the country. In view of this it was not difficult for Haine, even though he was a man of little imagination, to anticipate the headlines that would appear on papers published by the less responsible sections of the press. There would be talk of a plot, several plots, in fact, to silence the man who dared to expose things the establishment would prefer kept under wraps. It would be suggested that MI5 had organised the killing, or – and here Haine shuddered delicately – an under-cover member of one of the police forces. He was aware that both of these possibilities were highly unlikely, almost out of the question in his view, but one could not exclude private vengeance.

17

But, first of all, he had to break the news to a woman that her husband was dead.

There was money, it would seem, to be made from controversy. Haine and Ingrams drew up outside a house that had at one time been a barn and other farm buildings, now converted into a long, low dwelling with large picture windows surrounded by immaculate gardens. The man who tended these was raking the gravel of the drive when they arrived and moved a wheelbarrow to enable them to pass more easily.

'Very nice,' Haine commented dryly, observing a new planting of heathers mulched with dark, moist peat, each variety marked with a neat metal label. 'My garden just seems to grow weeds and stones.'

Ingrams didn't have a garden; he lived with his wife and two children in a flat over a hardware shop. A garden like this should be for kids to play in, he thought as they got out of the car, not for middle-aged people to stare at as they sipped their pre-dinner gins and tonics. Perhaps the Gilcrists had grandchildren. Somehow, he thought not.

The woman who came to the door, after they had waited so long that the Chief Inspector had had to ring the bell again, looked as though she had just got out of bed. Probably in her middle forties, she was wearing a short see-through négligé over what appeared to be an equally transparent nightdress.

'Oh, God,' she said. 'I thought you were the daily.' The voice was slightly hoarse as though she might be a heavy smoker.

'Mrs Amanda Gilcrist?' Haine asked.

'Yes.'

He introduced himself and Ingrams and asked if they might enter.

'Why, is something wrong?'

'I would rather talk about it inside if you don't mind.'

'As you wish.' She led the way into a living room that had not been tidied that morning, opened the curtains, gathered a couple of empty wine bottles and two glasses and took them from the room. 'Please sit down,' she said when she returned.

She had donned a long peach-coloured dressing gown which eminently suited her fair colouring.

'Your husband is Marvin Gilcrist?' Haine said.

'Yes, we are still just about married – the divorce hasn't gone through yet. Why, what on earth has happened?'

'I'm afraid that a body was found in the River Avon yesterday and we've every reason to believe –'

'Marvin! But that's impossible. He's at the cottage and won't be returning until tonight.'

Haine continued, 'A green Jaguar car registered in his name has been parked at the Crossbow in Broadstoke since Saturday night. Where is this cottage, Mrs Gilcrist?'

She still didn't seem to believe what she was being told. 'There, at Broadstoke. It's only about four miles from here.'

'Was he alone?'

'I've no idea who else could have been there. He goes there to be alone – to work. Look, this is simply ridiculous. There must be some mistake.' She stared at them both. 'You're saying that he's *dead*?'

Gently, for despite all his bluster and a tendency to slam doors Haine was a compassionate man, he said, 'There was no identification but your husband is well known. With a photograph we were able to . . .' He broke off sadly.

Amanda Gilcrist had sunk into one of the huge pale orange armchairs. 'In the *river*? What was he doing there? In summer you can walk along the riverbank to the pub – you just go up some wooden steps to the aqueduct and you're practically in the lounge bar. God, I can't *bear* to think of him blundering along there in the dark and falling in and dying like that – all on his own.' She snatched a paper tissue from her pocket and dabbed at her eyes with it. 'The fool, the big, stupid old fool. You know, I said to him on more than one occasion that if he carried on drinking the way he was . . .' She started to cry quietly.

Haine said, 'There were injuries, Mrs Gilcrist. We're treating his death as murder.' When she made no reaction he added, 'Is there someone we can contact for you?'

She did not appear to hear the question. 'I suppose you want me to come and formally identify him.'

19

'Unless there's another close member of the family who could –'

'Close?' she interrupted, her voice harsh. 'No one's close. There's no family either.' Bitterly, she added, 'Marvin Gilcrist was far too famous to have a family.'

'You mean he snubbed them?'

'As far as he was concerned they didn't exist. His parents are dead – have been for years – but he has a sister in Wales and a brother over in Ireland. They're both ordinary people insofar as the brother's a sheep farmer and his sister works in Boots. The world hasn't spoiled them yet as it did Marvin. I send them a card at Christmas but that's as far as it goes. He wouldn't have them here. Oh, and yes, you probably guessed it – we've no children.'

Haine asked her for the address of the cottage and sent Ingrams outside to radio his instructions to the scene-of-crime team to go there immediately. Ingrams had done this and was about to go back indoors when he saw a movement at the side of the house where the drive swept in a curve to some garages at the rear.

'Oi!' he shouted.

A man who had been about to get into a small Rover turned and glowered at him. 'Are you addressing me?' he asked, not actually adding, 'my man'.

His temper rising, the sergeant marched up to him and flashed his warrant card under the other's nose. 'Detective Sergeant Ingrams, Bath CID. Who are you?'

The man straightened and looked Ingrams up and down before replying.

'My name's Craxton. Blair Craxton. What the hell do you want?'

'So you haven't spoken to Mrs Gilcrist yet today?'

There was the merest hesitation. 'No, I've only just got up as a matter of fact. Is something wrong?'

'You were leaving without saying goodbye then?'

'No, of course not. I wasn't leaving – just fetching some music tapes from the car.'

'Have you been here all weekend?'

'Yes, I'm a friend of the family. Although what that has to do with you –'

Smoothly, Ingrams interrupted. 'Chief Inspector Haine and I are here in connection with the discovery of a body in the River Avon yesterday morning and we've every reason to believe it is that of Mr Gilcrist.'

'Marvin? Good God! I don't believe it.'

'When did you arrive here? Friday night?'

Craxton sank onto the driving seat. 'Look, this is a dreadful shock. What did you say?'

'I asked you what time you arrived for the weekend.'

'Oh, Friday night. It was latish. I arrived at about ten-thirty.'

'And where were you before that?'

'Surely you don't suspect that –'

'Just routine enquiries,' Ingrams broke in again, losing patience.

'I came straight from work. That's in Bristol. I run a small business – antiques. I'd been working late catching up with paperwork – all the VAT stuff.'

'Did you see Mr Gilcrist at all over the weekend?'

'No. He was at the cottage at Broadstoke. He goes there – went there – to work and hated being interrupted. He refused even to have a phone installed.'

'Did he often go to the Crossbow for a drink?'

Craxton wrenched open the glove compartment and took out a handful of music cassettes. 'Yes, quite a bit. Frankly, I think he spent more time there than on his precious work.'

'Did he normally drive or walk?'

'Marvin, walk? He'd take the car to the next corner to post a letter.' He stared hard at Ingrams. 'I see what you're driving at. He was found in the river?'

'Yes, and we're treating his death as murder. Perhaps you could give me the details of your movements over the weekend.'

'I stayed here. *Murder*?'

'All weekend?'

'Yes.'

'You didn't go out at all?'

'No.'

'What about Mrs Gilcrist?'

'She was here all the time too.'

21

'You can't be sure about that though, can you?'

'Yes. She would have told me if she was going out.'

Ingrams leaned one hand on the roof of the car. 'Did you like Mr Gilcrist?'

'No.' Craxton smiled bleakly. 'Now, is that all you want to ask? I'm hungry.'

Ingrams relayed this interview to Haine, who was on his own waiting for Amanda Gilcrist to get dressed.

'What's he like?' Haine grunted.

Aware that he was being asked for a full description, Ingrams said, 'He's in his thirties, fair hair with highlights –'

'Highlights?'

'Bleached bits.'

'I'm with you.'

'He's about five feet nine inches tall, has grey eyes that look a bit shifty and wears the sort of clothes that come with designer creases in them.'

'Her toyboy.'

'Definitely, sir.'

The DCI began to pace up and down the long room. 'I hope to God we have the PM soon. Trust John Butler to go and break his ankle yesterday. Who's standing in for him, do you know?'

'Sir Hugh someone.'

'Rapton?'

'That's it, sir.'

'We're honoured. He's professor of Forensic Science at Bristol University. Must be a friend of Butler's – he retired from the sharp end some years ago.' He chuckled at his own joke. 'Where the hell's that woman got to?' Ramming his hands in his pockets he continued, 'You appreciate that this is a very awkward one indeed. The press'll have us by the short and curlies as soon as Gilcrist's death's announced. I'm sure I don't have to remind you that over the past few years he's made it his business to rout out any hint of police corruption and plaster it all over the media. People like that usually have powerful friends and they'll be howling for blood – ours.'

With a swift look over his shoulder in the direction of the door Ingrams said, 'We might have a prime suspect already.

There seemed to be a few empty bottles around. Perhaps they were celebrating. And she said a divorce was going through. It's possible she might be better off a widow than whatever the court would award her.'

'It's a thought,' Haine muttered. 'And we can follow that up.'

Later that day, after Amanda Gilcrist had formally – and it had to be said, serenely – identified her husband, Haine and Ingrams went to Rampsons, the cottage at Broadstoke. They might have thought they had arrived at the wrong place as they fought their way through overgrown trees and shrubs to reach the front door, if they hadn't already seen several police vehicles parked outside. A constable stood at the entrance.

'It's like a pigsty, sir,' he commented as they went in.

'So it is,' Haine said loudly when he stood in the tiny living room, making several people who had not heard his arrival start violently. 'But someone's turned it over too, haven't they?'

Ingrams surveyed the devastation: the broken furniture, smashed ornaments, pictures thrown from the walls, a bookcase upended, the volumes and paperwork scattered all over the floor. 'Or Gilcrist in a bit of a frenzy?'

Haine said nothing but strode back into the narrow hall, through a room at the rear even smaller than the one in the front and from there into a kitchen of sorts. Everywhere was in the same state of chaos.

'Anything might have happened,' Haine said at last. 'And I don't suppose it would be much use asking his wife if anything's missing as I've a feeling she never sets a foot in the place. But ask her all the same. Find out if there was a wall safe or anything hidden under the floors.' He stared around with an air of bafflement. 'I think I've been long enough in this game to think that we've evidence here of a man who slummed it, threw a few things around when he'd had a drop too much and had a visitor before or after his death who did some more wrecking.'

'It's just as bad upstairs, sir,' someone called out from a cupboard in the hall, adding under his breath, and not for Haine's ears, that they'd be working in the house for a month.

23

'Even more evidence,' Haine said breezily. 'I mean, for God's sake, there must be something here that'll lead us to his killer.'

There was, but no one present found it.

Chapter Three

Joanna had decided to devote the whole of Monday, if necessary, to try to piece together what had happened to Carrick on Friday night. She had no theories and had abandoned the idea that he had offered to give someone a lift home and then, for one reason or another, lost control of the car. It seemed highly unlikely that any passenger would simply walk away from the accident without reporting it and if whoever it was had been much the worse for alcohol they would not have been able to.

Carrick's skene-dhu, the little dress dagger worn tucked into the top of one of the woollen stockings, was missing. Joanna thought it probable that it had been lost when he had been dragged from the car. Someone might have found it, perhaps the old man who had gone to his aid. Much more likely it had been trampled into the muddy field. She therefore decided to visit the scene of the accident first.

She had no trouble in finding the spot, for other than the gaping hole torn in the hedge, Wood Lane was as neat as a patchwork quilt. She left her car a good fifty yards downhill and walked back. Crows wheeled and quarrelled over nesting sites in a tall stand of elms in one corner of the field but otherwise it was very quiet, the only other sound the distant and intermittent hum of traffic on the main road high above on Lansdown Hill.

As she walked Joanna tried to recreate that evening in her mind. She could picture him with ease, a graceful figure in the Kennedy tartan kilt, the heavy fabric with its many pleats in shades of dark blue and green with thin cerise and gold stripes. Earlier that morning she had taken it to be dry cleaned, together with the green velvet jacket, one of the silver buttons of which was also missing. The silver-mounted white fur sporran she had carefully brushed herself, haunted by the look on his face when he beheld his heavily muddied Highland Dress. For it was part of the man himself, wasn't it?

A robin twittered softly in a hedge near to the place of the accident. Yes, he had tried to brake; even after the heavy rain of Saturday night the skid marks left by the left-hand side tyres could be clearly seen on the verge and there were skid marks on the road surface as well. Other vehicles, an ambulance and a police car presumably, had also left tracks; the night had not been cold enough to freeze the ground solid.

Joanna changed into the boots she had brought with her and negotiated the steep slope, following the wheel ruts and shorn-off roots and stems down to where the car's front wheels had come to rest in the mud. Then she closely examined the ground in an area of several square yards. She found two ten pence pieces and, squashed right into the mud, a yellow duster. There were several footprints, some elongated where people had slithered in the mud, but no sign of the skene-dhu.

'That's a pity,' Joanna said to herself. It had been handed down from his grandfather to his father, drowned at sea before James was born.

It seemed that there was nothing to be learned here, but her curiosity, or possibly professional tenacity, took her on up the hill. She wanted to see again the lane from the point of view of someone driving down from the top where it joined the main road.

There was a very wide grass strip – much wider than an ordinary verge and on the same side as the road junction – which extended almost as far as the race course. A narrow path ran along it that riders from nearby stables used in order to keep a safe distance from the traffic. The ground was broken and muddied where the two roads met, churned up as riders waited to cross to a bridle path on the other side.

There were tyre tracks too and deep grooves where wheels had spun in the soft ground. And something small and shiny.

Carrick's missing button.

Joanna cleaned the mud from it with her handkerchief, mind racing. From the broken threads on the jacket it was clear that the button had been ripped off. Until this moment, she had thought that it must have happened when James was being pulled from the car, but now she knew it had been ripped off *here*. There were two sets of tyre tracks: one nearest to the hedge looked very much like those left by Carrick's car in the field, the other, made by wider tyres, those closest to where she had found the button giving the impression that the vehicle had run onto the grass and then been driven off again at speed, the tyres spinning on the soft ground.

There were a thousand possibilities now. Had he stopped here for some reason, been waylaid and beaten up, tried to get away and then crashed? If that was the case there was still no explanation as to why he had left the hotel. A crime might have been committed near the hotel that he had witnessed and he had given chase. But there was a radio in his car – he would have reported what had occurred, not just rushed off like a one-man posse.

'But when Scotsmen don their kilts and their skene-dhus they become utterly different people,' Joanna told a Jersey cow grazing on the other side of the hedge. She had suddenly remembered tales that her mother had recounted about great-grandfather Mackenzie who had been the black sheep of his own rather wild family.

Like the time he had tossed the man from the Ministry of Agriculture into the burn behind the farm . . .

And how he always got into fights on market day . . .

'Fighting!' she exclaimed.

She went back to the car but did not get into it, as Harry Fuller's cottage was only a matter of twenty yards farther down the hill. Had James got into a fight? With fists and knives? It hardly seemed possible, but she followed through the train of thought. If he had lost then his adversary might have tipped him into his car and then James, fuddled, would have driven away.

She could not imagine him losing a fight.

But it might have been two, or even three, against one.

27

'That's right – 'twas me who found him,' said Harry in response to the query. 'Are you from the insurance? I saw you up the road just now.'

'No, just a friend,' Joanna said, introducing herself.

The door was flung wide. 'Come in. Kettle's on.'

The kettle was probably always 'on', simmering quietly on the hob of an ancient and battered Rayburn in the kitchen-cum-living room. Several shirts were drying over an old-fashioned clothes horse in front of it and, curled up amongst a sprinkling of ashes in the hearth, a battle-scarred tabby tom-cat dozed.

'I thought 'twere a girl to start with,' Harry said, shifting a pile of newspapers off a chair so Joanna could sit down. 'There you are, m'dear. Sorry about the washing and all. Have a warm. No, but when I started to lift him out I saw it was a man in a kilt. Is he all right?'

'Remarkably well, considering,' Joanna replied. 'He asked me to thank you.' She was sure that when Carrick was better his thanks would take a more tangible form.

'Well, it was fortunate I was late turning in,' Harry said. 'I thought I'd go out for a breath of fresh air and there it was. Can have only just happened.'

'What makes you think that?'

'Because the engine was still hot. That's what made me get him out in a hurry – in case it went up in flames.'

'Was he quite unconscious?'

Harry fetched a teapot. 'As good as. He muttered a bit when I was trying to disentangle his feet from around the pedals and so forth but was dead to the world really. That made me get a move on – I knew then there was a chance for him and I wasn't looking at a corpse.'

'Did you by any chance notice a small dagger in a leather sheath tucked into his right stocking top?'

'A dagger?' Tom snapped his fingers. 'I've got you now. We had a calendar once that Doris and Ernie sent us from Oban when they were on holiday. It had a picture of a chappie in full Highland rig with his bagpipes and all. And a little knife was in the top of one of his socks. But your friend didn't have one. I'd have noticed that.' He grinned at her, turning from pouring boiling water into the teapot with grave risk to his table. 'Does he play the pipes? It's a stirring sound, that it is.'

'Not so far as I know.' Now *that* would ginger them up at Manvers Street at New Year.

'Well, I'm sorry, m'dear, but I didn't see no dagger. Just a purse on his belt like a badger's backside. And I hope they haven't been saying he was drunk – plenty have gone off that road stone-cold sober.'

'He was over the limit.'

'Pah! You're only allowed a teaspoonful these days. When I remember what my brothers and I used to get up to in an old Austin . . .' He grinned again, reflectively. 'We all used to get in when we'd been down the pub and drive the bits that we fancied. I might take the pedals and George steered while Stan waved his arms out the windows because the trafficator things didn't work.' He chuckled. 'But don't get me wrong now. There was no harm in us and we didn't have no more than half a mile to go with nothing much to miss other than the oak tree on Mile Lane Corner and a pony trap or two. These days . . .' He sighed. 'Milk?'

'Please.'

A milk bottle was found on an overflowing dresser. Harry sniffed the contents. 'Yesterday's – but it's all right.'

'Was the seat belt fastened?'

'No. That's what surprised me rather. He wouldn't have been thrown forward and hit his head if it had been. Clouted it on the driver's mirror, most likely.' He unearthed a bag of sugar. 'Sorry about the mess – I can't keep the place as nice as Tilly did. Thank God she can't see it now.'

'Your wife?'

Gamely, he smiled. 'Been dead a twelvemonth now. Cancer. But the end was a mercy really, for it happened quickly. They gave her several months but she died three weeks later. She said herself it was better like that. Tilly was a proud sort of woman – she couldn't have stood what she called fallin' to bits.'

'I'm afraid that our Functions Manager is at a meeting,' said the receptionist, languidly examining her bright red finger-nails.

'That's all right,' Joanna told her. 'I'll wait. Tell me, were you on duty last Friday night?'

The girl took her time to reply. 'No. I do only mornings or afternoons. That was Margo.'

'And where can I find her? At home?'

There was the merest flicker of interest. 'Are you from the police?'

The denial still hurt. 'No.'

'Only we've had them already. Asking about someone who was involved in a car accident.'

'That's what I want to talk to Margo about.'

After a pause the receptionist said, 'You might not get much joy from Margo – she's a discreet sort of person.'

Speaking more quietly Joanna said, 'I'm not from the press either – the accident happened to a friend of mine. He can't remember what happened so I'm trying to find out.'

'Was it Mr Campbell?'

'No.'

The receptionist looked around quickly before speaking. 'Look, I'm quite careful what I say too, but it was no secret that Mr Campbell had far too much to drink and his sons had to take him home. And they'd been drinking too.'

'Did they have far to take him?'

'I've no idea.'

'His address would be in your records though, wouldn't it?'

'I'm sorry, I can't help you. I've probably said too much already.'

This was the real penalty of no longer being in the job. Joanna left with only Margo's address in reward for her efforts, since Grayson's meeting was apparently likely to go on for some while.

Margo might be discreet, but she had a rather different outlook on life from her colleague's. Although she had only just got up and was padding around barefoot in her flat wearing a crimson towelling dressing gown that was approximately five sizes too large for her but which presumably fitted her boyfriend perfectly, she greeted Joanna warmly.

'Would you like some tea? I'm absolutely gasping.'

Although she had just consumed a half-pint mugful at

30

Harry Fuller's, Joanna accepted.

'Take a seat – I'll put the kettle on.' Through the open kitchen door Margo called, 'I've never had a visit from a private eye before.'

'This isn't a proper case,' Joanna said. 'And I'd be really grateful if our conversation goes no further. I'm doing a favour for a friend, that's all.'

'I'm all ears,' Margo said, returning to the living room.

'I understand you were working at the Crawford Hotel last Friday night.'

'That's right. I volunteered actually – I love the music that accompanies Scottish dancing.'

'Did you see James Carrick during the evening?'

'Yes, of course. He's a policeman, isn't he? He recited "Tam O'Shanter." Completely from memory, of course, which is a real feat as it's so long. I was watching from the doorway. I spoke to him later when everyone was leaving. He said he was turning in as he wanted to get up quite early and have a swim before the pool got busy.'

'Did you actually see him go upstairs?'

'Well, I saw him go in that direction. But there were a lot of people in the foyer so I can't be too sure what he did. Why, has something happened to him?'

'He was involved in a car accident that night.'

'But that can't be right! He was booked in for two nights. He said he was looking forward to a couple of days off.'

'Nevertheless at some time before midnight, when he was found, he left the hotel, got into his car and drove away. I'm trying to find out why because, as you might imagine, policemen who drive when they're over the limit and crash get into a lot of trouble. And he can't remember.'

The kettle shrieked and Margo hurried into the kitchen. 'I can hardly believe it,' she said when she came back. 'He was there as large as life saying goodnight to me. The Campbells were in the Appin Lounge – that's through an archway near the bottom of the main staircase – and he spoke to them too. They were a bit squiffy, frankly. I saw him leave there and then the phone rang or something and I was distracted. We had another function on that night as well.'

'Are you quite sure you didn't see him later?'

'No, I didn't. But I was off duty at eleven-thirty and went home. The night porter takes over then.'

The Crawford Hotel was only a ten-minute drive from the top of Wood Lane. So if Harry had found Carrick almost immediately the accident had occurred, Carrick need not have left the hotel until eleven thirty-five, a time when the reception desk might have been left unattended.

'Are there any other ways out of the hotel?' Joanna asked.

'Yes, there are fire doors at the rear and one at each side in the dining room and the residents' lounge. But they're not normally open – the car park's at the front, as you know. Oh, and of course there's a rear door from the kitchens and another for deliveries, but why would he go out that way?'

'These people, the Campbells, who are they?'

'I don't know them at all, really, and it's only the father, Graeme Campbell, who lives in the area. He bought Hinton Grange about three months ago. His two sons Fraser and Bruce live in Scotland and were down for the weekend visiting him. I don't think either of the sons are married – at least, they didn't have any ladies with them.'

'Not even the father?'

'No, he's a widower. He told me when I checked their tickets – I'm not quite sure why. Perhaps he's lonely. He said he'd moved south and bought the Grange to make a new start.'

'And at the end of the evening they were a bit merry?'

Margo went away again to see to the tea. 'Mr Campbell senior was plastered,' she said from the kitchen. 'There was a bit of a commotion and his sons took him home. He didn't want to go – you know how they get. I think Fraser was angry with him for making a scene.'

'Fraser's the eldest?'

'Yes, he's more like his father: big, blond and with a loud voice. Bruce is quieter and not so tall. I think he's in one of the Scottish regiments – he piped in the haggis. He didn't seem to have had so much to drink and I got the impression he was fed up with the pair of them. But he helped Fraser get their father outside and to the car.'

'Was Inspector Carrick's room at the front or the back?'

'Number thirty-one, at the back.'

32

And as Margo had just said, the car park was at the front. So he couldn't have heard Campbell shouting and, ever the copper, gone down to investigate. Damn.

'Milk and sugar?'

'Just milk, please.'

Moments later Margo returned with two large mugs on a tray. 'Sorry about these potties. I really must get myself some proper cups and saucers one day.'

Joanna said, 'I didn't see any security cameras in the car park.'

'No. They've been talking about having them for ages but it's the same old story, expense. A house like that costs a small fortune to run.'

There seemed little that Joanna could do except talk to the night porter. There had been hundreds of people at the hotel that night, any one of whom could have witnessed Carrick leaving it. But she had neither the time nor the resources to trace them all and interview them.

So, in short, she had let him down.

Some people, she knew, would scorn any feeling of guilt on her part. Because of James Carrick she had had to give up a promising career – he had made no attempt at an appeal on her behalf, for which lapse he had since apologised – and working as a private investigator was not proving to be as interesting or as remunerative as she had hoped. That this was making her increasingly bitter and angry, no matter how hard she tried to tell herself the contrary, was also a complication. The man loved her and had asked her to live with him on several occasions but this did not compensate, if she was really honest with herself, all that much. Perhaps that was the real reason for the feeling of guilt.

Sometimes, in dark moments, she asked herself why she continued with the relationship when it came hand in hand with giving him her views on the cases which he discussed with her – almost all of them – those opinions eagerly sought by him as though they were both still working in the same team. She was still his assistant, it appeared, but unpaid, unrecognised and unsung. Sometimes she wanted to storm into her old workplace and tell them all precisely what she thought of them. But what was the use? The man who had forced her to resign, he who had thought that women were better employed at home, was long retired.

So perhaps it was only her pride that kept her with Carrick, so she could keep proving that she was just as good a police officer as he.

'Damn his gorgeous blue eyes,' she muttered.

Chapter Four

Marvin Gilcrist, it appeared, had taken a lot of killing. According to Sir Hugh Rapton, the pathologist, there had been an attempt to strangle him, possibly after some kind of tussle, as there was bruising to the victim's face and also to his knuckles, suggesting an exchange of blows. The bruising and marks on the throat were more serious and pointed to a pressure severe enough to make Gilcrist lose consciousness. Water and mud in the throat and lungs suggested that he had fallen face down at the edge of the river whilst still breathing; fibres of vegetation, sedges and reeds, had been discovered between the front teeth, evidently forced there. In Rapton's estimation the murderer had stood on the victim's head to keep it below water level. The serious injury to the back of the head had, Rapton thought, resulted from a blow with a rock, tiny fragments of which were embedded in the skull, which had been fractured. Rapton could not say definitely whether Gilcrist had still been alive when the blow had been administered but thought it likely. For his age, fifty-four, Gilcrist had been a strong, healthy man even though his liver showed signs of damage caused by heavy drinking. On the night of his death he had consumed only a moderate amount of alcohol, though it was enough to put him well above the legal limit for driving.

Haine's team found the scene of the crime and the rock, a small round sandstone boulder, very quickly. Gilcrist had met his death some five hundred yards north of the Crossbow at a point about a hundred and fifty yards south of the cottage, Rampsons. Trampled grass and nettles, in a clump of which

35

the stone was discovered, and a small area of crushed reeds told their own story. But heavy rain later that night and the resulting rise in the level of the Avon had washed away any footprints, and indeed much of the mud where presumably Gilcrist's body had lain. Later that night the water had taken him away too and carried him downstream until the weir in the centre of Bath had arrested that progress.

As to the murder weapon, to which human hairs still adhered, it had fortunately been sheltered from the worst of the weather by the plants. Haine had immediately taken it to Sir Hugh. He had then ordered a wider search to be made of the area, to include the river (by divers) and the pastureland adjacent to the riverbank path. For Gilcrist, surely, had not blundered along here in the dark. He must have had a torch of some kind to light his way. Haine thought it likely that, as Sir Hugh had reported the murder victim not to be in a state that could be described as drunk at the time of his death, Gilcrist had been on his way back to the pub to buy whisky. There had been only empty bottles at the cottage. But where was Gilcrist's wallet? There had been no money on the body at all. Surely robbery had not been the reason for the killing.

A wide search during the rest of that day and continuing into the next – daylight hours being of course extremely short – revealed nothing but rather a lot of litter, two rusty horse-shoes, one small, the other larger, a broken lavatory pan, white, hosting about two and a half dozen hibernating snails, and a dead (very) hamster in a plastic bag. The DCI then interviewed Amanda Gilcrist again, spurred on by the thought that when a woman has a man other than her husband with her during that husband's murder then policemen have a duty to ask difficult questions. Blair Craxton indeed was her only alibi, as she was his.

Haine had spoken to the landlord of the Crossbow before, too, but there were several more things he wanted to know. He thought it sensible to call in there with Ingrams at lunchtime on Tuesday on their way to have a look at Craxton's antique shop and ask the owner even more difficult questions. For Haine did not believe either him or Mrs Gilcrist.

The landlord, Tim Brockenhurst, was an ex-Royal Marine

well over six feet in height whose French wife's excellent cooking had added considerably to his girth since his service days. He prided himself on running a very tidy establishment and there was never, ever, any trouble: miscreants of the young, noisy, male variety were likely to find themselves taking a cold bath in the canal, which was only fifteen feet from the leaded windows. There was a long pole kept handy to assist those who could not swim. Haine knew about this, of course, and had ordered muted warnings to be issued after a couple of complaints had been made. In truth, all those on the side of the angels were only too pleased that this charming country pub was not on their list of regular calls to prevent youths brawling.

The DCI had this at the back of his mind as he entered the saloon bar. He wanted to find out if the deceased had caused any trouble in the pub that night – those who over-indulge tending to get into arguments – and whether he had been seen with anyone.

Brockenhurst emerged through a doorway carrying an enormous, creaking basket of logs. He dumped it down near the inglenook fireplace, placed a few logs on the fire, his sausage-like fingers handling them with amazing delicacy, and then noticed that he had visitors, the room being otherwise empty.

'I take it this is business, gentlemen – or are you having lunch? It's venison and mushroom pie today as the chef's special.'

Haine had already decided that it would be business *and* lunch. He had been in his office very early that morning and other than a cup of canteen coffee – a beverage that one of the probationers had described as having a three star 'yuck' rating – had consumed nothing and was famished.

Brockenhurst took their order and it was decided that Haine would have salad with his, and Ingrams, chips. The landlord, asked about Gilcrist, said that as far as he knew he had always been on his own, had spoken to no one, had usually drunk about three doubles of whisky, which he took with water, and had definitely not got into any arguments that night. Aloof, in Brockenhurst's opinion.

The sergeant noted this down. He was enjoying working

for the DCI, even if one ignored the business of having a proper lunch. Usually he had to content himself with a snatched sandwich, with lots of greenery in it if Carrick had bought it for him. Carrick, he knew, was trying to make him lose weight, which was natural he supposed, the inspector being a rugby-playing fitness freak. This had paid off when suspects did a runner, for the man was like greased lightning on his feet and had an awesome line in tackles. But Ingrams could not concentrate when his insides were hollow and making growling noises and he was looking forward to his pie and chips with childlike glee. His wife's cooking could never be described as user-friendly.

Haine suddenly spoke, jerking him out of his reverie.

'The office of the film company's in East Street, near the theatre. As soon as we've finished in Bristol I intend to go there and talk to a few of Gilcrist's associates. They've been informed, of course.' He cleared his throat and spoke quietly. 'There's an angle to this that I don't like at all. Gilcrist's most famous production, as you probably know, was about the Fulton Bridge case up at Wemdale. A local hoodlum by the name of Jones was sent to prison for life for the murder of a little girl but released on appeal after Gilcrist showed that the evidence was shaky: the usual business of seemingly altered notes and statements and Jones's own allegation that a confession was thumped out of him. A CID sergeant by the name of Terrington resigned – on the grounds of ill-health.'

Ingrams, whose ears were tuned mostly to the rattle of plates in the kitchen, said, 'And you think he might have had it in for Gilcrist, sir?'

'The grapevine,' Haine whispered, 'has it that his temper was always on a pretty short fuse.'

'Yes, but it's not as though Gilcrist was in Terrington's back yard, is it? Terrington would have had to make a conscious decision to get on a train or whatever for quite a long journey. That would be more than just lashing out on impulse. And if Jones was stitched up then Terrington's boss must have been in on it – and probably *his* boss too.'

If this was intended to soothe Haine's fears it failed. He said, 'If we have to talk to Terrington – and it'll probably come to that – I'll do it with the utmost discretion. It would only take one newspaper reporter to . . .' It was really too ghastly to contemplate.

This train of thought was interrupted by Brockenhurst bringing their lunch. He had just placed their loaded plates before them when the door that led into the public bar opened and in walked James Carrick.

'Didn't realise you were here, sir, until Tim mentioned it,' he said blithely. 'May I join you?'

Somewhat grimly, they made room for him.

Carrick peered at what was on Ingrams' plate. 'That's just the sort of thing you shouldn't eat,' he said rudely. 'However, I'm starving – I think I'll have the same.' He got up and went into the other bar again, reappearing almost immediately with a pint tankard of beer.

'You don't look too bad,' Haine said grudgingly, eyeing the purple bruising and stitched cut on Carrick's forehead. 'But I hope that you're not jeopardising your recovery by gadding about.'

Carrick, who was endeavouring to forget that every bone in his body felt as though it had been unscrewed and put in again back to front, said, 'Not at all, sir. As a matter of fact I'm engaging in a little light detective work.'

Haine gave him a long, hard look but found no trace of insubordination or insolence.

Carrick went on, 'And I'm really glad I bumped into you. I don't know yet whether it throws any light on what happened to me on Friday night but Joanna Mackenzie found one of the buttons from my jacket at the top of Wood Lane where it meets the main road. And my skene-dhu's still missing.'

Two forkfuls of food came to a stop in mid-air.

'My skene-dhu,' Carrick said. 'The Gaelic for it is *sgian-dubh* if you're interested. It's the little knife you tuck into the top of your sock. I've been back to the place where the car went through the hedge – so has Joanna – and there's no sign of it. I also searched the car and asked the hospital if it had been found in the ambulance. No luck.'

With what he felt was admirable patience Haine said, 'And what do you think is the significance of the loss?'

'Well, it was there when I decided to go up to bed.'

39

Looking as thunderstruck as he felt, Ingrams burst out, 'You were wearing a *kilt*?'

'Of course. It was Burns Night,' Carrick replied, conveying that he was less than enchanted by the question.

'Was this skene-dhu valuable?' asked the DCI, still puzzled.

'It was my father's and his father's before that so I suppose it could be described as being of sentimental value. That's not really the point. Being old and not one of the shiny toys they give you in dress hire shops ...' He shrugged. 'The thing's a real weapon, small but pretty sharp.'

The Chief Inspector was still trying to get his thoughts in order. Carrick's father, he knew, had been drowned off the east coast of Scotland before his son's birth in what Haine had always assumed to have been a fishing boat accident. He rather felt that fishermen didn't wear kilts, not even on special occasions. Perhaps he was wrong. He said, not at all seriously, 'So you think someone might have attacked you with a view to stealing it?' and then had to give all his attention to his lunch when the chilly blue gaze came to rest on him.

'No, of course not,' Carrick said. 'I'm just trying to reconstruct what happened. I still can't remember anything. That and the button are just pieces of evidence, that's all.'

Haine sighed. 'James, look ... You have my support on this, believe me. When I first heard about it I admit I was very angry. But I understand that, sometimes, everyone ...' He tailed off as the blue eyes blazed with anger.

'Something *else* happened to me,' Carrick said. 'I've far more bruises than seems natural in the circumstances. And how the hell did my jacket button come to be at the top of the hill?'

'Someone could have found it farther down, at the scene of the accident, and then thrown it away again,' Haine said lightly. 'A child, perhaps, on its way to school.' He dissected a section of pie. 'As I said, James, you have my support. I'll sort something out somehow. But meanwhile I have a murderer to find. I was hoping that Brockenhurst would be able to throw a little light on Gilcrist but it seems that the man kept himself very much to himself while he was here.'

Carrick said, 'No, I don't suppose Tim would know about Gilcrist's girlfriends if he didn't bring them here – or to be more exact, the young woman he was having an affair with and might have intended to marry. Not that his wife was blameless with Blair Craxton practically living with her.' He thanked Brockenhurst, who had just come in with his lunch, waiting until he was out of earshot before resuming. 'Craxton's from a completely different background too. A public school education followed by a commission in the Guards. Now he's running an antique shop and dabbling in interior decoration. Stony broke too, by all accounts.'

'Who told you all this?' Haine demanded.

Carrick embarked hungrily on his meal. 'Mrs Gilcrist's daily help. A Mrs Ripley. I called at the Gilcrist's house on my way out here for a bite of lunch – she was the only person in.'

'Well?' Haine blared when nothing more seemed to be forthcoming.

Carrick dealt peaceably with his pie and chips for a few more moments and then said, 'According to Mrs Ripley the Gilcrists haven't been living as man and wife for some time – Gilcrist was spending most of the week at his office and in pubs in Bath and the weekends at the cottage. When they were filming he sometimes went away for weeks at a time. The young woman in his life is Leonora Kelso, a freelance researcher. Gilcrist brought her to the house once when his wife was on holiday. Mrs Ripley – who lives in Broadstoke, incidentally, and cleans the cottage too – sniffed meaning-fully at this point and referred to the lady in question as "being of the long legs and no knickers variety".'

'And the wife knows about her?' Haine asked eagerly. 'That's why there's been a rift between them?'

'Yes, that and for other reasons. He's had affairs in the past, too.'

'What about Craxton? How does he really fit into all this?'

'When they moved in to the house about four years ago Mrs Gilcrist bought several pieces of antique furniture from Craxton's shop in Clifton village, Bristol. He became a friend of the couple and on one occasion took them to a country house sale and bid for a few things for them. I presume the

41

close friendship with Mrs Gilcrist developed from there.'

'Did you get any names with regard to Gilcrist's previous affairs?'

'No, Mrs Ripley didn't know about those.'

'Any idea how she knows what she does?'

'They shouted at each other a lot, apparently, and didn't care who heard them.'

'It seems to me that Craxton and the woman might have acted together on this. Thank you, James. But there's no need for you to bother yourself with it any further – you're still not well. And don't worry about Friday night, I'll fix it.'

Woodenly, Carrick said, 'There were people drinking in one of the lounges who invited me to join them. I refused. I can remember refusing and leaving the room.'

'You could have dreamed you did, sir,' Ingrams said, without thinking.

Turning to Haine, Carrick said, 'One thing, sir. Before I officially return to work perhaps you'd be so good as to arrange a new assistant for me. I can't work with people who have no faith in me.' And with that he got up from the table, collected his plate and tankard and returned to the other bar.

'That was stupid and tactless of you, Ingrams,' Haine hissed. 'I tend to agree with you in principle but one of the most useful attainments of a good CID sergeant is to know when to keep his mouth *shut*.'

That he too could be included in Carrick's *cri de coeur* quite escaped him.

Sir Hugh Rapton gazed down at the still form on the mortuary table before him. He beheld a man aged thirty, six feet one and a half inches in height, weighing slightly over twelve stone. The body was wiry, with a faded tan, and gave every indication of a good healthy lifestyle.

There was plenty of bruising, on the torso in particular, and Rapton already knew that there were two cracked ribs. The arms were marked with bruises and light lacerations and grazing. The worst injury was to the head, a gash on the brow about an inch long that had been skilfully stitched and was almost hidden by a lock of the thick blond hair. The most intriguing injury, as far as he was concerned, was a severe bruise to one side of the neck.

He picked up a scalpel and touched it lightly against the breastbone. Instantly, the eyes, which were blue, focused on him.

Rapton chuckled. 'You know, you're the first customer I've ever had with goosepimples.'

'I hope the cover's on that thing,' Carrick said.

Still smiling broadly, the Professor of Forensic Science laid it aside. 'Most certainly, laddie. It's that sharp even its own weight would fillet a kipper.' He sighed. 'I'm disappointed though. It's such a shame to stop now.'

Carrick sat up. 'I'll go and find you a kipper.'

'I've not finished yet. Turn over. So you'd been to a Burns Supper?'

The corpse grunted.

'Drunk a few drams, no doubt?'

Carrick smiled into his sweater, having been permitted to use it as a pillow. 'Not too drunk to remember "Tam O'Shanter".'

Sir Hugh prodded carefully, eliciting a muffled groan. 'I know what you mean. That would probably mean a couple of glasses of wine with the meal plus one or two small drams afterwards. Sufficient to put you over the limit as far as driving's concerned but just enough to oil the wheels of the brain so your recitation went with a swing.'

'Precisely,' Carrick mumbled.

'And after that you stripped the willow until bedtime. Then you remember nothing?'

'Nothing.'

'Amnesia. It happens all the time. It'll almost certainly return to you eventually.'

'By which time I'll be pounding the beat.'

'Ach! Get your clothes on. You'll live yet.' He watched as Carrick went over to where his clothes were piled on a chair. Rapton always looked well groomed, but he was looking particularly elegant this evening, since he was attired in evening dress, ready for a dinner engagement. A close friend of John Butler, currently simmering at home in plaster, he had agreed to the odd request with alacrity. So here was a man who had been involved in a car accident but who seemed to have bruises in all the wrong places.

'I can't make this into anything official, you understand,' Rapton said, very businesslike now. 'There's no existing procedure for it.'

'No,' Carrick replied, pausing in buttoning his shirt. 'And I'm most grateful, Sir Hugh, for your time and trouble.'

'You might not thank me when you are walking the beat.'

'So you think I had some kind of rush of blood to the head and forgot what —'

'No,' the other interrupted. 'But proving it will be the difficult part. What I think is that you were set upon in some way. Are you right-handed?'

'Yes.'

'There are the sort of bruises on your right hand, on the knuckles, that I've seen on murder victims who have tried to defend themselves. Not only that, I think someone fetched you a crack across the side of the neck with something hard. Not his hand, unless he was a martial arts expert; something with a hard narrow edge to it along the lines of a cricket bat. You'd have fainted from the pain of it if it hadn't rendered you senseless.'

Carrick had sat on the chair.

'Well, you're the policeman so you must solve the problem,' Sir Hugh continued. 'But it seems to me that you must have gone to your car, otherwise whoever else was involved wouldn't have known which was yours. Unless of course they knew you very well indeed. Any godfathers present?'

'No, *they're* all Sassenachs.'

Rapton laughed. 'And colleagues?' he asked blandly.

Carrick looked up from putting on his shoes. 'You mean I might have been stitched up by someone on the job?'

'It's happened before.'

'I don't think anyone hates me that much.'

'What puzzles me is that no one seems to have seen what happened. Surely, after a do like that there would be any number of people milling about.'

'The car park is actually L-shaped with a small area at one end that you approach through a narrow neck planted with shrubs. I'd parked in there but can't remember anything about other vehicles.'

'How many cars can you park in this small area?'

'About eight – perhaps ten. I didn't take much notice.'

'It might pay you to go back. Wander around. Try to recreate that evening in your mind. Talk to people who were there and who you know saw *you*.' He took his evening jacket from a peg in a cupboard. 'And if you wish I can have a word with Chief Inspector Haine – if you think it would do any good. I'm ninety percent sure that the bruise on your neck isn't there as a result of the car going through the hedge. I don't think it can have been going at any speed, either, otherwise it would have turned over.'

Carrick prepared to leave. 'Perhaps I'd better find a little more evidence first.' He held out his hand. 'Thank you, sir. I'm indebted to you.'

'Can I give you a lift anywhere?'

'No, but thanks. A friend brought me over.'

'I hope you're going to have a few more days in which to recover.'

'It probably depends on how many more people go down with flu,' Carrick replied with a wry smile. 'And how Haine progresses with the Gilcrist case.'

'I performed the PM. Someone must have hated *him*. When strangulation and drowning failed they smashed his head in with a rock. So you're likely as not looking for someone weaker than the victim. Otherwise they'd have made a better job of it.'

They parted and Rapton left for his college dinner. He paused for a moment, on his way to his car, to wave as Carrick got into the vehicle waiting for him. The interior light illuminated the driver, a red-haired girl. Ah, so that was the one-time CID sergeant whom that old gossip Butler had mentioned. Sir Hugh hoped that she properly appreciated a man who could recite 'Tam O'Shanter' from memory.

Chapter Five

Blair Craxton's antique shop was exactly the kind of establishment that Ingrams had expected. It was situated on the unfashionable side of Clifton at a junction of two roads where the houses, terraced and once genteel, had been split up into flats and any number of bedsitters. Flanked by a shabby-looking Italian restaurant on one side and a newsagent on the other, the shop's window held merely a marble-topped washstand with a ewer and basin set on it and a long, red, draped velvet curtain. Ingrams stared at the chinaware for a moment before he followed Haine inside. He wanted to learn about such things; there was an inner, burning, secret desire to acquaint himself with all the aspects of life that a solid working-class background had denied him in his youth. In his view it was a *good* policeman who could sort the chaff from the wheat, whether that happened to be people or inanimate objects: the guilty from the innocent, forgeries from the genuine.

He sniffed dismissively. He was sure that the ewer and basin were modern reproductions.

The interior filled him with even more suspicion. This was not to say that Craxton was passing off the small carved lamps with brightly coloured silk shades as antiques. Nor even telling people that the Chinese dragons made of what looked like plaster and crudely painted in sploshy gold with green eyes and lurid crimson tongues were artefacts dug from an ancient tomb. But there were far too many of them. Somewhere in downtown Hong Kong there must be a shack housing modern-day slaves who turned out millions of the ugly things to be sold at a vast profit for their employers. And old ladies in Guildford thought they had bought something exotic. Perhaps they had, he reasoned; perhaps a foreign sweatshop was exotic enough for some.

To be fair there were better things on offer and he mooched about the shop, one ear cocked for what Haine, very much on edge after another phone call from the Super, was saying. Yes, that little table with patterns on the top made from different woods was rather attractive. His wife would like that. The stuffed owl in the glass case would give her the horrors, though – she wasn't too keen on birds.

Unaccountably, Ingrams found himself thinking about Carrick. He was still smarting about what Carrick had said in the Crossbow and there was the real worry that Haine would act on the request. Not now, perhaps, when the DCI was so put out about his subordinate's escapade, but later. The Scot was stubborn enough to refuse to work with him and that wouldn't look too good on his *own* record.

'I don't see what it has to do with the police how business is going,' Craxton was saying.

'I'm just interested to know, sir,' Haine replied, deliberately polite.

'Well – I can't say that it's all that special but times are still tough, you know, and –'

'So in other words it's bad.'

'Slow,' Craxon replied defiantly.

'Had Mr Gilcrist departed for the cottage when you arrived on the Friday?'

'I'm not sure that he'd even been home.'

'Did he know that you'd be spending the weekend at his house?'

'I've no idea.'

'You don't think Mrs Gilcrist would have mentioned it then?' Haine asked silkily.

'God knows. Why don't you ask her?'

'I intend to. Did you go out?'

'No.'

'Not even for a walk?'

'No. Amanda didn't feel like doing anything. She was a bit under the weather actually.'

'Oh. Why was that, do you think?'

'I don't know. She just was. People don't always feel a hundred percent, do they?'

'The Gilcrists are getting divorced, I understand. Was that a result of Mrs Gilcrist having men friends in the house when her husband was away?'

'No, of course not. You've got everything wrong about last weekend. For all I knew Marvin would be there. Sometimes he was and sometimes he went off to the cottage to work. He was that sort of person and if anyone minded it was their own tough luck. But things have been difficult lately and Marvin has been using the cottage as a bolt hole. Until recently they tended to have friends around all the time – neither of them wanted to be rattling around in that big house by themselves. Not unless Marvin needed some peace and quiet to work. It was unusual for Larne not to be there but –'

'That's Larne Painswick? I was told he was a freelance researcher.'

'Yes.'

'What about Leonora Kelso? She's employed on the same basis.'

'I've never heard of her.'

'Please continue with what you were saying.'

'Oh. Yes, that's right, Larne. He went to Torquay for the weekend. To see an aunt or something like that. And, as I was saying, he would usually have been there for dinner on the Saturday. This weekend it was just Amanda and me.'

'Are you having an affair with Mrs Gilcrist, sir?'

'No, I'm not.'

Ingrams still didn't believe him. The voices droned on.

Brockenhurst hadn't been able to tell them anything really useful either. He had never engaged in conversation with Gilcrist, the man making it plain he had no wish to talk, and could offer no explanation as to why Gilcrist, having been given a lift back to his cottage, should apparently set off again from home back in the direction of the Crossbow. The local farmer's son who had taken him to Rampsons that night had been interviewed by the police. Haine had talked to him again on the way to Bristol, and he had been virtually eliminated from the inquiry. He insisted that he had no idea who

Gilcrist was, even though he had seen him in the Crossbow on several occasions, and that he'd dropped him outside the cottage without incident, not a word having been exchanged between them. There was a witness to their parting: the organist from the parish church, who had been returning from practice on foot. He knew Gilcrist's Good Samaritan well and was also given a lift to his home, back in the direction of the pub. The organist had actually noticed Gilcrist blundering in through the cottage's front door. There had been no lights on within and no other vehicles parked outside. The scene-of-crime unit had found no tracks of vehicles other than Gilcrist's in the overgrown driveway and although there were plenty of fingerprints within the cottage they were mostly smeared and useless, only Gilcrist's and those of Mrs Ripley, the cleaner, distinguishable.

'Who says she only ever went there on Monday afternoons,' Ingrams muttered to himself, having been sent to talk to her in the light of Carrick's revelations while Haine had interviewed the farmer's son. Mrs Ripley had gone on to say, in the monotonous, grumbling tone that seemed to be her normal manner of address, that Rampsons was always a pigsty, whatever she did to it on Mondays. Gilcrist had been the messiest individual she had ever come across. Ingrams didn't believe her; he had an idea she'd done the bare minimum as far as cleaning was concerned. Certainly her own house was nothing to be proud of.

'So you didn't really like him?' Ingrams had asked.

A thin-lipped, pale woman in her fifties, Mrs Ripley had drawn herself up to her somewhat modest height and said, 'It wasn't my place to like or dislike him. And someone hated him, didn't they? Really hated him. Perhaps you'd better go and find them instead of bothering me when I'm cooking.'

Sour-faced old bag, Ingrams had thought, leaving. But she was right, someone had hated Gilcrist enough to half-strangle him, half-drown him and then smash his head in with a rock. The photograph that Gilcrist's wife had given them hinted at why he might have inspired such loathing. It depicted an arrogant face with a hooked nose, the mouth set in an amused and superior smile: the sort of man who would have treated a CID sergeant exactly the same way as Craxton did. Like dirt.

49

'I quite liked those little lamps,' Haine said when they were outside. 'Made over a hundred years ago, you know.'

It occurred to Ingrams that Carrick, who was interested in antiques and occasionally bought things at auction, might not have agreed.

Carrick had regretted his lunchtime sortie and had returned to his flat with a thumping headache. He had dropped into an armchair and fallen asleep immediately. When he was awakened by the phone ringing he floundered out of a nightmare in which he was being chased around the garden of a country house at night by men waving cricket bats with whirling metal blades attached to them.

'Sorry, were you in bed?' Joanna said in response to the grunt in her ear.

Another grunt.

'Look, it might not be relevant but can you remember anything about a Graeme Campbell on Friday night?'

'Graeme? Yes, he was there. He usually is. Why?'

There was a polite silence on the other end of the line that told him that more was expected of a police inspector.

'Yes,' Carrick said, after due thought. 'He was one of the people drinking in the Appin Lounge who asked me to join them.'

'Well, I know you declined and went up to bed because the receptionist heard you say goodnight and saw you go up the stairs.'

'That's great,' Carrick whispered. 'Thank you.'

'But you must have come down again, mustn't you? Unless someone followed you and hauled you down the fire escape. The girl also said that Campbell was taken home by his sons because he was getting a trifle troublesome. I was working along the lines of you hearing a bit of shouting and going down to see what was the matter. But apparently your room was at the rear of the hotel so you wouldn't have heard anything.'

'Not unless the Campbells went round the side of the building. But I'm afraid this doesn't ring any bills with me at all.'

'Do you know him well?'

'Not really. He used to be in Bath a lot on business but now he's bought himself a house in the locality and runs his small company from home.'

'I was wondering if it would be worth your while going to see him and asking if he remembers seeing you and if anything odd happened when he was leaving that night.'

Carrick had woken up properly now and so had his headache. 'From what I know of Graeme getting drunk he makes rather a good job of it. That's why I didn't want to get involved.'

'James, it can't do any *harm.*'

'No, I suppose not,' he agreed. 'I've wheels now – my insurance company's arranged the hire of a car.'

'I happen to know you're not supposed to drive. Shall I take you?'

'No, it's okay. It's not far – he lives at Hinton Littlemoor.'

Carrick knew exactly where Hinton Grange was situated as he had been to the house before when it had been the home of the Chief Constable, Sir Eric Framley. Framley was now retired and had bought a riverside cottage near Fowey in Cornwall. Upon his retirement there had been a party. He was a popular man and always keen to raise money for charity, so he'd decided that invitations would be on a lottery basis, tickets priced at a minimum of one pound each. So it was that the rawest probations had found themselves rubbing shoulders with Chief Superintendents, the large lady who served behind the counter in the canteen at Manvers Street had told Lady Framley all about her gall bladder operation and a police charity had benefited by several thousand pounds.

Some four miles south east of Bath, Hinton Littlemoor was a picture-postcard village: thatched cottages with neat gardens bounded by hedges of rosemary and box, the winding main street overshadowed by enormous ancient chestnut trees. The road curved around the church, St Michael's – which was of Saxon origin – the rectory and the Ring O'Bells public house and then swooped down to where a shallow ford crossed a river. Those who continued on this

51

journey found themselves in a maze of narrow lanes, mostly unnamed and unsignposted, that lost themselves in deepest Somerset.

On this, one of the last days of January, the village was wreathed in mist that hung in the valley like smoke. Above it, all was in bright sunshine where the slight warmth had lifted overnight frost, but here hoar frost clung to every branch and twig and when Carrick got out of his car the cold air went into his lungs like liquid ice.

Hinton Grange, which was reached by a private drive that had its entrance between the church and the pub next door, dated from the sixteenth century and was built of the local honey-coloured stone. But on this particular morning, drained of colour by the freezing mist, it looked merely grey.

All noises were deadened too. As Carrick walked to the front door, the crunching of his shoes on the gravel was somehow muffled. Not a bird twittered in the clipped beech hedge. It was as if the house had never been lived in. There was silence even when he pressed the bell push and he wondered whether it was working and if he should use the knocker instead. Then he heard footsteps approaching inside.

A woman wearing a checked nylon overall opened the door and gazed at him suspiciously. Campbell's daily, no doubt.

Carrick introduced himself. 'Is Mr Campbell in?'

'No, he's gone up to Scotland on business.'

'When are you expecting him back?'

'I really have no idea. He usually rings me when he's returning. There's nothing amiss, is there?'

'No, not at all. I'm just hoping he can help me on a private matter.'

'I can give you his son's number. Fraser, that is. He might know.' She hesitated. 'You'd best come in for a minute.' In the wide hallway she cleared a vacuum cleaner to one side and took a thin booklet from beneath a telephone on an oak chest. 'Have you got a bit of paper?'

Carrick wrote down the two numbers on the back of his cheque book. Both were in Scotland; one in Helensburgh, presumably Fraser's home number, the other belonging to a branch of a well-known Scottish estate agency. A further

52

enquiry confirmed that the woman was indeed Campbell's daily and that her name was Betty Smithers. He thanked her and turned to leave.

'Oh, by the way . . . when did Mr Campbell travel up to Scotland?'

'Well, it must have been Saturday morning because there was no one in when I called round for my wages. He usually says when he's off again but he must have forgotten this time.'

'Couldn't he have gone shopping?'

'But there was plenty of food in and I *thought* he'd said he was looking forward to a quiet weekend at home. Something must have cropped up.'

Carrick thanked her again and left. He was aware of doing these things automatically: speaking, writing and smiling almost as though it was someone else performing these actions. The real James Carrick, the one hidden beneath the seeming normality, could think only of the sheer horror of the gap that was now in his life, that short period of time when he had been oblivious of everything. Perhaps he *had* drunk more than was good for him and then gone for a late-night spin through the countryside. Perhaps he ought to resign.

Haine was still working on the theory that Gilcrist had been on his way on foot back to the Crossbow having forgotten to buy himself a bottle of whisky in the distraction of being given a lift home. This was perfectly possible; the Avon ran past the bottom of the small overgrown cottage garden and then over a natural rocky weir before flowing under the aqueduct near which the pub was situated. All someone on foot had to do was follow a well-beaten path along the riverbank and then climb some wooden steps set into the earth ramparts of the aqueduct itself. It was a much more pleasant walk than along the road, which had no pavements or lights despite the often heavy traffic.

The site of the murder, still cordoned off, was hidden from view both from the top of the aqueduct, along which a path ran on both sides, and from the road. This was due to thick clumps of alders and willows – as good a place as any, Haine thought, to lie in wait for someone. But how had anyone

53

known where Gilcrist would be? There were still no clues as to whether the murderer had followed Gilcrist or met him at the spot, all footprints having been obliterated by the rain.

Only empty bottles had been found at the cottage, quite a few of them. Several used glasses had been found in various parts of the building, all with the victim's fingerprints on them. Very little food was in the kitchen cupboards and refrigerator – just a few bread rolls, a couple of tins of soup, milk, tea and coffee. Sausage wrappers had been found in the dustbin, together with a plastic package that had held smoked salmon, and there had been the remains of crisp packets in the ashes in the fireplace. Tim Brockenhurst had said that very occasionally he had known Gilcrist to have a bar snack. So that must have been what the man had lived on at weekends – snacks.

Followed by Ingrams, Haine prowled along the riverbank, his hands rammed into his trouser pockets. It was impossible to tell if anything had been stolen from Rampsons – he was thinking along the lines of papers connected with Gilcrist's work – as sheaves of notes in Gilcrist's untidy handwriting had been strewn everywhere. None of the little they had been able to read had made much sense. And until he could talk to Larne Painswick, delayed from his weekend in the West Country by a problem with his car but due to arrive in an hour or so, he could not discover what Gilcrist had been working on. If indeed, he mused gloomily, it was even relevant.

Startling Ingrams from an unaccustomed reverie, Haine suddenly said, 'What day is it?'

'Wednesday, sir.'

'Good God! I'm supposed to be catching the one-thirty train to Birmingham for the confounded Law and Order Conference. I'd forgotten all about it. There's no getting out of it either – now that Hadley's ill there'll be no one from Avon and Somerset there if I don't go and the Super would never forgive me.' He strode off back in the direction of where they had left the car, Ingrams having to run in order to catch up. 'Find out if Inspector Carrick's fit to resume duty. Damn it, this couldn't have come at a worse time. And you'll have to talk to Painswick. Make sure he really went to

54

wherever he said he's been. And ask Carrick to do a little *quiet* checking on that poor sod Terrington whom Gilcrist steamrollered in his film about the Jones case. He is *not* to go dashing off up north raising hell. Tell him not to go upsetting anyone senior up there.'

Ingrams knew that even if he had time to sit down and think about it he wouldn't be able to put the instructions into tactful words. His heart sank; the next few days were not going to be happy ones.

As it happened when Ingrams tried to phone Carrick he was out and before he could really start tracking him down Larne Painswick arrived.

'This is the most appalling shock to me,' said Painswick when he had seated himself. 'Amanda rang me with the news and then I got stuck in Exeter for most of Monday and yesterday while someone fixed the car. Trouble is it's a Morgan and I had a hell of a job getting spare parts.'

'So Mrs Gilcrist knew where you were?' Ingrams said, closing the door of the interview room and pulling up a chair.

'Yes, it's company policy for people to be easily contactable. I'd rung her and told her where I was staying. But what the hell's this about Marvin? He's *dead*?'

'Murdered,' Ingrams said, sitting down and subjecting Painswick to a look that he hoped was as effective as the gimlet-eyed stare Carrick gave those he was interviewing. 'Where do you live, sir?'

'I've a pied-à-terre in Walcot Street, just a cubbyhole really. Perhaps I ought to explain further. I used to live with the aunt I visited over the weekend. She brought me up when my parents were killed in a plane crash when I was five years old. She's in her eighties now and her health isn't too good, so she sold her house and we found her a place in a really good nursing home in Torquay. It's a beautiful place set in large grounds and she's very happy there. I got this small flat and I've bought a cottage at Bathford to restore in my spare time. So I sort of commute between the office, a cupboard and a ruin.'

Despite his avowal of being deeply shocked Painswick appeared composed enough. He was about thirty years old but possessed the gravity of someone older. Not that he had a dismal manner, far from it, Gilcrist's death notwithstanding. Nevertheless he had himself very much under control and Ingrams felt that the brown eyes were summing him up carefully whilst no clues as to his own inner feelings were permitted to show.

Ingrams said, 'Did you buy the cottage so you could be nearer to the Gilcrists?'

Painswick looked surprised. 'No. But they had invited me to their place a couple of times and I fell in love with the area. The cottage was advertised in the paper and was going cheap due to the condition it's in. So I bought it.'

'Did you ever go with Mr Gilcrist to Rampsons?'

'No. He didn't like being interrupted when he was writing and thinking things over. I'm freelance but Marvin always called on me – I've worked for him for years.'

'Perhaps you'll give me an account of your movements over the weekend.'

Painswick grimaced. 'Yes, well I suppose everyone who knew him is a suspect until proved otherwise. Let me see . . . I left Bath at about three-thirty on Friday afternoon – you beat the rush if you get away early enough – and arrived in Torquay at about seven. I'd taken my time and had a bite to eat in Honiton to avoid the rush hour in Exeter. I went straight to the hotel – the Ardley, I quite often stay there – unpacked, had a shower then a quick drink in the bar and went out for a meal. It was too late by then to visit my aunt that day – I hadn't planned to, anyway – so I had another couple of drinks in the bar and went to bed. On the Saturday morning I had a bit of a lie-in, until eight-thirty – that's late for me as I'm an early riser – and then had breakfast. I had a bit of shopping to do, some flowers and chocolates for my aunt and a couple of shirts for me from a very good little tailor's I know. After that I went along to the nursing home.'

'Your aunt was expecting you?'

'Oh, yes. You can't just drop in on the old, you know. If she expects me she has her hair done and puts on one of her best dresses. She likes to make an occasion of it. Poor old lady doesn't get many visitors now that most of her friends are dead.'

'Are you her only surviving relative?'

'There's a sister in the States, but she's over ninety. Where was I? Oh yes. I stayed to lunch, which we had in her room, and I left at about two as I know she has a nap in the afternoons. Then I got in the car and drove out to Dartmoor for the afternoon. I'd taken my boots and went for a five-mile hike.'

To Ingrams this seemed a very staid sort of weekend. And wasn't Painswick just a mite too doting on his aunt? If he wanted an alibi, however . . . He noted down the rest of it: Painswick had gone to a film theatre in the evening to see a Russian film with English subtitles and then had an Indian meal. On the Sunday morning he had attended church – 'St Hubert's still uses the old prayer book, you know, and the music's always excellent' – before calling to have coffee with his aunt. After lunch he had driven to Plymouth to look at a couple of locations – business, rather than pleasure. The weather had been bad.

The sergeant stifled a yawn. Gilcrist had been killed on the Saturday night, the pathologist was certain about it. Later that night and through the early hours of the following morning it had rained heavily and the river had risen sufficiently to carry the body downstream. He questioned Painswick again about that night but the man stuck to his story and gave him the address and phone number of the Ardley Hotel and the name of the Indian restaurant where he had eaten. He still had the ticket stub for the cinema in his pocket.

On the Monday, early, Painswick had set off home only to break down on the outskirts of Exeter. He had been forced to stay in an hotel until today, Wednesday morning, while a new distributor was fitted to his car.

'So it was the hotel in Exeter where you learned of Gilcrist's death,' Ingrams said.

'Yes. Sorry, I should have made that clear. I phoned Amanda as soon as I checked in and she rang me back with the news as soon as the police had left the house. She didn't really believe it just then – she hadn't been to identify him or anything at that stage.'

'Did you like him?'

'Not particularly. But he was all right to work for.'

57

'Isn't that a bit of a contradiction in terms?'

'Not at all. I didn't care for him as a *person* but he was very good at his job. Working for him will stand me in good stead as he was highly regarded in the industry. I know that sounds mercenary but I can assure you, sergeant, that the TV world is a cut-throat sort of environment.'

'So would you say he had many enemies?'

'Oh, probably hundreds. But he didn't care a damn.'

Ingrams was not to be sidetracked. 'And yet you met with the Gilcrists on a social basis. You bought a house nearby.'

'It's not that close – about six miles away, actually. And you must understand that both Amanda and Marvin are sociable people – at least Marvin was when he wasn't working. I think I felt sorry for Amanda really – she doesn't have a happy life.'

'Do you know Blair Craxton?'

'Lord, yes.'

'He was at the house when Chief Inspector Haine and I went to break the news to Mrs Gilcrist.'

'That would figure. I think she used to ring him as soon as Marvin had gone to the cottage. For one thing she hates being on her own. She's been like that ever since the house was burgled a couple of years ago.'

Ingrams made a note of that. You never knew . . .

'Are they having an affair?'

'I thought you'd have realised that. Yes, Amanda sort of collects men.'

'Did he mind?'

'Marvin? He was too busy to mind.'

'Would you include yourself in Mrs Gilcrist's – er – collection?'

'No.'

'No?'

'No. I don't make a habit of making love to other men's wives.'

'Tell me why you didn't like Gilcrist.'

'It's to do with what I've just said. He was too busy for almost anything. Too busy to be polite, to worry about other people's feelings, to buy his staff a round of drinks or remember his wife's birthday. And frankly, seeing as you ask, he was the sort of man who would almost literally kick out of the way those whom he regarded as excess baggage.'

Painswick's eyes were glittering with anger as he spoke.

Chapter Six

'I've been thinking about your car keys,' Joanna said. She had called round to Carrick's flat to find him on the point of going out.

'What about them?'

'Did you have them with you during Friday evening?'

'No. If you keep things like keys, or loose change, in a sporran while you're dancing, they jangle around.'

'That's what I thought. So when you came down from your room you must have taken them with you or you wouldn't have been able to start the car – or someone else wouldn't.' She glanced at him sideways. 'That suggests to me that you went to the car to fetch something you'd forgotten.'

'Damned if I know what,' Carrick answered gloomily. 'Everything I needed was in my suitcase.'

'And you still can't remember anything?'

Carrick shut his eyes for a moment. 'No.'

'Is it possible that you noticed your keys weren't in your room and you went down to see if you'd left them in the car?'

'I tend to be a bit careful about things like that. Anyway, you need the keys to set the alarm.'

'It's interesting though, isn't it? What Rapton said, I mean. That someone might have hit you with some kind of blunt instrument.'

'It's also possible that I tripped over something and clouted myself on the car.'

'That's silly. From what I've seen of that bruise the blow would have rendered you quite unfit to drive.'

'It's only conjecture on his part. Haine will say that it

60

happened when the vehicle went through the hedge.'

Joanna realised that there was no point in continuing this line of conversation while he was in such a negative mood. 'It's a shame that Graeme Crawford's gone to Scotland.'

'He must have a good cure for hangovers – he was totally plastered when I last saw him.'

'Can I drop you off anywhere?' Joanna asked, eyeing his working shirt.

'At the nick, if you wouldn't mind.'

'James, you're not going back to work!'

'I have to. Haine had forgotten all about a conference and has shot off to Birmingham. Everyone's going down with the flu so the walking wounded have been called in. I'll be okay though. Ingrams can do all the driving.'

'What do you want me to do now?'

He smiled. 'Just like old times, eh? Nothing, thanks – not at the moment.'

She made him promise that he was to call her as soon as there were any developments, then took him down into the city. As Manvers Street, Bath, is the last place on Earth where you can stop a car long enough to whisper sweet nothings to your front seat passenger, she had to be content with a swift peck on the cheek. Waiting for a gap in the traffic she spared a glance in his direction as he went into the building: a pale, earnest figure doing a very good job of not looking as though he hurt all over.

'This Painswick character strikes me as odd,' Ingrams said, consulting the copious notes he had made during the interview.

'In a nutshell, why?' Carrick asked.

'He seems too good to be true, that's all. Went to see his old aunt, goes to church, enjoys long walks on his own. I asked just as he was leaving if he had a girlfriend down in Torquay, if he met anyone there and – well, you know, invited them back to his hotel. He said no. Seemed shocked that I should suggest such a thing.'

'So where is he now?'

'Gone to the cottage he's bought at Bathford to get on with some DIY – so he said.'

61

'Was he upset about Gilcrist's death?'

'No, not very.'

Carrick held out a hand for the notebook, murmuring moments later, 'Your bloody handwriting. As though a tipsy hamster with ink on its paws ran all over the paper. So was Gilcrist seeing other women? Besides Leonora Kelso?'

'Don't know, guv. I forgot to ask him. But according to him Gilcrist didn't have time for anyone.'

'Most blokes find time for *that*,' Carrick said and there was a short silence – a disapproving one, Ingrams thought – while he read. 'I'll go and see him,' he announced, flatly.

The phone rang and Carrick snatched it up. He listened briefly and then promised to ring back the caller in five minutes.

'*You* go and see Painswick,' he said. 'Ask him about Gilcrist and this Kelso woman, and see if he knows about any other women in Gilcrist's life. Lean on him a bit. Ask him what size shoes he takes, whether he's left- or right-handed and have a look at his car. Make it sound as though we've some evidence in connection with those things. And I want the name of his auntie and where she's staying.'

'That's over the page, guv. She's a Mrs Baxter, his mother's sister. The nursing home's address is there too.'

'Good,' Carrick said, flipping over the page. 'Oh, and take a good look at the cottage while you're there. Yes, I know he's just bought it and it's in a bit of a mess. Look at it from the point of view of what he told you and make up your mind if his lifestyle fits what he led you to believe. I mean, if there are big piles of porn magazines and books on black magic we won't be so keen to go along with the prayer book and church music story, will we? Use your *eyes*.' Instead of prejudices and preconceived ideas, he almost added. 'Then go and see Amanda Gilcrist. Ask her if she knows of any bust-ups her husband had with anyone recently. Then check with the SOCOs to see if they've come up with anything new.'

'And where will you be if I want you, sir?' Ingrams asked stolidly, assuming that Carrick was going home and to bed.

'Here. For a while anyway. That was Alan Terrington on the phone – the ex-copper who was taken to the cleaners by Gilcrist.'

'Inspector Haine –' Ingrams began.

'I know. He doesn't want me to upset Dalesland Police. I'm not even going to approach them. I'm going to persuade Terrington to come here so we can talk.'

'I think I'd have it in for some poncey film producer who dug dirt on me.'

'I'll forget you said that,' Carrick said tersely. 'What you must remember is that Gilcrist was *right*.'

Ingrams went away. He wasn't feeling too good.

Carrick had no trouble in talking Alan Terrington into coming to see him, Terrington not being in the least inclined to discuss the subject over the phone. He said he had read about the film producer's death in the paper and, as he put it, 'wanted to put the record straight'. He didn't 'want people coming looking for *him*' – there had been enough of that in the past.

For a long time after this Carrick sat reading all the evidence that had been collated so far about the Gilcrist murder. All the staff at Gilcrist Productions, as the company was rather unenterprisingly called, had been interviewed, with the exception of Leonora Kelso who was on leave and not at home either, and nothing any of them had said was of much help. They were not in the habit of seeing Gilcrist socially during their spare time or at weekends, except for Painswick, whom of course Carrick knew about. They had all provided accounts of their movements over the weekend and other than one sound assistant who had admitted not seeing a soul, having spent most of the time asleep, all had been in the company of other people who could vouch for them.

'Which can all be gone into in more depth if necessary,' Carrick muttered, tossing the fat file to one side. At six-thirty he left a message for Ingrams that he could be contacted at his flat and caught a taxi home.

Joanna, to whom he had given a key some time ago, was in the living room watching the TV news. She was wearing an outfit he had bought for her birthday, a softly draped dark blue velvet top and matching trousers.

'Have you anything on under that?' Carrick asked lightly.

She turned off the television and came over. 'Of course.'

'Pity.'

She grinned. 'I'd hardly set out to seduce you when you're

not very well.'

He put his arms around her and pulled her close. 'Not up to it, eh?'

'James, that statement has rather unfortunate nuances of meaning.'

'Don't go all schoolmarm on me, Miss Mackenzie,' he whispered into her ear with a chuckle, his hands roaming beneath the soft material. Small lacy undergarments were twitched aside, Joanna marvelling, as always, when all her clothes lay on the floor seemingly moments later, at his pure genius in undressing her without any real pause in the proceedings. Not to mention himself: one moment dressed, the next naked and lifting her astride his hips, heaven commencing.

'He's got *what*?' Carrick barked into the phone at seven-forty the next morning.

'Mumps, sir,' said Sergeant Woods. 'His wife reckons he caught it off the kids.'

Carrick groaned, thanked him and rang off. Then he dialled Joanna's number.

'Ingrams has the mumps,' he said without preamble when she answered.

'That can be quite nasty for adults.'

'Really?' Carrick contendedly pictured all sorts of gruesome and excruciatingly painful complications that might beset his sergeant but kept them to himself, saying instead, 'I was wondering, if you haven't much on at work, whether you'd take a drive out to Hinton Littlemoor and ask if neighbours heard anything of the Campbells' return home on Friday. I've a funny feeling about them.'

'No problem.'

'It's a house called Hinton Grange and it's sort of tucked behind the church and rectory.'

Joanna had come across Carrick's 'funny feelings' when they worked together; once again she experienced that tingling sensation, as if the tiny hairs on the back of her neck were standing on end.

She called in at the office first. Since the death of Lance Tyler, her partner, and taking on Greg Perivale to assist her,

64

Joanna had made quite a few changes. For one thing, she didn't expect him to do all the donkey work.

'Had a call,' he said laconically, his mouth full with a large bite from a Sally Lunn, thickly buttered, that was on a plate before him. 'Sorry. Bloke with a strange squeaky voice who reckons his wife's having it away with the man over the road. Wants me to keep watch on her.'

'Name of Dobbs?'

Greg nodded.

'He's bananas. He isn't married at all, he has a crush on the woman across the street. Don't touch it. He's been warned off once before by the police but if he carries on pestering her he's in trouble. Just make a note of it in the day book.'

'It's really handy you having contact with the Bill,' Greg said with the smile he always wore when Carrick's name was in the air. It was his mild form of revenge for having to take orders from someone young enough to be his daughter.

'Well, I'm going to return a few favours to the Bill this morning,' Joanna told him. 'That's if pressure of work can stand it.'

'All we've got is a woman who's lost her labrador. I am to leave no stone unturned, she said. She thinks it's been stolen.'

'Try the park. They're nearly always there.'

'We're not really a lost dogs' home though, are we?' It was a sore point with a man who had spent his police career chasing criminals.

'Fifty quid is fifty quid,' Joanna said on her way out.

As with so many English villages these days – the school closed and converted into a 'desirable residence', the post office-cum-general store shuttered and up for sale, the cottages sold to incomers because the local people can no longer afford to buy them – Hinton Littlemoor was as quiet as if it were a Sunday, most of the residents away at work in cities. Joanna parked her car in the wide lay-by in front of the church and gazed around, enjoying the sunshine. Outside the Ring O'Bells a man shuffled along morosely, prodding at the pavement with a worn broom. Man and broom had more than a passing affinity. He acknowledged her greeting with the merest nod of his head, a picture of total exhaustion.

'Such a *lovely* place,' Joanna enthused. 'I suppose you

65

wouldn't know if any houses are for sale?'

'Can't say as I do,' muttered the man. He was actually the landlord of the Ring O'Bells and recovering from the all-pervading flu. His wife had sent him out to get some fresh air.

'I mean, I know how reluctant people are these days to have a board outside. Everyone knows your business then.'

He stopped sweeping and leaned on the broom. Dredging up some energy he said, 'They say there's a few bungalows going to be built on the railway station site.'

'I was hoping for a cottage. But nothing grand, not like a mansion or grange. Not that little places like this have such things.'

'We do that,' he retorted. 'Hinton Littlemoor ain't that small. The Grange is up that drive yonder. Behind the rectory. But it's not for sale.'

'Oh, I couldn't *possibly* afford a big house like that,' Joanna said with a horsey laugh. 'The upkeep of big houses is frightful. You have to be a millionaire at least.'

'Mr Campbell ain't no millionaire.' A triumphant smile appeared on the somewhat battered features. 'He told me hisself that he's always wanted an English country house. Ever since he was a lad. It's right strange that, seein' he comes from Scotland. He told me he likes the weather down here too – better for his rheumatics.'

Joanna nodded sagely. 'No doubt. But you'd think he'd miss the pipes and porridge and curling and all that.'

'Ah, but there's a society that he belongs to that had a dance last week. He came over here for a quick one before he left and what a grand sight he was in his kilt and so on. I allus thought that kind of thing was a bit sissy until I saw Mr Campbell that night. It makes yer suits and trousers seem real drab somehow.'

'Did his wife go too?'

'She's dead. It's just him and his two sons although neither of them live with him. I reckon' – and this with a leery wink – 'that he's looking for a lady to share that big house with him.'

'I expect he was pretty late getting home.'

'No doubt. Long after we'd shut up shop and gone to bed. I wasn't feeling up to much – had the dratted flu coming on.'

'So you didn't hear any skirling and hooting then,' Joanna

66

said with a broad smile.

'When I sleep it takes the Devil hisself to wake me.'

'Well, I hope he never does,' Joanna said.

The gates to the rectory drive were wide open and a builder's pick-up was parked about halfway down it. The sounds of hammering and sawing were coming faintly from the direction of the house. Joanna squeezed past the vehicle, for it had been parked slightly askew and the drive was not very wide, and walked up to the front door. She knocked and when no one came rang a bell she had not previously noticed but the racket within was presumably making it impossible for either to be heard. Never one to give up easily, Joanna went round the side of the house, wriggled by a skip almost filled with what looked like rotten floorboards and found herself in a medium-sized yard.

There was a garage, the doors of which were open to reveal the front end of a dark blue BMW, next to it an old stable and, glimpsed through a wide archway, a large garden. An extensive lawn bordered by trees and shrubs surrounded the house and here, at the rear, there was a fruit and vegetable garden. A man was forking over the soil.

Joanna ignored the fact that the back door was wide open and went across the grass towards him. He noticed her before she was halfway there and stopped work.

She introduced herself and then said, 'I'm looking for the rector. Do you know where he is?'

'Sure now,' said the man. 'Himself and his good lady are in Devon to see the new grandchild. It was a good time to go too with the builders knocking all hell out of the place.' Joanna's disappointment must have shown for he added, 'But if it's spiritual help you're after I've the phone number of the vicar at Wellow who's taking over while —'

'Oh, no,' Joanna interrupted. 'It's nothing like that. I'm on rather a strange errand really after something that happened to a police inspector friend of mine last Friday night.' When she had spoken she was not sure why she had come straight to the point but it might have been something to do with the keen way he was regarding her.

'Care to talk about it over a cup of coffee?' Without waiting for an answer he rammed the fork into the ground and set off towards the house. 'The name's Patrick.'

'I say, they won't mind, will they?' Joanna asked anxiously.

He chuckled. 'Not for a moment. I'm sort of looking after the place, you see, and making sure it's properly secured at night. The good lady said to make myself at home.' He turned to beam at her.

By the back door Patrick fastidiously brushed loose soil from his jeans and a dead leaf from his old army 'woolly-pully' and removed his boots. One of his socks had come off inside the boot and he placed the bare foot on the floor while he retrieved it. Joanna's gaze drifted momentarily in that direction and she was shocked to see that the foot was an artificial one, a very good replica as it happened, with proper 'toes' but the ankle joint constructed of stainless steel. She busied herself making sure that there was no mud on her own shoes in case he realised she had noticed.

'The kitchen's warmest,' Patrick announced, waving her in. 'I lit the Rayburn.' He shut the door that led into the hall and the sound of hammering was slightly muffled. 'Dry rot in the floor of the rector's study and under the cloakroom and creeping up the stairs. He's thanking the good Lord that the diocese is paying.'

'And the baby arrived right in the middle of it all, so to speak?'

'No. She was born early in October but was premature and so poorly that it wasn't thought she'd survive. But after weeks in an incubator she's now at home and everyone can breathe again. And the poor rector went all the way to Plymouth on the day she arrived to christen her because it wasn't thought she'd live the night.'

'How awful for the mother. I don't think I could cope with that.'

'Ah, she had plenty of support. And the rector John Gillard's such a good man that the Almighty always gives him an ear.'

Joanna glanced at the speaker to see if a joke was intended but he was solemnly spooning instant coffee into two mugs. She said, 'So no one was on the premises on Friday night?'

'Yes, I was. I'm sleeping here.'

'I suppose you didn't hear the Campbells next door come back from a do they'd been to?'

Patrick sat opposite to her at the kitchen table and pushed across a mug of coffee and a tin of biscuits. 'Suppose you tell me the whole story.'

Against her better judgement Joanna did. As before, it might have been because of his disconcerting grey eyes or even the easy smile that invited confidence. Whatever the reason, she recounted what had occurred with the thoroughness with which she would have made a verbal report, in her police days, to a Chief Superintendent.

He seemed to sense her worry that she had been indiscreet. 'This'll go no further than me, I can assure you of that. But I don't think I can be of much help. I didn't hear a thing on Friday night or early Saturday morning and I do tend to be a light sleeper. There's a pretty tall clump of trees between the two properties though.' His eyes lit up. 'There's also the possibility that Campbell wasn't in a position to make a fuss by that time.'

Joanna said, 'Yes, you're right. He could have been out for the count by then.' She was wondering what had happened to the Irish accent.

'I'm interested in Carrick's loss of memory. It'll return, I'm sure – I've had a bit of experience of that kind of thing. But you're right to be concerned because it might be years before it does. It might be worth trying to recreate the evening – take him back to the Crawford Hotel and sort of walk him through the time he was there.'

'Sir Hugh Rapton suggested that. But it would be very difficult seeing that we don't know what took place.'

'No, but we could find some staff who were on duty – or even play a tape of the sort of music he danced to.'

'You do believe him then?'

'Why not? Don't you?'

'Yes, of course but . . .'

'At the back of your mind there's the nasty sneaking thought that he's cooked up the memory loss story because of being drunk in charge of a car?'

'Not *consciously*. He couldn't. His integrity –'

Patrick butted in blithely. 'Integrity tends to inhabit the

subconscious too. More coffee?'

'No thanks, I've wasted enough of your time.' Joanna was bitterly regretting telling him everything, despite his assurances. In a small village like this it was madness.

'I can't really help you with Campbell either. We've only met once. He told me that his youngest son Bruce is in the Highlanders. He was a bit dismissive about Fraser, though. I've no idea why.'

'Perhaps because he works for an estate agent.'

Patrick looked thoughtful. 'I shouldn't have thought that was too much of a disgrace.' He paused, twirling his empty mug round and round on the table. '*Gossip* has it that he's a bit of a bastard. Fraser, that is.'

'And the source of that gossip?'

'Betty Smithers, Campbell senior's cleaning lady. She helps here too.'

'I might go and talk to her,' Joanna said, getting up to leave.

'Rosebank Cottage,' Patrick informed her serenely. 'That's down towards the ford on your right. You haven't said how you fit into all this.'

Well, he knew everything else. 'I used to be in his team,' Joanna said. 'Someone tipped off those in charge that we were more than just friendly and Carrick was married at the time. I'm a private investigator now.'

'Ah, that explains the mailed fist manner. Tell me, would you and the inspector who was undoubtedly worth throwing up a promising career for care to join me for a drink tonight?'

'At the Crawford Hotel you mean?'

'Why not?'

'I'll ring you here if for some reason James can't make it.'

He levered himself to his feet. 'That's if my back doesn't give out from gardening.' When she had gone he poured himself another mug of coffee and paced restlessly up and down the room. 'You're bored, Gillard,' he severely told his reflection in a small mirror on the kitchen door. 'Just because you've worked undercover for MI5 and your mother asked you to tidy up the fruit garden it doesn't mean that you have to go all out for an Oscar nomination.'

70

Chapter Seven

Carrick had decided to make up his own mind about Larne Painswick. Really, he had no choice as he could hardly trouble the stricken Ingrams and, anyway, had no desire to call upon the mumps-infested household as he had no idea whether he himself had had this particular malady as a child.

Others were conducting house-to-house enquiries in Broadstoke, continuing to sift riverside soil and hacking down undergrowth along the eastern bank of the Avon in the direction of the Crossbow. The latter exercise had soon proved worthwhile, Gilcrist's wallet having been found lodged amongst the roots of a tree in a clump of nettles. It was at a distance from the path that suggested it had been tossed where it had come to rest after any money it contained had been removed. Gilcrist's credit cards were still inside together with a season ticket for the car park near his company's offices and sundry receipts, most from Oddbins. As Carrick set out for Bathford the wallet was being examined for fingerprints.

Painswick's cottage was in the oldest part of Bathford; a tiny terraced property in a lane that meandered up a steep hillside and which was so narrow that it obviously dated back to the time of horsedrawn vehicles. Carrick, having been forced to abandon his car in the centre of the village and seek out the house on foot, arrived at 44, Beck Street wondering if a bang on the head could really make you feel so weak or whether he was appallingly unfit despite having been, until the previous weekend, in hard training for playing rugby. The Ferrets would have to do without him for the next couple of

71

matches.

'Come in,' Painswick said after taking a quick look at the warrant card. 'I was expecting someone after Sergeant Ingrams rang to say that he was unable to see me again as he'd been taken ill. Please excuse the mess – I've just knocked a wall down.'

There was thick dust everywhere in the room that the front door opened directly into but Painswick ushered Carrick into another room at the back. He appeared to live in here when he was working at the cottage and although bare and spartan it was reasonably habitable. There was a large sofa with blankets folded on it, a microwave cooker on a shelf and things for making tea and coffee.

'I mostly eat at the pub at the moment,' Painswick said, clearing a space on the sofa for Carrick to sit down. 'But when the guy's been in to do the plumbing in the kitchen I'm creating by knocking down the wall between the old scullery and the wash house life will become a little more civilised. How can I help you, Inspector?'

Carrick sat down. 'For a start you can tell me about Leonora Kelso.'

'Leo? She works with me really. I can't see how she's involved in any way with Marvin's death.'

'Well, as you might imagine, policemen are fed a lot of gossip. Someone said that she and Gilcrist were having an affair – more than that, that she was the woman in his life.'

'The woman in his life?' Painswick echoed wonderingly. He sat down opposite Carrick, grinning from ear to ear. 'I'm sorry but someone's been having you on. Leo's just a sweet kid – one of those girls who go around in Doc Martens, a dress with fringes on and about a ton of beads. She thought Marvin was *gross*.'

Carrick always listened carefully to the way people spoke. 'So he'd made a pass at her then.'

'You could say that,' the other acknowledged evenly. 'She threatened to leave.'

'You're sure she wasn't seeing him in secret?'

'Not a chance.'

'Is she married?'

'She was for a short while. I think it was one of those

72

teenage mistakes. She's twenty next birthday – as I said, she's only a kid.'

'So there was a divorce?'

'Er – no, officially she and Brian are still married. He won't agree to a divorce.'

'You seemed to give my sergeant the impression that Gilcrist simply couldn't be bothered to get involved with women. And yet someone who can be described as being close to the Gilcrists insists that a young woman she understood to be Leonora Kelso went to the house when Mrs Gilcrist was away and also insists that Gilcrist had had other affairs.'

'I've no idea what Marvin got up to,' Painswick said with a dismissive shake of his head.

'I don't believe you,' Carrick said softly.

'Ask *her*,' Painswick snapped. 'But if your source of information was old Ma Ripley, the Gilcrists' cleaning woman, then I feel I ought to warn you that a more spiteful gossiping old bag never walked the Earth.'

'If it wasn't Mrs Kelso where would she have got the name from?'

'Any number of sources. Marvin left notes pinned up for people when he was working. Stuck them up all over the place – in his office, I mean. So he might have done that at the cottage. Or left bits of paper around with people's names on at home. Mrs Ripley might have overhead telephone conversations when Marvin phoned from home – he didn't exactly speak quietly. He didn't care what time of night or day he rang too if he'd forgotten to tell someone something. Leo told me he used to ring her in the early hours of the morning sometimes.'

'Did she turn you down too?'

'No, she . . .'

'What?' Carrick barked when Painswick bit off the rest of what he had been about to say.

'All right,' Painswick groaned. 'For a time – she and I . . .'

'But not now?'

'No.'

'You broke up because she was seeing Gilcrist too?'

Silence.

73

Carrick said, 'Perhaps we ought to continue this conversation down at the –'

'All right, damn you! Yes! Yes! The bastard told her he'd see she never worked in TV again if she didn't ...' He dropped his gaze.

'Why the hell didn't you tell me the truth in the first place?'

Looking up, Painswick said, 'Because I'm still very fond of her. I didn't want her to be mixed up in this filthy mess.'

'Did *she* tell you Gilcrist was blackmailing her?'

'No, as a matter of fact it was her husband, Brian.'

'You know him then?'

'Yes, of course. He's just about the best cameraman in this part of the world. Marvin uses him whenever he's not signed up for something else.'

'I understand you have a Morgan car. That must motor.'

'It's pretty good. Not that I go in for burn-ups.'

Carrick got to his feet. 'Just the sort of car to get you back from Devon on Saturday night while you were ostensibly in your film theatre. You could have bought a ticket but left after five minutes and driven back to Broadstoke. You knew where Gilcrist would be and had a nasty suspicion that Mrs Kelso was with him. There's nothing like knowing that another man's screwing the woman you're still fond of, is there?'

'No!' Painswick yelled. 'You've absolutely no evidence to back up what you're suggesting. So that's how it is, eh? You're going to pin this on me.'

'Had you confronted Gilcrist about him and Mrs Kelso?'

'No.'

'It seems to me that she might be more happy with the situation than would appear. Young women these days don't have to put up with that kind of bullying.'

'You didn't know Marvin,' Painswick muttered.

'I take it that your break-up with Mrs Kelso was fairly acrimonious,' Carrick continued relentlessly.

'Well, I was hardly overjoyed about it, was I? But we don't let it affect our work.'

'She doesn't appear to be at home. Do you know where she is?'

'No.'

74

'Don't leave the district until I say you can.'

For several minutes after his visitor had departed Painswick sat still, staring sightlessly at the wall. Then he went over to the phone and, having obtained a number from directory enquiries, dialled.

'Leo? It's me, Larne. Yes, I guessed you were staying with Val. Look, we've got to talk . . . Yes, of course I'm upset, I've had the police here . . . No, for God's sake, you know it wasn't me . . . What do you mean, it could have been? You little cow . . . Look, Leo, I'm warning you, if you tell the police you saw me that night I'll –'

He stared at the receiver. She had rung off.

Deliberately, Carrick had not made Painswick go over his account of his movements over the weekend, preferring instead to wreak a little havoc with his peace of mind. A quick scan of the titles of the books carefully stacked in one corner of Painswick's living room had done nothing to refute the impression he had given Ingrams. There had been *Understanding Bach*, *The Turin Shroud – A New Study* and an entire set of volumes devoted to the architecture of Rome.

This was not to say that Carrick believed everything Painswick had said, however. It was he who had thought Gilcrist gross and at no time when Gilcrist's name was mentioned could he conceal his hatred, a loathing that seemed undiminished even though the man was now dead. Oh, yes, Painswick had hated him all right.

Carrick was studying the pathologist's report when the phone rang.

'No, I'm sorry, Jo,' he said after listening for a few moments. 'I haven't the time to have a drink with a gardener from Hinton Littlemoor who doesn't seem to have heard anything on the night in question . . . No, be your age, of course I'm not being snobbish. I simply do *not* have a free evening as Alan Terrington is coming down from Wemdale to talk to me about . . . fine, you know about him. Why do you think this Patrick is so important? Do you fancy the bloke or something? . . . You do! Well, *you* go and have a drink with him.'

Carrick crashed down the phone.

Amanda Gilcrist was waiting to see him in number two interview room, nervously tapping her fingers on the table before her. Although soberly dressed in a dark green silk suit with black shoes and bag she had offset the dark colours with an amber and gold necklace, bracelet and earrings and was carefully made up.

'There's just one or two points I'd like to clear up,' Carrick said, having greeted her and seated himself. 'What time did your husband go to the cottage on Friday?'

There was a pause before she answered. 'At about six-thirty. But I can't be quite sure as he didn't tell me he'd come in from work and he didn't say goodbye. I was just aware that he was in the shower and then later I heard the front door bang.'

'So he didn't speak to you at all?'

'No. But that wasn't unusual.'

'And you had no contact with him over the weekend at all?'

'No, but that wasn't unusual either. Perhaps I ought to explain a little more. Marvin was very fond of the cottage. He used to go there with his family for holidays as a child and just after we moved here he found out it was on the market and bought it. It was his den, his bolt hole really.'

'We've found his wallet by the way.' Carrick went out for a few moments and returned with it in a plastic bag. 'Unfortunately only your husband's prints are on it so finding it hasn't been much use.' He placed it down before her. 'I can't let you have it back yet, I'm afraid.'

Amanda Gilcrist gazed at it as if the bag contained maggots. 'I don't want it back, thank you. Besides, there might be a photo of *her* in it.'

'Mrs Kelso?'

'Who else?' She opened her bag. 'May I smoke?'

Carrick fetched her an old saucer that doubled as an ash tray from the window-ledge. 'Would you say that he had been drinking more heavily lately?'

'Yes. Over the past few weeks it's been really bad. I tried to talk to him about it but . . .' She shrugged. 'He'd stopped listening to me really.'

'Are you aware of any particular reason for it, the drinking

76

I mean?'

'Why do men drink heavily?' she said when she had lit up and blown a cloud of smoke towards the ceiling. 'Because he was bloody miserable, I suppose. So am I. I've been miserable for as long as I can remember.'

'Was Leo Kelso the cause of his misery, do you think?' Carrick asked.

She gave him a wan smile. 'You're different, you know that? Most men would assume that *I* made him unhappy. Yes, I think she was a sort of drug. He needed her to try to kid himself that he was just the same devil-may-care Marvin but I can imagine that when they were together she would just make him feel past it.'

'He must have known about you and Craxton though.'

She drew on her cigarette, exhaled slowly and then said, 'Look, I know this must be difficult to believe and you probably think we're the sleaziest bunch of no-gooders you've ever had the misfortune to deal with but once upon a time Marvin and I were really happy. But the more famous he became the more he surrounded himself with young, talented people who kept telling him how fantastic he was. It happens all the time. Marvin no longer wanted to be with a woman of his own generation – I reminded him how old he was. And Blair?' She gave Carrick another smile but a big bold one this time. 'He's *my* little bit of make-believe. He's more sensitive than Marvin ever was, we have really good conversations helped along with a couple of bottles of wine. And if he wants to go to bed with me then I regard that as a bonus. Blair's around your age, Inspector. Would you go to bed with a woman of forty-nine?' When he did not immediately reply she said, 'You look like an honest man so the answer must be no.'

'You denigrate yourself,' Carrick said. 'I like intelligent conversations with women too. Not to mention a bottle of wine and what happens afterwards.'

She laughed.

'And Larne Painswick?' Carrick asked.

She laughed again. 'We have a joke, Larne and I, and it is, quite simply, that I can't seduce him. I've never tried, bless the dear boy, he's simply too good to be true.'

77

'But he was going with Leo Kelso too.'

'He thought he was. Oh, I've no doubt she took him to her bed, realised that he had nothing particularly spicy to offer and cast him aside. He doted on her for a while.'

'He did mention to me that you – what was the word he used? – *collect* men.'

'Yes, well, he led a very sheltered life with that aunt of his. If he sees a woman like me, having a little fun with a younger man, he thinks that's very, very wicked. But the boy's full of Christian charity. We get on fine. He'll be all right when he's a little older and a bit tarnished.'

'When I spoke to him his Christian charity didn't seem to extend to Marvin.'

'No, Marvin offended Larne in every way – just by being himself.'

'Have you any idea if your husband – I'm sorry, this is perhaps an offensive question – gave Mrs Kelso money?'

'Presents,' she replied briskly. 'Yes, you're right, there had to be something in it for her. A car, I believe. Only a small second-hand one.'

'Can you tell me if he was in the habit of walking along the riverbank to the Crossbow?'

'Only sometimes. I can remember remarking that it was probably the only exercise he ever took. He went for whisky when he knew he was too sloshed to drive.'

'Even in the winter, in the dark?'

'Yes, he had a powerful torch.'

'We haven't found it, even in the river. Can you describe it?'

'It was a rechargeable one. Red, oblong with a handle. The usual sort of thing. But if he was really drunk he might have gone out without it. You don't think he just fell in the river and hit his head on a rock?'

'No, the rock that killed him was found some distance away from where we think it happened. There were other injuries too. Someone had tried to strangle him first. Are you aware of any threats he might have received?'

She shook her head. 'No, but there hasn't been a lot of communication between us lately. He must have upset people though – he got a pretty nasty letter from that policeman he exposed.'

'Terrington?'

'Yes, that was the name.' Sharply, she asked, 'Will you be speaking to him too?'

'Of course.'

'He came to see Marvin, you know – when he found out he was investigating the Jones case.'

'Was that before or after he wrote the letter?'

'After, I *think.*'

'Did Marvin meet him?'

'He had no choice. The man burst into his office and started shouting.'

'Tell me something . . . Why did your husband do this kind of work? Did he feel he was a sort of crusader for the truth?'

'I'm afraid you wouldn't have liked him at all, Inspector. He did it for the money. He pandered to the current British thirst for more and more examples of corruption in high places and police injustice.'

'What will happen to the company?'

'God knows. I don't care a lot. I certainly won't be carrying on with the good work. I might ask Larne if he wants to run it until certain projects are completed. After that, who knows? He hasn't Marvin's naked aggression and greed so it will probably sink without trace.'

Casually, Carrick said, 'There are substantial life insurances, I presume.'

'I don't know. There used to be but whether I'm suddenly a rich woman as a result of my husband's sudden demise I couldn't tell you. That's what I hope to find out later today when I see my solicitor. May I go now?'

'Yes, but please contact me before leaving the Bath area.'

'My solicitor's in Bristol.'

'I think I can stretch to that,' Carrick said with a smile.

She rose to go. 'I might get on the phone and ask you over for a drink – a progress report and all that. Would you accept?'

'I think it might be a bit inappropriate at the moment, don't you?'

'Umm, I suppose you're right. You're Scottish, aren't you? There's a slight accent now and again.'

'Yes, but my mother was from Orkney.'

'*That* explains your Viking good looks.'

He was a little ashamed of the warm inner glow that this remark generated. It lasted for hours.

Chapter Eight

Chief Inspector Haine, it appeared, was returning that night from the conference – Carrick had an idea that those in authority had ordered his return – and hoped to arrive at work first thing the following morning, Friday. Meanwhile, Carrick commandeered as many personnel as could be spared and organised another search of the river banks and fields in the vicinity of the murder site, this time in the opposite direction to the Crossbow. This was carried out until lack of daylight and heavy rain forced it to be abandoned for the day. Nothing was found but a woman's handbag, which was taken back to Manvers Street as Carrick had an idea that it might be connected with the mugging of an elderly woman in Bradford on Avon the previous week.

Frozen, wet to the skin and famished with hunger he gained entry to his flat – although a controlled explosion through the door into it might more accurately describe what took place – stripped and headed for a hot shower. When he reached around the curtain for a towel it was placed in his hands.

'Oh, hi,' he said without real enthusiasm.

'I've made a chicken casserole,' said Joanna.

'I thought you had a date with an Irish gardener.'

'There's beer too and I've bought a bottle of wine. No, that's not until eight-thirtyish.'

'So he's too mean to give you something to eat?' Carrick said, towelling furiously.

'You were invited as well, you know. I think it's really you he wants to see. I told him what happened to you.'

Thunderstruck, Carrick emerged from the towel. 'You told ... Thanks a million. Now the whole world'll know.'

She kissed an exposed bit of shoulder. 'No, I don't think so.'

'You realise that this is just a ploy to get a couple of people to buy him a few pints?'

'No again,' Joanna said coolly and proceeded to kiss him on the throat and from there to nibble his ear. 'Anyway, you're talking to Terrington tonight.'

'No, I was given a message. Due to what he called personal circumstances he's had to postpone the trip for a couple of days. He has a dreadful cough so perhaps he has the flu along with just about everyone else.'

Joanna was burrowing under the towel. 'James! You've gone all –'

'Auto-pilot,' he interrupted. 'How about that beer?'

'Yes or no?'

'Yes or no what? Woman, I warn you if you carry on doing that I will not be held responsible for my actions.'

Joanna sighed regretfully and went away to fetch the beer.

'Sorry to be such a miserable old sod,' he said when she returned. He kissed her on the tip of the nose as thanks for the beer. 'Tell me why you're so taken with this bloke. How can he help?'

'Well, for a start I don't think he's really Irish even though he told me his name's Patrick. I'm not too sure he's a gardener either – not for a living, anyway – his hands were too smooth for that. When he dropped the brogue he was well-spoken and there's something about him that tells me he's either very senior Bill or connected with the military. Probably the latter as he seems to have an artificial right leg or foot. What interested me is that he said he'd had experience of loss of memory and from the way he said it I gathered he meant not personally but among his men.'

Carrick was looking at her in total admiration. 'God, you never lose your touch, do you?'

'Jackpot? You know who he is then?'

'Yup.'

'Who?'

'Is he about my height and build and has dark wavy hair

going grey?'

'Yes.'

'I met him and his wife at the Framley's party. He's the rector's eldest son.'

'Patrick – er – Gillard then.'

'Correct. Lieutenant-Colonel, no less. Ex-Special Services, ex-MI5, ex just about everything hair-raising.'

'So was it *his* baby the rector and his wife had gone down to see in Devon?'

'Must be. His wife's Ingrid Langley the novelist and I seem to remember she was expecting when I spoke to her at the party. It would be their second child – they've already got a little boy.'

'He's probably bored with just looking after a house and wants to get involved in something interesting,' Joanna said reflectively.

'From what I've heard about him, heaven help us!' Carrick retorted.

There was no hint of the Irish gardener now, Carrick thought, when he first glimpsed Gillard in the Lovat Lounge, a smaller, more private bar than the Appin, adjoining the restaurant. Not that he looked like a soldier either.

When Gillard saw them he gestured encouragingly in the direction of a table in a window recess and followed them over.

'I told Joanna who you are,' Carrick said to him when they had shaken hands.

He turned to her with a wide smile. 'Sorry about the theatricals. But you weren't really taken in, were you? Otherwise neither of you would have come tonight. What will you have to drink?'

'Ouch,' Joanna said quietly when he had gone back to the bar.

'What you must understand,' Carrick said out of the corner of his mouth, 'is that they turned him loose on what used to be referred to as traitors. If we switch our brains into super-overdrive we might just scrape by. And don't say I didn't warn you.'

'What else do you know about him?'

83

'Well, he's only just been promoted and I gather this was a little long in coming because he doesn't play by the rules. You'll notice that he drinks Marston's Pedigree – he's not a G and T man. I gather he's the sort of bloke who goes in the public bar and plays darts with the locals if he feels like it. According to Ingrid – I had quite a long chat with her at the party – he lost the lower part of his right leg following injuries he received during the Falklands War.'

'I assume you're working on the Gilcrist murder case,' Patrick said when he returned. 'It might not help much but I ought to tell you that about two and a half years ago he was given a hefty warning-off for planning some kind of film that would suggest that MI5 was about to mount a sleaze campaign against the then Leader of the Opposition.'

Carrick said, 'You gave the warning?'

Patrick came up for air from his pint. 'Gardening gives you a hell of a thirst. Yes, it was felt that I had a suitable repertoire of warnings.'

'And one of your men had fed him the story in a pub, just to see whether he'd take the bait?'

'What a nasty suspicious mind you have, Inspector,' Patrick murmured. Then he smiled like a shark. 'Yes, of course. But seriously, I want you to know that there aren't any odd bods wearing trench coats with the collars turned up involved in this.'

'As far as you know?' Joanna said.

'No, it's gospel. As a matter of fact I checked up this morning. Not that the security services are in the habit of pushing people who get up their nose into rivers.' He fixed Carrick with his keen gaze. 'As a matter of fact I'm much more interested in what happened to *you*.'

'Campbell's still in Scotland,' Carrick said. 'But I'm only clutching at straws. He was far too drunk to have noticed anything that I might have done. I rang Fraser's work number and was told he was away on holiday, skiing somewhere in the Highlands.'

'His father didn't pack a suitcase when he went north,' Patrick said evenly.

Carrick set his drink carefully down on the table. 'I must insist you tell me how you know that.'

'Sure and there's no need to wave the boiling oil and flaming arrows in my direction,' said Patrick liltingly. 'And here's me desperate to help the good officers with their enquiries.'

Carrick chuckled at himself. 'Sorry.'

'There's nothing complicated about it. Mrs Smithers is Campbell's daily help and she also helps my mother at the rectory. I went round to see her to tell her that there's no point in her coming round while the builders are making such a mess. I'm making damned sure they clear up most of it themselves, but that's beside the point. She's worried about Campbell as he normally rings her when he's away to tell her of his plans to return. I gather she does more than cleaning for him; does a little baking, washing and ironing and cooks him meals on some evenings. What's really worrying her is that the case he normally uses is still in his room and he doesn't seem to have taken shaving gear or any clothes. All that's missing as far as she can tell is his Highland Dress. But she did say that she might be wrong and he's bought another suit that she doesn't know about and taken his evening rig to the cleaners.'

Carrick said, 'But there'd be the shoes and his sporran and belt and any jewellery.'

'I didn't ask about that. I didn't really feel that I ought to really. She gave me all this information quite spontaneously when I went to see her.' He smiled. 'So please don't think I've been interfering.'

'I don't mind *that* kind of interference,' Carrick told him.

'Yes, but I do,' was the reply. 'And many's the time the police have barged in on one of my set-ups.'

'Mrs Smithers wasn't in when I called round,' Joanna said, thinking that she might have to act as some kind of buffer zone between these two men.

If Carrick was irritated he showed no sign of it. He said, 'I can't really justify doing anything about this – my hands are tied until some kind of official complaint is made.'

Patrick said, 'Did you speak to the man during the evening?'

'No, I'm fairly sure I didn't. But I was aware of his presence. You are with Graeme – he's a big man in every sense of the word.'

'And you've remembered nothing more?'

'No.'

'What time did you go to your room?'

'At just after eleven-thirty. The dancing finished at eleven and I had a coffee with a couple I was talking to and made my way upstairs. After that, nothing until I woke up in hospital.'

'Joanna said that you saw all three Campbells on your way upstairs.'

'Yes, they were in the Appin Lounge near the main staircase.'

'Were there any other people in the room?'

'I can't remember seeing any.'

'Could you see right into the room from where you were standing?'

'I'm not sure.'

'Shall we go and have a look?'

Carrick hesitated fractionally and then said, 'Yes, why not?' He drained his glass and got to his feet.

As Margo, the receptionist on duty that night, had told Joanna, the entrance to the Appin Lounge was a wide archway just off the main reception area. Directly facing anyone entering, in the left-hand corner of the room, was the bar, a rather resplendent edifice well-decorated with shields, broadswords and swathes of tartan material. A large ornate fireplace was set into the same facing wall, surmounted by a gilt-framed mirror with wall-lights on each side.

'They were seated there,' Carrick said, pointing to one of the room's circular tables placed between the fireplace and the bar.

'They saw you and spoke with you?' Patrick asked. He went and sat down in one of the chairs set around the table, which was unoccupied. 'I'm Graeme Campbell. What was he doing?'

'Sitting in the chair to your right but slightly turned about so that he faced me,' Carrick said. He had remained standing in the archway. 'Bruce had his back to me and Fraser was standing leaning on the bar. He was the one who spoke.'

Patrick moved to the next chair. 'What did he say?'

'He congratulated me on my efforts with "Tam O'Shanter" and then asked me to have a drink with them.'

'No, his exact words.'

Brows knitted, Carrick said, 'I can't remember.'

Patrick leapt to his feet and went over to the bar. 'What you need is a little cerebral lubrication.' To the barman he said, 'Two doubles of The Macallan if you please.' He smote his forehead. 'I forgot the lady. What will you have, Joanna, Sheep Dip?'

'Being as you're asking I'll have Highland Park,' she said coolly.

He grinned at her. 'Touché.'

When they had been served Patrick said, 'I know I'm banging on about this but I think it's important because it's the last thing, James – and I hope we're on first name terms now – that you remember. So, what did Fraser say to you?'

Carrick had remained where he was, scared, almost, that if he moved he would somehow break the fragile hold he had on the events of that evening. There was something about the encounter that had always been in his mind but he had failed to mention it because it made no sense, as though the memory was completely out of context. He said, 'I *might* have refused to drink with them because I was angry.'

In response to this Patrick leaned negligently on the bar with a superior smirk on his face. Joanna, about to protest, desisted when she saw the effect it was having on Carrick.

'Yes!' he burst out. 'That's it! He was a bit tight and very full of himself. He drawled something along the lines of, "Watch out, it's Jimmy Carrick. With a memory like his they don't need a records department. But very well done, Inspector. Care to have a dram with us?"'

'With an invitation like that who could refuse?' Patrick said. 'But you haven't answered my other question. What was Graeme doing?' He sat down again.

'Nothing. He was just sitting there, an empty glass before him, staring straight ahead, eyes sort of glazed.'

Patrick commenced to look horribly drunk. 'Like this?'

'More or less. His mouth was slightly open.'

'Did you go over to their table?'

'Yes, I did. I've remembered now.'

'Do it.'

Carrick slowly paced into the room, aware that a couple at the far end, the only others present, were watching with great interest.

Patrick said, 'Joanna, go and sit down at the other corner table. Now, James, did you look around and notice anyone else?'

'No, I don't think I did.'

'Okay, what did you say?'

'I spoke directly to Fraser as he had addressed me. I was polite though and declined, explaining that I planned to get up early and go for a swim.'

'What was Bruce doing?'

'Sulking.' Carrick froze. 'God, yes, he was too. He just glanced up at me and then away again.'

'So who out of these three drunkards had brought their car?' Joanna asked from the other end of the room.

'Don't bloody interrupt his train of thought!' Patrick rapped out.

'No idea,' Carrick said. 'I only know it was dark in colour.'

Patrick laid a finger to his lips, looking at Joanna. 'Go on,' he whispered.

'I don't know what made me say that,' Carrick admitted. 'I've no idea whose car it was.'

'Never mind. Go back into the lobby and in the direction of the stairs. What was your room number?'

'Thirty-one.'

'Did you have the key with you or had you left it at the desk?'

'I'd left it with reception as I hate things jangling around in my sporran when I'm dancing.'

'Don't we all?' Patrick said, getting to his feet. 'Off you go then.' He grinned inanely to allay any offence.

Margo was on duty at the desk.

'Might we,' Patrick said to her winningly, 'borrow the key to room thirty-one – provided of course that no one is booked in there? We are trying to reconstruct a *happening* last weekend when the good inspector here left his head in the wardrobe and –' He broke off and ducked a blow that Carrick had not aimed at him.

'You've got someone then,' Margo mouthed at Joanna, handing over the key. 'Good,' she added, giving Carrick a huge smile. 'There you are, inspector.'

Entering into the spirit of the thing Carrick clasped the 'suspect' and marched him towards the stairs, Margo making circling movements with a forefinger to her temple in their wake.

'It's not my local,' Patrick muttered. 'I need never show my face in here again.'

Joanne smiled to herself; things were going better than she had expected.

'Right, and when did you first realise that you'd left your head behind, officer?' Patrick was saying, wandering down a corridor on the first-floor landing.

'No, up to the next one,' Carrick said.

'Bejabbers, he remembers all along,' Patrick chortled and carried on. At the top he stopped. 'I suppose you didn't take the lift?'

'No.'

'I thought not.'

Carrick took a left turn at the top, walked down a short corridor, turned right and went up three narrow stairs to a tiny landing off which opened two doors. He put the key in the lock of the left hand one of the two.

'Wait!' Patrick said urgently. 'Was it locked or open?'

'Locked,' Carrick answered, turning the key.

A steely grip closed around his wrist. 'Are you sure? Think!'

It was as if a fog was swirling in his mind, or rather in a tunnel in his mind that he had not yet entered. This side of the darkness, though, a few things were clear. 'Yes,' he said, 'it was locked.'

'Was it quiet? Any sounds coming from this room or from next door?'

'No – Wait a moment . . . Someone was talking next door.'

'Was it people in the room or a TV?'

'Someone in the room. A woman spoke. But I don't know what she said.'

Patrick released his grip. 'That's all right then. Folk don't usually do that when they're about to ambush someone close by.'

Carrick walked into the room and came to a halt. 'This is where it all stops. I can't remember coming back in here.'

'You're doing very well. Can you remember getting ready?'

'Yes.'

'What colour is the bathroom?'

'Pink and white.'

Patrick took a look. 'Ten out of ten.'

Joanna said, 'Wander around a bit. And who knows? your skene-dhu might be under the bed.'

'It's missing?' Patrick said.

'Yes. Sorry, I forgot to tell you.'

'That bothers me. Especially as you found the button in a rather strange place.'

Carrick had shoved the bed to one side to reveal a little fluff and two salted peanuts.

'Yours?' Patrick asked, picking up the latter.

'Negative. I don't eat peanuts in bed.'

'Just peppermint lumps,' Joanna said without thinking, then went a little pink. She busied herself feeling down the sides of the cushions on the armchair.

Patrick sat on the end of the bed. 'Could you have *used* the knife for anything? A jammed suitcase lock? To peel an apple perhaps? To free the window catches that you can never shift in these centrally heated places? Let's picture it. You came upstairs, and if you're anything like me after dancing you're hot and thirsty. You strip off your evening jacket or whatever and make for the bathroom where you probably have a pee and a long drink of cold water.'

'It's no good,' Carrick said after a long silence had elapsed. 'I simply can't remember.'

'Don't worry about it. Show me where you have this bruise that Joanna mentioned.'

Carrick sketched a line across his neck and shoulder.

'Would you very much mind removing your shirt so I can see for myself? Joanna, either avert your gaze or ring room service and ask them to send up some peppermint lumps.'

Laughing at her discomfiture Carrick pulled off his jacket and shirt and his audience breathed in, hissing, through their teeth.

'And you're walking about and being as nice as pie to us,' Patrick said wonderingly. Gently, he traced with a finger the long purple-black bruise and then set the edge of one hand against it, measuring. 'Well, unless he had hands almost twice as large as mine you weren't chopped across the neck martial arts style. There's a nasty transverse ridge too, as though whatever it was had a metal knob on it.'

'Someone mentioned a cricket bat,' Carrick said.

'No, it wasn't a cricket bat. I think whatever hit you was made of metal. I had a look at the lighting arrangements in the car park on my way in and they aren't too good. There are a lot of deep shadows and dark corners where half an army could hide.'

Carrick got dressed again. 'So what do you think?'

'There's bruising to your chest and stomach. I think you were hit in the body with fists and when that failed to floor you someone grabbed something that did. The bruising isn't severe enough to suggest to me that you were kicked when you were down. The motive probably wasn't just to beat you up. Did you have any money on you, do you know? What about your watch?'

'All back in my room. My watch and loose change as well as my wallet were among the things the hotel packed up and sent along to my flat.'

'We could go outside if you like and take it from there.'

Carrick shook his head. 'Not tonight, if you don't mind. Look, will you forgive me if I make for home? I'm really grateful to you for trying but until I remember what happened everything's conjecture. The DCI's back tomorrow and if he's anything like he usually is when he gets back from one of these conferences it'll be a very long day.'

'I'll drive,' Joanna offered quickly.

'No, you stay on, I'll get a taxi. I insist,' he called over his shoulder as he went away.

'I ought to go with him,' Joanna whispered to Patrick. 'He's really not too well.'

'Of course. Sorry we didn't achieve anything.'

91

'Thanks very much anyway – and for the drink. Can I keep in touch?'

'I was going to ask if you would.'

When they had gone Gillard thoughtfully retraced his way down to the lobby where he returned the key.

'I thought you were under arrest,' said Margo.

'No. He's forgiven me,' Patrick said absently.

Outside, he took his time walking to his own car. 'Damn,' he said under his breath. 'I forgot to ask him where he parked that night. And what would anyone have in the boot of a car that would be a handy weapon? A jack or a spanner,' he said to the stars. 'Now those are nasty lumps of metal if ever there were.'

He fetched a torch from his BMW and spent quite a long time searching the ground under the trees and bushes. Then he went back into the hotel and engaged the barman in the Appin Lounge in conversation. This man, he soon discovered, had not been working on the night of the Burns Supper as he had been at home ill with the flu. His replacement had been someone the hotel had obtained through an agency which specialised in emergency staffing.

'Thou shalt not be bored,' Patrick said and went back outside, leaving the man looking a little nonplussed.

He was quite convinced that there was no deception on Carrick's part. Latterly in his army career he had become involved with deciding whether people were telling the truth or not. Prior to this, when those in authority had discovered certain aptitudes he possessed for mimicry, living off the land, leadership and an instant rapport with whatever weapon was handed to him, he had worked undercover. Over the years, and mostly because of an almost charismatic ability to bring those under his command through hell, high water and worse, his superiors had learned to ignore his sometimes incandescent bad temper, insubordination and regrettable habit of allowing his heart to rule his head. Right now they were wooing him in the direction of merging his small MI5 department with a new international force against terrorism.

Gillard had no illusions about himself and as the son of a clergyman was not proud of having lied, killed and maimed in the cause of Queen and country. But an awesome reputation can sometimes bring odd rewards and some weeks previously this had come in the form of a horse. The event had been so bizarre that he still smiled to himself every time he thought about it.

The invitation to spend the weekend at the Devon estate of a very senior officer had come right out of the blue. His family – yes, they really were a family now with Justin *and* Victoria, at home and thriving – had been included in the invitation too, and as the house in question was only a matter of twelve miles from where they lived he had accepted with alacrity. Ingrid had more than deserved a break.

They had arrived on the Saturday morning to discover that a shoot was planned and Ingrid, who did not enjoy, in her words, the sky raining dead pheasants retired indoors to admire their hostess's collection of Coalport plates and Inuit artefacts. She had a good excuse: the newest edition to the family was already demanding lunch. Justin Patrick took with him, against his better judgement.

There was just a small favour the host asked of him first. Handing him a hunting rifle and taking him to a small field at the rear of the stables where everyone was setting off for the morning's sport, he had indicated an aged, bony hunter which when it saw their arrival set off with a whinny in their direction. It was lame on a near foreleg.

'I know you're a good shot,' said the man. 'It's knackered.'

'I don't have to be a good shot,' Patrick had muttered as the animal busily commenced to frisk him for sugar over the fence.

'No, but you know what I mean, man. The bloody thing's been retired for years and I'm fed up with looking at it. Maggs'll dig the hole tomorrow with the JCB – either that or I'll let the hunt have it for the hounds.'

Patrick had looked down at Justin. 'I don't think my son ought to see this.'

'No, you're right. Although it's never too early to make a man of them, is it?'

He was given into someone's charge and sat in the front of a Range Rover.

No one but the horse witnessed what happened next but when the two men rejoined the party, a single shot having

93

rung out, it was perceived that their host was white and shaking, having, it was rumoured afterwards, lost his breakfast in the grass. Patrick had then borrowed a Land Rover and trailer without asking, loaded the horse, collected wife and baby from indoors and departed for home.

Following attention to its hooves and teeth, Polar Bear, for it was a grey, was now sound and beginning to fill out satisfactorily. Kept at livery with others of its kind for company, it was very happy with life and on increasing occasions could be seen conveying its saviour with serene enthusiasm around quiet country lanes.

No, Gillard did not shoot horses.

Chapter Nine

Not at all to Carrick's surprise, Chief Inspector Haine was already at work when he arrived at a little after eight the following morning and again predictably, the entire premises was reverberating to his presence. But Carrick had not expected the DCI to be in his, Carrick's office, most of the paperwork connected with the Gilcrist case spread out before him.

'You don't seem to have got very far with this.'

Carrick decided against pointing out that Haine had been away for less than forty-eight hours and said instead, 'Alan Terrington's promised to phone at about nine to confirm when he's coming down for a chat. Oh, and although we've found Gilcrist's wallet it didn't provide any leads. Personally, I think the murderer wore gloves, not necessarily because he was well organised but on account of the weather. And I've initiated a much wider search to be made of the area between the scene of the crime and Rampsons, which is resuming about now. We had to call a halt last night.' A little humility, perhaps, was good for the soul.

'But it was very closely examined at the time.'

'I've particularly asked that everything be searched within the distance that a man might be able to throw a small heavy object.'

'Like what, for instance?'

'Gilcrist's torch. Even if he was blind drunk, which he wasn't, he wouldn't have tried to walk even a short distance without one. For the same reason I don't think the murderer lay in wait for him or met him on the riverbank. It was too dark to see anything and he'd have had no idea surely that Gilcrist would return to the pub.'

'So where does that train of thought lead to?' Haine said, baffled.

'I think he'd been at the cottage *with* Gilcrist. Perhaps he was there when Gilcrist was dropped off by that bloke who gave him a lift. He said he saw no lights within but there are rooms at the back where someone could have been present with or without Gilcrist's knowledge. The murderer might even have rolled up shortly after Gilcrist got home.'

'The man who gave him a lift saw no other vehicles outside, remember.'

'No, but someone who was familiar with the property would have known about the small drive and would have expected Gilcrist's car, a big Jaguar, to be parked there taking up all the space available. There are cottages about fifty yards away with parking space in the road outside.'

'And you think they walked to the pub together?'

'I don't see how else it could have been. There had to be illumination of some kind and that must have been provided by Gilcrist's torch. It's bloody difficult to kill someone in the pitch dark.'

'It would also explain the several desperate attempts to finish him off and the way the vegetation was all trampled. A dreadful thought, really – the pair blundering around, one trying to kill the other.'

'Sir Hugh Rapton's of a mind that the murderer is not a strong man. That rather points us away from Larne Painswick: the sledgehammer he was using to knock down a wall at his cottage wasn't a toy. He could have strangled Gilcrist easily without all the business of the rock.'

'It was a savage attack, though,' Haine mused. 'Someone was beside themselves with temper. Frenzied. Do you really suspect Painswick?'

'Yes, sir, I do. He could easily have driven back from Torquay on the Saturday night and then returned without compromising his alibi. He *did* go and see his aunt, I checked, but the whole weekend seems to have been planned so carefully that I can't help but feel a bit suspicious.'

'Has the Kelso woman surfaced yet?'

'According to colleagues at work she's due to return today.'

'Where's she been?'

'No one seems to know.'

'I always have doubts about people who do a bunk.'

'Especially when they do it *after* the crime's been committed.'

'I'd like you to make her a priority. I'll speak to Terrington when he rings.'

'With all due respect sir, I think that as I've made contact with him I ought to continue.'

Haine opened his mouth to evoke his authority but saw the stubborn set of his subordinate's jaw and realised that he would have a fight on his hands. Besides, if subjected to stress Carrick might get a headache and go sick again. And that, in the present circumstances, would be a disaster. 'All right, James,' he said, as sweetly as he knew how. 'But if he says anything really controversial, for God's sake tell me before you get on the blower to Dalesland Police.'

Priority or not, it was lunchtime before Carrick was free to talk to Leonora Kelso. Over the phone Alan Terrington had said, laconically, that he would be in Bath that night. Carrick gave him his home number.

It appeared that Mrs Kelso was in the pub. By this Carrick assumed that she was lunching in the Green Lanterns, an establishment much frequented by those connected with the arts, it being close to the Theatre Royal, various galleries and a school of music. The decor was probably the draw, he had decided some time previously, as the beer was awful. Posters of film stars, mostly deceased, adorned the walls, and high ledges were crammed with dusty valve radios, cinema memorabilia and oddly, a collection of old chamber pots. Eight stuffed bats, probably the props from a horror film, hung from the ceiling on dark thread and went round and round in the draught from several creaking wooden fans. For some reason – and nothing to do with beer or bats or the fact that the landlord hated policemen in any shape or form – the place always made Carrick feel slightly uneasy.

He had been told by one of the two typist-cum-receptionists at the film company's headquarters – the pair of them in a kind of stupor of inactivity – that the person he sought had blonde hair and was wearing black jeans with a white blouse and 'lots of silver bracelets'. And here she was, just inside the door sitting on her own: a tall, strong-looking girl with large hands and feet, a lioness with a tawny mane and green eyes. What had Painswick said? 'She's just a kid really?' Rubbish – she was all woman with beautifully manicured red claws to prove it.

'Mrs Kelso?' he asked mildly.

'Who wants her?' The voice was quiet and as he might have expected, almost a purr.

He introduced himself.

'I've been expecting someone. You want to talk about Marvin.'

'That's right.'

'I don't really want to discuss him in here. Do you?'

'It's up to you. If you're having lunch . . .'

She glanced at her watch. 'I was supposed to be meeting Brian – he's my husband only we're separated. He's late, so to hell with him.' She stood up. 'Let's go somewhere else, shall we?'

Outside, it was just starting to rain.

'We'll talk in Marvin's office,' Leonora decided and led the way with long strides. 'Marvin hated that place,' she said when they had gone about fifty yards. 'He loathed anything that he thought was phoney. Perhaps it reminded him what a sham *he* was.' When Carrick remained silent she went on. 'I'm glad you came, in a way. Brian and I were going to talk about divorce. Are you married, Inspector?'

'Was,' Carrick said, adding before he got involved in the wrong sort of conversation, 'my wife's dead.'

Strangely, she stopped and regarded him wide-eyed. 'That's really sad. You think when you're young that death's for other people, don't you? That it can't come and spoil everything for you and that only little old ladies and racing drivers die. And then you realise that children get cancer and babies die at birth and you start feeling insecure.'

'I think that's called growing up, Mrs Kelso,' Carrick said.

She carried on walking. 'Is it?'

They did not speak again until she had shown him into the film producer's office. Carrick had not actually set foot in the room before, Haine and Ingrams having done the groundwork while he was in hospital.

If he had anticipated a brash, glitzy room, successful film producer writ large, with massive furniture, expensive prints and a shelf full of awards he would have been disappointed. The room was sparsely appointed: a plain, scuffed desk, a swivel chair with a pronounced list to port and knockabout shelving loaded with files, books and folders in all sizes and colours. The carpet looked as though cigarettes had been ground out into it for twenty years and instead of framed prints the walls were host to more than slightly pornographic nudes, the posters held up, just, with strips of masking tape.

'This is his private office, you understand,' Leonora Kelso said. 'And please call me Leo. There's another room that's grandly referred to as the boardroom, with a big table and chairs and a coffee machine. Marvin didn't usually bring what he called VIPs in here. Sit down, Inspector. Yes, go on, in his chair. You might get a feel for the bastard he really was.' She seated herself opposite him and surveyed him with her wide, artless gaze. 'No, you don't give off the same greedy, uncaring vibes. You can be ruthless, but you're not in the same league when it comes to sheer nastiness.'

'Thank you,' Carrick said soberly.

Expansively, she waved an arm. 'See that door? It opens into a large walk-in cupboard. Marvin kept stationery in there. That's where he screwed me when he felt like it. When he wanted sex he wanted it *pronto*.'

'You didn't want to talk about it in the pub,' Carrick said, needing to be certain about the relationship between the two. 'Why?'

'I like the pub.'

'Don't women have a say in things like that these days?'

'No, not as far as Marvin and my career in television were concerned.'

'A little bird told me that he bought you a car,' Carrick persisted gently.

She pouted. 'I bet they didn't tell you why. He ran into the side of my old banger in the car park when he'd had a few and wrote it off. The one he bought me was an even older old banger.'

'You went to his house too.'

'Only once. That was the time he was hinting that I might be Mrs Gilcrist number two. You're shocked at female fickleness? Call it stupidity on my part. I think it was merely Marvin wanting to make love to me in bed instead of in a cupboard standing up.'

'Your husband found out?'

'He'd guessed, but didn't care a lot. He'd already left me for some trollop who serves behind the bar in a pub in Chippenham. You see, nice Inspector, I'm divorcing *him*.'

'Tell me what you did last weekend.'

'Well, I didn't waylay him in the dark and beat his brains out.' There was silence for a few seconds and then she said, 'What happened to *your* head?'

'I was waylaid in the dark and someone tried to beat my brains out,' Carrick replied. 'Who gave you the black eye that make-up hasn't quite hidden?'

'That was *before*' she said under her breath.

'Before last weekend? Yes, it must have been because it's fading nicely. Was it Gilcrist?'

She looked frightened. 'Look, I didn't –'

'Just tell me about it,' Carrick interposed.

'It was at the cottage the previous weekend – the Saturday. He rang me at home and said he'd left a shooting script at the office and needed it. He said it was here, in the top drawer of his desk. He wanted me to drive out with it. I started to refuse. It was late, ten forty-five so he said he'd come for it. I knew he'd be well over the limit by that time of night so I caved in.'

'Where do you live?'

'Just round the corner from here. Sheridan Street. I've a flat over a florist's.'

'So you called in here and drove over with it. Was it the real reason for him asking you to go there?'

'You're quick off the mark, aren't you? No. I realised the truth as soon as I arrived. He just wanted a roll in the hay. But I wasn't going to play, I'd had enough of him. He hit me.' Her eyes filled with tears and she dashed them away with a fierce jangle of bracelets.

'Did you stay?' Carrick whispered.

'No. I think he was actually quite shocked by what he'd done – he didn't stop me leaving. I don't know how I got home. No one has ever hit me before, not in all my life.'

'Did you tell your husband?'

'I had to say something because we'd arranged to meet on the Sunday morning to visit his mum. She's in hospital and we're both very fond of her. Well, I could hardly say I'd walked into a door.'

'What was his reaction?'

'Brian's a bit of a cynic. His attitude has always been that people get what's coming to them. But he was angry, I could tell. He went quiet.'

'Did you go to the cottage last weekend?'

'No!'

'Okay, so tell me what you did and where you were.'

'I was at home last Saturday and Sunday. The weather was foul and I didn't feel like going out. All I did was go down to Sainsbury's on Saturday morning. I wasn't feeling all that good, hadn't been all week – perhaps it was shock.'

'Did Gilcrist apologise?'

'No. But I only saw him once during that week – I had to go and look at a couple of locations.'

'Did you have any visitors?'

'Last weekend? No.'

'Not Larne Painswick, for example?'

She shook her head, avoiding his eye.

'*He* must have been pretty angry when he saw –'

'He's a real pain – thinks he's some kind of knight on a white charger. I told him to mind his own business.'

'But you have had an affair with him.'

She rounded on him angrily. 'Is that what he told you? Are a couple of quick cuddles in a car an affair? Perhaps they are to him. No, what happened between Larne and me wasn't an affair – it was just nice to be in the company of a sympathetic man for once.'

'Did he say he was going to confront Gilcrist with what he did to you?'

'No.'

101

'Where did you go after news of the murder came out?'

'I took some leave that was owing to me. It seemed a good moment. As a matter of fact I stayed with a friend in Brighton – a female friend.'

'I suggest to you that you were scared that you might be implicated because Gilcrist assaulted you. You're still scared, aren't you? But that's mainly because you haven't told me the truth.'

She shrugged, looking at her hands clasped nervously in her lap.

'Is someone threatening you?'

'No.'

'Where can I find your husband?'

'At the flat of his trollop, I expect.' She caught his gaze then and wished she hadn't, finding herself giving him the address. 'I'm scared of the dark. I couldn't have killed him in the dark,' she added in a mutter.

Carrick got to his feet. 'And Marvin Gilcrist certainly walked into the dark, didn't he? He was with someone he knew well, though – I'm certain of that. The pair of them had walked along the riverbank from the cottage in the direction of the Crossbow and I shouldn't be surprised if they quarrelled every inch of the way. And what could they have been so upset about? I wouldn't mind betting, Mrs Kelso, that it was you.'

She was shaking her head, mouth trembling, eyes brimming as he spoke.

'Perhaps it was in connection with the assault on you,' Carrick continued. 'Gilcrist might have felt he had no case to answer. He probably felt that it was a lot of fuss about nothing. That attitude would have made the man he was talking to even more angry – or was it a woman?'

'I didn't –'

He cut in ruthlessly. 'Amanda, for example. Now although he'd been committing adultery for years Amanda might have heard from someone in the company what he had done to you ... It might have struck a chord of feminine sympathy?' Carrick smiled bleakly. 'Yes?'

Slowly, Leo said, 'Marvin did once tell me that she'd said if she had an axe she'd bury it one night in the middle of his

102

back.'

'Really? How bloodthirsty of her.'

There was a very long silence.

'I lied,' Leo said at last. 'I did go out on Saturday night. I drove out to the Crossbow. It was late, almost closing time, and I felt that if I didn't see other people I'd go mad.'

'Why the Crossbow? There are plenty of pubs in Bath.'

'I didn't want to see Marvin, if that's what you mean. I didn't know he went there until I read about it in the paper. It's a great pub. I used to go there a lot with Brian when everything between us was all right. I just wanted to go somewhere where I felt *happy*.'

'What was Gilcrist's latest project?'

'He'd just completed the filming of an investigation into the way the government treats illegal immigrants.'

'Then why was he working at the cottage?'

'He liked it there, regarded it as home. And he wanted to stay out of Amanda's way.'

'There was a lot of paperwork there. I'd like you to have a look through it all if you wouldn't mind. Are you quite sure that there's nothing he had planned, something of a sensitive nature? The place had been ransacked, you see, and it's impossible to tell if anything's missing.'

Leo waved an elegant hand at the bulging files. 'All the important stuff's here. Your lot have been through everything. Marvin told me he didn't keep anything of significance at Rampsons – he was worried about burglars. It was pretty isolated, that cottage.'

'We found a briefcase there, empty. But the contents could have been scattered all over the floor.'

'God knows. He was a secretive man. If he'd had anything special in mind he wouldn't necessarily have told *me*.'

'Who might he have confided in?'

'No one, probably. He didn't trust anyone.'

'But people would have to know eventually – the people who worked for him.'

'Yes, but he wouldn't go public until he was good and ready. Until he was certain what he had to say would hold water. He hated looking like a fool.'

'Did you work on the Jones case? The one involving Alan

Terrington?'

She shook her head. 'No.'

'Did your husband?'

'He might have done,' she answered cautiously.

'Where did that story come from? Was it inside information?'

'I have absolutely no idea.'

When Carrick got back to the office he telephoned the
address she had given him. A sleepy-sounding woman told
him that Brian Kelso was in Egypt.

Chapter Ten

A little later Carrick received a message: the team searching the riverbank had found a torch. He drove straight out there.

A thin, cold mist hung over the Avon valley, the vegetation by the river dank and rotting, the ground underfoot slimy mud with the occasional loop of bramble stem to trip the unwary.

'There, sir,' said the man who had made the find, pointing to the rear of a small ruined farm building of some kind, possibly at one time a pigsty. 'It had been chucked into all the nettles behind – must have hit the wall to get that sort of damage.'

The torch was smashed, the batteries in danger of falling from the outer casing, all the glass of the bulb and reflector knocked out and now no more than glittery shivers amongst the nettle stems.

It was the wrong torch: cylindrical, silver in colour.

'Well done,' Carrick murmured, turning over the plastic bag and its contents. 'But I'm afraid you'll have to carry on looking as it doesn't fit the description of the one that's missing. Get someone to take this to the forensic lab – no, on second thoughts I'll take it and I can show it to Mrs Gilcrist on the way in case it does belong to their household.' He glanced around to get his bearings and saw that they were only about seventy yards from Rampsons. 'Carry on the search up to the cottage and a stone's throw beyond and then call it a day.' It was probably in the river, he concluded, slithering down into the lane where he had left his car.

A dark blue BMW was parked right behind it.

'They said you were here,' Patrick Gillard called, winding down the driver's window. 'I don't want to stop you working but I think I know the sort of thing you were attacked with.' He got out of the car and opened the rear door, picking up something from the back seat.

The monkey wrench was about fourteen inches long, had the remains of blue paint on the handle and looked as though it had been in service for many years. Carrick took it from Gillard in the hand not holding the plastic bag and gazed at it wonderingly. A dark car . . . No, a *black* car . . .

'Ring any bells?' Gillard asked after what seemed like hours had elapsed.

'I'm not sure.'

'I found this one in the old stable at the rectory. But it was the adjusting nut that caught my eye – it just about corresponds with the shape of your bruise. It's the sort of thing someone would have in a car, too. I take it there wasn't one in yours?'

Carrick shook his head. A black car . . . shadows on the ground . . . long shadows . . .

'Keep it for a few days,' Gillard suggested. 'If it helps.'

Carrick remembered the torch. 'Thanks. I really appreciate your taking time to –' Suddenly trees, road and the man he was talking to spun sickeningly. The next thing he was aware of was sitting sideways in a car that wasn't the one he had arrived in, his feet on the road, head between his knees, a strange ringing in his ears. Then the door behind him opened and he found himself effortlessly lying back on the BMW's back seat. Icy cold water followed by an equally cold cloth passed over his face and brow.

'It's river water, I'm afraid,' said the clothbearer cheerfully. 'Stay where you are for a moment.' He went away.

Carrick manoeuvred the sodden, still-folded handkerchief, a fine white lawn one, from where it had been left parked on his forehead to his temple, where the pain was worse, and held it there. He would not reprimand Woods for telling a complete stranger where he was when he was working. What was the point? Everyone obeyed that voice.

'I've fixed it,' Gillard said, returning briskly. 'I told your man in charge that you weren't too well and that I'd take you wherever you have to go with that piece of evidence. Someone will take your car back to your flat when they've finished here. Have you eaten today?'

'No,' Carrick muttered.

'Neither have I. I'm sure you can think of a very good reason to call at the Crossbow to have a further word with the landlord – a late lunch wouldn't do you any harm at all.'

Handing over his car keys Carrick had no choice but to submit to being organised. He felt too shaky to do otherwise. But he did move into the front passenger seat of the BMW as he had a marked disinclination to be ferried, as it were, as cargo. When they arrived at the Crossbow he took the torch inside with him.

'No, it was a red one,' said Tim Brockenhurst emphatically. 'He always had it with him.'

'And you're sure he had it last Saturday night? Even though he'd brought his car?' Carrick asked.

'Positive. He used to put it down on the bar in front of him, that's how I know. He'd left it on the floor once and gone without it. Yes, always. There are no lights in the car park, see? I have to have planning permission to put them up as it's what they call a heritage area and so far the planning bods aren't too keen. I keep telling them it's dangerous and I don't want people taking a wrong turning and ending up in the river or even the canal.'

'And you haven't seen *this* one before?'

Brockenhurst stared at it balefully as though it had been directly responsible for one of his clients' demise. 'Can't say as I have. But Gilcrist wasn't the only one to bring a light. Some folk walk from Broadstoke along the road regularly as they don't want to drink and drive. And that's a ten-a-penny kind of thing, isn't it? Probably came off a market stall.'

A large portion of steak and kidney pie later Carrick felt a new man. And so, apparently, did his companion for he suddenly said, 'It would be interesting to know if the batteries are flat because then you could work on the theory that the person who killed Gilcrist acquired his victim's torch because his own wasn't much good. When he walked back to the cottage he chucked the other one away.'

Carrick had not had the chance to discuss the case with

107

Gillard at all that day, other than to mention that the item in his possession was not what everyone had been looking for. 'It occurred to me too that the murderer had possibly walked along the riverbank with Gilcrist. But we did find Gilcrist's wallet in the *other* direction – not far from here.'

Patrick shrugged. 'That could have been either a deliberate ploy to make the police think that Gilcrist had been mugged by someone in the vicinity of this pub or he might have panicked, forgetting for a moment that his wheels were back at the cottage. If he was unfamiliar with the area or really worried about being spotted he'd have gone back that way anyway.'

'Is that what you would have done?' Carried enquired.

Patrick smiled peaceably. 'No, because all my efforts in that direction have been properly planned in advance. This killing wasn't, surely. Only Gilcrist could have known he would wander back to this place for some booze that night. I mean, no one can have been lurking around in the dark on the offchance that he would – it wasn't as though he did that kind of thing on a regular basis. No, I think the murderer was waiting at the cottage and agreed to walk back to the pub with him. Either that, or Gilcrist stormed out in the middle of an argument and the person he was arguing with was forced to accompany him or forget it and go home. Perhaps the argument got out of hand. But to answer your question properly, no, I'd have gone across the fields.'

Carrick poured a little milk into his coffee. 'You know more about this than was printed in the papers.'

'Yes, well, my department did undertake a little investigation. I'm not the sort of bloke to issue warnings if I haven't satisfied myself that one is necessary. And if your next question is is there a file on Gilcrist the answer's yes – not that I can allow you to have a look at it.'

'I'm sure you have a very good memory, though,' Carrick murmured.

'Of course. What do you want to know?'

Carrick was wondering what kind of connection this man had now, if any, with the security services. And perhaps in gentle revenge for no .mention of files having been made previously, he said, 'Tell me about Alan Terrington.'

'The one-time CID sergeant? He's dying from lung cancer.'

'That would explain the appalling cough,' Carrick said.

'He's had a lung removed but won't stop smoking. I understand that he's very bitter, but I can't see him thumping Gilcrist over the head on a dark January night. Officially it was his ill health that forced him to retire from Dalesland Police, not the Jones case. A profitable line of enquiry as far as you're concerned might be to discover how Gilcrist got to hear of Terrington's handling of the case. That wasn't really our brief.'

'What about Brian Kelso?'

'All I know about him is that he sometimes works for Gilcrist's film company.'

'He's married to a girl Gilcrist was having an affair with.'

'Ah, well, do remember that I got caught up in this a while back – just over two years ago. It goes without saying that you've spoken at length with Gilcrist's wife. She's a wealthy woman now he's dead.'

'She told me she didn't know how things stood in that direction.'

'Really? Then perhaps circumstances have changed. At one time she had a very substantial life insurance policy in his name. She's the daughter of Mick O'Reilly by the way, a gentleman well known to the Metropolitan Police until someone put three bullets in him in March '79.'

'A stolen car racket, armed robbery and taking away post office safes without the owners' consent if I remember rightly.'

Patrick grinned. 'But a wonderful family man. Perhaps a fond father gave his daughter an allowance to help pay large insurance premiums.'

'She doesn't strike me as that kind of woman,' Carrick said reflectively.

'I'm sure you're right. Nothing useful comes from prejudging people.'

There was a short silence broken by Carrick saying, 'You don't have to try so hard not to tread on my toes.'

'It's your case,' Patrick pointed out. 'Okay, tell me about the car you saw instead.'

'It was black, the boot lid was up and . . .'

One dark eyebrow lifted enquiringly. 'And?'

But the mists had swirled into Carrick's mind again and the tantalising glimpse had been blotted out. He shook his head.

'You'll remember. It's only a matter of time.'

'The car might be totally irrelevant.'

'I very much doubt it. For one thing Graeme Campbell has a black Ford Granada.' He stretched his arms, wincing. 'Bloody gardening. Are you ready?'

'It might be in his garage,' Carrick said, staying put.

'It is. Mrs Smithers said so. But Campbell doesn't usually drive north, he flies.'

Carrick slowly got to his feet. 'I just can't go nosing around. There are no grounds – I've absolutely nothing to go on.'

'I did ring the airport – Bristol, that is. He got the nine-thirty flight to Glasgow on Saturday morning.'

Carrick didn't speak until they were outside. He said, 'Then until I hear otherwise I'll have to accept that he's in Scotland. I'm sorry, Patrick, but I can't operate under your kind of mandate. I've a feeling that given a little encouragement from me you'd get into that garage and go over it with your own personal forensic lab. Don't. If you do and the whole affair goes pear-shaped I'll have no choice but to throw the book at you. But I'm really grateful, believe me I am.'

Gillard said, 'I'd have been more than a little worried if you'd encouraged me in the slightest way. And you're right really about how I'm used to operating. I've been given *carte blanche*. But there was always the knowledge at the back of my mind that they had a cupboardful of very sharp nails with which they'd crucify me if I got it wrong.'

'You've a gut feeling that something's very wrong as far as Campbell's concerned?'

'Would he have cultivated such a good hangover if he knew he was flying north on business the next morning?'

As he had promised, Patrick gave Carrick a lift to the building that housed the Path. lab and, as Carrick insisted he could get a taxi from there to Manvers Street, left him. Thoughtful, he then drove back to Hinton Littlemoor. He wasn't sure he could justify meddling with something that was, strictly speaking, none of his business. There was an uncomfortable feeling that here was a man in his early forties who still couldn't resist playing at soldiers.

Nonetheless, later, after some discreet surveillance, he made a phone call to an office situated above a certain herbalist's shop in Milsom Street, Bath.

Carrick, in fact, was quite glad to see the army officer go. Much more of his company and he would get involved in unprofessional, irresponsible, questionable and utterly entrancing behaviour. Every ounce of his being, he had to admit, yearned to crawl all over Graeme Campbell's Ford Granada looking for bloodstains, monkey wrenches and God alone knew what else.

'Bugger everything,' was the only muttered grumble he permitted himself, realising he had forgotten to ask Amanda about the torch.

He couldn't face the nick, nor Haine for that matter, and despite the fact that he still felt weak at the knees, went for a walk, trying to get his thoughts in order. His stroll took him to Kingsmead Square, where he bought a local paper, and paused for a moment, scanning the front page. Glancing up, he saw Leonora Kelso and Larne Painswick walking on the other side of the road.

They did not see him; in fact, they were hardly looking where they were going, such was the intensity of their argument. Carrick followed them, with his paper ready to hide his face. But they were so involved with what they were saying to each other it was doubtful if they would have noticed a brass band in their wake.

Fifty yards from the square they turned right through the entrance of a small park, Leonora walking even more quickly now, giving the impression that she wished to finish their conversation. Painswick was gesticulating furiously by this time and seized his companion by the arm to bring her to a halt. She furiously shook off his hand and continued on her way. Painswick shouted something, Carrick did not hear the exact words, and then set off after her, having almost to run to keep pace with her long strides.

111

The park was deserted. An early dusk had been brought on by low, murky-looking clouds, and the air on Carrick's face was raw cold, with snow in the offing. He slipped behind the trunk of a plane tree when the couple halted, Painswick having once more caught the girl by the arm. When she tried to struggle free, he shook her hard. She started to scream that he was hurting her, her cries sending up a flock of pigeons that had been pecking at the grass.

Painswick saw Carrick when he was some twenty yards away and ran. He knew that, in the eyes of the law, his behaviour would be open to only one interpretation. He was sorry that he'd hurt Leonora – but he'd done quite a few uncharacteristic things lately and regretted them afterwards. If Carrick did catch up with him – which was unlikely, for he was pretty fit, what with all the country walks he enjoyed – he could risk it all, lash out, then make for Heathrow and the nearest country that had no extradition agreement with Britain. He glanced back. The cop had stopped to see if Leo was all right and was accompanying her to a park bench. Painswick slowed down. He'd just cruise to that little side exit that not many people seemed to know about . . .

It was a horrible shock then to be run down like a hapless gazelle by a cheetah, slammed face down into the mud, all the breath knocked out of him.

'You're not allowed to do things like that,' Painswick gasped when he could speak.

Carrick was suffering the consequences of his tackle and said nothing. It wasn't the first time he had heard those words from a suspect. He simply hauled Painswick to his feet and marched him back the way he had come.

'Okay, I hurt her,' Painswick shouted when seated in number two interview room, back at the Manvers Street headquarters. 'I'm sorry I did it now but at the time I could have . . .' He broke off, biting his lip. There was dog's mess on his best sweater where he had hit the ground and although he had taken it off he could still smell it. It was making him feel sick.

'*Killed* her?' Carrick enquired softly.

'Don't put words into my mouth.'

'Mrs Kelso has made a statement to the effect that you've

112

been threatening her, trying to stop her from revealing to the police that you were in Bath last Saturday night.'

'I'm not saying any more.'

'Silence won't help you, and you know it. I suggest to you that you planned it all quite carefully. You drove back from Devon, intending to go and visit Marvin Gilcrist, and teach him a lesson for blacking Mrs Kelso's eye. Did you lose your temper?'

'Go to hell.'

'It's quite a temper, too – Mrs Kelso's arms are severely bruised. Do you keep a torch in your car?'

'Yes, although what that –'

'What colour is it?'

'Greenish, one of those rubber, waterproof things. I once had to change a wheel in the pitch dark and I wanted to be prepared in future.'

'Had it long?'

'Years. Look –'

'Have you ever possessed a silver-coloured one?'

'No.'

'What time did you get back from Torquay?'

Painswick looked mulish.

Carrick said, 'You must have intended to do Gilcrist real harm, otherwise you wouldn't have gone to such lengths to provide yourself with an alibi.' When there was still no response he asked, for the second time during the interview, 'Would you prefer that your solicitor be present?'

'That's an admission of guilt,' Painswick muttered.

'Well, you're guilty of *something*. Assault? House-breaking? Murder?'

'I didn't *kill* him!'

'I can't even begin to believe you until you decide to co-operate. You said in your statement to Sergeant Ingrams that you went to a cinema on the Saturday night and then had an Indian meal. Is that true?'

Painswick took a deep jerky breath. 'Yes, damn you.'

Sergeant Woods, not normally much involved with CID work, but present due to lack of staff, looked on impassively. In truth, he was enjoying himself. Someone now ought to say for the benefit of the tape, he thought with amusement, that

113

the inspector was regarding the suspect in a fashion which conveyed that, given half a chance, he would have Painswick taken somewhere private where he would paste hell out of him.

'At – at least . . .' Painswick stuttered. 'In reverse order. I had the meal first.'

'Then you went to your cinema, bought a ticket but left straight away via some kind of emergency exit.'

'If you bloody know so much, then why ask?' Painswick shouted.

Carrick gave him a bleak smile. 'I just want you to confirm my suspicions. I suppose that even with the weather so bad you could have made the journey in a little over two hours – if you'd broken a few speed limits, that is. What time did you leave Torquay?'

'At just after eight-thirty,' Painswick answered sullenly.

'And you got here when? Come on, I've a headache and I'm fed up with dragging the truth out of you.'

'I – I think it was about a quarter to eleven. Look, Inspector, I'm not normally a violent man – far from it. I'd already taken Gilcrist to task over what had happened and he'd laughed in my face. Asked me what I was going to do about it. Asked if I was going to beat him up, said at least that would prove I was a real man. He liked to do that to people – wind them up. And despite what you said I didn't go away for the weekend with it all planned in advance, it just worked out that way. I was scared that you'd try to pin the murder on me, I had to lie.' He looked Carrick straight in the eye. 'And don't you dare pretend to be shocked by that – it wouldn't be the first time that someone's face has fitted.'

'It would be the first time as far as I'm concerned,' Carrick said quietly.

'I'd seen the film before,' Painswick continued. 'It was by a Russian director. In the first scene an officer in the Politburo rapes a girl, beating her when she resists. Just seeing it advertised made me think of what had happened to Leo and I started to seethe with anger. It was then that I decided to do something about Gilcrist. Not to kill him, just to teach him a lesson that he wouldn't forget. I didn't care a damn about my job – I'd already decided never to work for Gilcrist again.'

114

'You went straight to the cottage?'

'Yes, it was afterwards that I called in on Leo and told her he'd leave her alone from now on.'

'Those were your words – your exact words? Didn't you go into any more details?'

'No. I – I wasn't feeling too proud of myself by that time.'

'She thought you meant you'd killed him,' Carrick told him calmly. 'At least she assumed that when she heard he was dead. Go on.'

'He wasn't at the cottage. That really knocked me sideways after having driven all that way. I'd come off the boil by then a bit, too, especially after I'd hung around in the garden for another ten minutes or so. Then I wandered back to where I'd left the car, a bit farther along the road. When I reached it I heard a car coming – there'd been hardly any traffic up until then. It stopped outside Gilcrist's place and someone got out. I recognised Gilcrist's outline in another car's headlights. I made up my mind then to do *something* even though I was soaked practically to the skin – I'd accidentally left my waterproofs in my hotel room.'

'It wasn't raining in Devon?'

'No. Had been but it was fine when I left.'

'What sort of car had given Gilcrist a lift?'

'A dark pick-up of some kind. It stopped again when it had been turned round and gave a lift to someone else.'

The farmer's son who had taken Gilcrist home owned a dark blue Mazda pick-up.

'And then?' Carrick prompted.

'Just seeing him got me mad again. I went back and just walked in – the look on his face made it all worth while. He was a bit tight but not too drunk to know that I meant business. It was then that I found I couldn't do it.'

'You didn't touch him?' Carrick asked sharply.

'No. I smashed up the cottage instead.'

'You didn't lay a finger on him *once*?'

'Just pushed him away a couple of times when he tried to stop me.'

'Did he fall?'

'Tripped over a chair and fell to his knees. Seeing him crouched there, I realised he was just an obnoxious old man.

115

I left. I was in a bit of a state myself – I was sick outside.'
Painswick swallowed hard. 'I don't feel too good now,
actually.'

Carrick switched off the tape recorder and opened a
window. Then he asked Woods to fetch Painswick a cup of
tea.

'What was he doing when you left?' Carrick said when
they resumed about ten minutes later.

'Still sitting on the floor, swearing at me.'

'Did you see anyone outside when you left?'

'No. But I was in such a daze, I wasn't really looking.'

'Then what did you do?'

'I went back to the car and sat in it for a couple of minutes
– I felt very shaky. Then I headed for Leo's flat. She'd just
come in and wasn't pleased to see me. Later, I had a snack in
an all-night transport café. It was near Taunton but I don't
remember the name of it. When I heard on Monday that
Gilcrist was dead, I flipped. I thought I must have hurt him in
some way and he'd staggered outside and fallen in the river.'

'I'm not at all sure why you told Mrs Kelso what you'd
done.'

Painswick's lips curled in self-mockery. 'I was the big
avenging hero, wasn't I? I'd bearded the wicked baron in his
castle and taught him a lesson. At least, that's what I'd
convinced myself of by the time I reached Bath. I realised
afterwards how stupid I'd been to tell her anything. But it's
not true that I've been threatening her.'

'You say that she'd just come in when you arrived. Did she
say where she'd been?'

'No, and I didn't ask.'

Carrick took him through it all again but Painswick stuck
to his story. It was plausible; Carrick was inclined to believe
him. But he had him locked up in a cell all the same.

Chapter Eleven

When Hinton Grange was built, some time during the sixteenth century, a door had been put in the high boundary wall between the grounds and the rectory garden next door. This, no doubt, had been done to enable the squire and his lady to attend church without having to endure the stares of the villagers or the mire of the lane, there being a gate on the other side of the rectory garden that led directly into the churchyard. In modern times, at least while the Gillards had been living there, the door had been left unlocked to allow Elspeth Gillard and her friend Jane Framley easy access to one another's homes for coffee, or to retrieve the Framleys' overweight dog, Roz, who always seemed to turn up at the rectory at mealtimes. When Graeme Campbell had bought the Grange it was agreed that both parties should continue to hold a key.

On this particular night there was no grating sound when the key was turned in the lock nor did the hinges squeak when the door slowly opened, the reason for this being that both had been diligently oiled some two hours previously. Utter silence continued as the man passed through the opening and closed the door behind him again. He did not lock it. A few leaves rustled but this might have only been those which still clung to the lower branches of a beech tree as a slight breeze wafted through them.

It was going through Patrick Gillard's mind that he ought to be resolutely indoors, in front of the log fire he had lit in the sitting room, not lurking in his neighbour's garden, the first flakes of snow brushing against his cheeks. But Fraser

Campbell was at the Grange. He had arrived in the late afternoon and one of his first tasks had been to clean his father's car, thoroughly, vacuum cleaning the interior as well.

'A rude, unpleasant sort of young man,' Mrs Smithers had said when Patrick had intercepted her on her way home later in the day and steered the conversation round to Fraser, adding in a whisper, 'I know I shouldn't gossip but I heard them rowin'' – Fraser had asked for money and Mr Campbell said no.'

'When was this?' Gillard had enquired.

'The night they all went out – I'd been asked to go round and fix them a bite of tea.'

Fraser had been too busy with his sponge, bucket of soapy water and vacuum cleaner earlier to notice that one of the branches of an ilex tree that leaned over the wall from next door was dipping a little lower than usual. Even if he had walked considerably closer it was doubtful whether he would have noticed the tree's temporary inhabitant who sat, utterly motionless, clothed in dark grey tracksuit trousers and a matching sweater.

Patrick, whose attention had been drawn to activities at the Grange by the noisy revving of the engine of Campbell's car when it was taken out of the garage, slipped silently between a group of young silver firs, at one time Jane Framley's pride and joy, and blended himself inconspicuously with the deepest shade near an ivy-covered wall.

He had been wrong. This wasn't fun and games, a means of staving off boredom. Someone had tried to kill Carrick. That person was still at large.

At about the same moment as Patrick slipped noiselessly into Campbell's garden, Joanna rang the bell at the front door of Hinton Grange, switching on a big bright smile when the door was opened.

'Yes?' Fraser Campbell said in offhand fashion.

'Sorry to bother you,' Joanna said when she had introduced herself. 'I'm a friend of James Carrick's and I was wondering whether you could spare me a few moments.'

'Another time?' he said, already starting to close the door.

'Only he had a serious accident last week and I understand

118

you and your father and brother were the last to see him.'

'Is the man dead?'

'No.'

'Then how could we have been . . .?'

'The last to see him before it happened,' Joanna explained. 'You must remember, it was at the Crawford Hotel.'

'Oh, yes – of course. The Burns Night supper. But I don't see how I can help –'

'I just wondered if you could tell me what happened after he left you at the hotel.'

'You mean later, out in the car park, when he appeared at the run and drove off in his car?'

'*Anything* you can tell me,' Joanna said, hoping that she was still smiling. 'He's forgotten, you see – he had a bang on the head and he's suffering from amnesia.'

'Oh, I see. Perhaps you'd better come in and I'll tell you what I can remember.' In the hall he added, 'You'll probably be wondering why I've come south again. I had a phone call from a business friend of my father's who said the old man hadn't turned up for a meeting they'd planned. We put him on the plane last Saturday morning so he flew up to Glasgow all right. So where's he gone? I've called a couple of hotels where he might have been staying but he's not there. I'm beginning to think that the old scoundrel's gone to see his lady-love in Aberdeen and abandoned business to the four winds.'

'So why did you come here?' Joanna asked.

'Because he was supposed to be taking some hellishly important signed contracts north with him and the bloke who rang me asked if they were here. Mrs Smithers wouldn't know what to look for, so I came down. At extreme inconvenience, I might add.' He flung open a door. 'Sit down.'

Joanna perched on the edge of a chair in the overheated room. 'You actually saw Carrick leave the hotel, get into his car and drive off?'

'Yes, I don't think he saw us, but I suppose it's possible. Bruce had opened up the boot of the car to change his shoes. He was driving and always says it ruins his evening shoes. But don't ask me why Carrick left. He'd told us that he was staying at the place for a couple of nights. Drink?'

119

'No thanks,' Joanna said. Her task of causing a diversion with regard to the occupant of the house was turning into something else entirely.

Fraser wrung the top off a bottle of whisky and splashed some of the contents into a glass. He was a big, blond-haired man with a florid complexion. In his early thirties, he exuded an air of healthy, well-fed prosperity and was clearly conscious of this, flexing his broad shoulders as he seated himself in an armchair, smiling charmingly at his visitor, gazing upon her with his large china-blue eyes.

'Perhaps it isn't quite correct to say that Carrick was running,' he said. 'He was in a hell of a hurry, though – seemed to have a bee in his bonnet about something. He actually collided with a chap who was just about to go in through the front entrance.'

'Any idea who the man was?'

'No, not a clue. It was too dark and I was too far away to see properly. All I know is that he'd come to pick up someone – he'd left his car with the engine running not far away.'

'A taxi driver perhaps?'

'Could have been – I didn't take much notice. I was too busy getting the old man in the car – he'd had a few too many.'

'So you'd parked in the main part of the car park, not the smaller L-shaped area just round the corner?'

Glass halfway to his mouth, Fraser frowned. 'Why do you ask?'

'The latter's where Carrick's car was. I'm just trying to build up a picture of what happened.'

'Is it so important, seeing the man's still alive and kicking?'

'Mr Campbell, policemen who drink and drive tend to get into a lot of trouble.'

His brow cleared. 'God, yes! Sorry to be so thick. Yes, we were parked in one of the first slots in that area you mentioned. From where I was standing – arguing with Dad and telling him he couldn't stay for yet another drink – I could see the main entrance.'

'So after he collided with this man he must have come towards you.'

'Er – yes.'

'And then walked right past you, got into his car and drove off.'

'That's right.'

'Were there any other witnesses to this?'

'Not that I know of. Are you sure you won't have a drink?' Fraser asked, picking up in encouraging fashion the whisky bottle by the neck and waggling it.

See if you can stretch it to fifteen minutes, Patrick had said. 'Perhaps a very small one,' Joanna said. 'I'm driving.' She endeavoured to appear relaxed. 'Didn't Carrick speak, offer some kind of explanation as to why he was leaving?'

'No. But, as I said, I wasn't paying much attention, just saw him out of the corner of my eye as he went by.'

He handed her a drink and she took a sip. 'You must be worried about your father.'

Fraser smiled broadly. 'No, I'm not really. The old so-and-so's done it before. Unfortunately the lady in question is married so he can only go and see her when her husband's away working on oil rigs in the North Sea. I don't know why she doesn't just up and leave and come down here – her other half treats her pretty badly according to Dad. Perhaps that's what he's up to – giving her the persuasion treatment.'

'He must be lonely here, all on his own.'

'I think he always intended to get married again – but the right woman never came along. Mother died when Bruce and I were small.'

'So he brought you up single-handed?'

'There was a female relative who helped when we were very young. This, er – business of Carrick . . . Will he lose his job?'

'It's possible, I suppose. It depends upon those in charge. Unless he can prove he was innocent – or his memory returns.'

'Don't the facts speak for themselves?'

'I think everyone needs to know why he left. Perhaps I can trace the man you saw him bump into.'

'It was a hell of a collision. The guy went sprawling.'

A few minutes later Joanna left. She did not drive directly up to the rectory but left her car outside the church and made the rest of the journey on foot, worried that if Fraser was

121

outside he might hear the vehicle's progress on such a quiet winter's night. She was not unduly alarmed when a man-sized section of deeper shadow appeared from by the hedge and accompanied her up the drive.

'Go round the back,' Patrick instructed softly. 'We can't use the front door yet as there's still a large hole in the floor of the hall.'

'I hope I gave you enough time.'

He chuckled. 'Long enough to do what I wanted to and then lurk around out here to guide you round the pile of rubble the builders left for everyone to fall over.' He took her arm and steered her sharply to the right and then left.

'You have cat's eyes,' Joanna murmured.

'No, mine are merely used to the dark as I've been out here for quite a while. What did you make of Fraser?'

'I must admit, he was plausible. I found myself believing him when he said he saw Carrick leave the hotel and drive off in his car. Which is dreadful news for James, of course.'

'The bit about him colliding with someone was open to question, don't you think?' In the darkness Patrick unlocked the back door and switched on an interior light. 'After you.'

'So you have cat's paws too,' Joanna said when she had removed her coat and been ushered into a long, narrow room lit by the leaping flames of a log fire.

Patrick switched on a lamp. 'I'm not in the habit of sending young women into potentially dangerous situations without providing a little back-up. It didn't take very long to find the dust bag from the vacuum cleaner in the bin, together with a couple of dusters he'd chucked away with it.'

'It took all my willpower not to ask more about the woman in Aberdeen. When you've been in the job . . .' She shrugged. 'So he'd thoroughly cleaned the car. Does that make him a criminal?'

Patrick had stripped off his heavy dark sweater to reveal a blue silk shirt. Running his fingers through his tousled hair, he said, 'No, but it sounds as though you're a mite depressed about things in general. Coffee?'

'Yes, please. Is it that obvious?' She removed the miniature tape recorder from her bag and placed it on a low table.

'That you're still fighting mad about being made to resign? Yes.'

The coffee was all ready in a thermos jug on the hearth.

'Perhaps I ought to wear a paper bag over my head.'

'Or decide what you want to do with your life,' was the calm response.

She wrapped her hands around the mug of coffee she had just been given. 'You're right, of course. I'm just raging around blaming everyone but myself. And I'm not going to say anything really wet like he'll always need me. When they get round to giving him a decent sergeant I shall be able to direct my energies elsewhere.' She glanced up, giving him an angry look. 'No, that's living in cloud-cuckoo land, isn't it? Perhaps I can't face the fact that I'm not good at anything else.'

Patrick clicked his tongue reprovingly.

'Or perhaps I should marry the guy?' Joanna asked tautly.

'Has he asked you to?'

'Sort of.'

'Then marry him and come and work for me. I can promise that your mind will be too stretched to carry on feeling sorry for yourself.'

She shook her head. 'I don't think I could cope with two such men in my life.'

He controlled his amusement.

'Back to the matter in hand, what do you make of Fraser? James said you were an expert in truth and lies.'

'It helps to be able to see those you're trying to assess but I would say that he seemed very assured and had his tale off pat. Just the way you'd expect an estate agent to be when he's enthusing about the Victorian fireplace so the punters don't notice the dry rot in the opposite corner.'

'What did you do with the things you found in the bin?' Joanna asked when they had listened to the tape right through.

'They're in a clean plastic bag just inside the back door. I think James ought to have them – and this tape.'

'It seems hopeless,' Joanna said, suddenly feeling extremely weary. There was not the smallest piece of evidence to back up Patrick's rather wild theories.

123

'There is one thing we can do. If Carrick really did collide with someone on his way out, that person can be traced. Fraser might have made a point of telling you about it because he chucked Carrick's skene-dhu in the shrubbery somewhere in that area.'

'We don't even know if he found it.'

'Carrick might have tried to defend himself with it. If he did it had to be tidied away somehow in a fashion that would fit the story Fraser was already cooking up – especially, of course, if he noticed the knife on the ground just as they were leaving.'

'I'll go and look for it in the morning,' Joanna promised, stifling a yawn.

'No, this is too interesting to delay,' Patrick said, leaping up. 'I'll drive out and take a look. It'll take me about an hour but please don't go. If I find it we can plan the next move.' And without drinking the rest of his coffee he hurried out, Joanna staring after him disbelievingly.

The room was very cosy in the soft lamplight, the fire having settled down to a rosy glow. Which was why the Reverend John Gillard, his wife Elspeth and their daughter-in-law Ingrid, who was carrying a baby in her arms and had a tired four-year-old clutching her skirt, discovered that they had a sleeping and rather beautiful redhead on the settee.

'I'm sure there's a perfectly logical explanation for it,' Elspeth whispered, shooing her family from the room. Nothing that her eldest son did ever flummoxed her.

Alan Terrington, one-time Sergeant in Dalesland CID, coughed resoundingly and lit another cigarette. He was a thin, round-shouldered man of medium height, his face tanned and prematurely lined. He looked ill but when he gazed at Carrick through the smoke wreathing around his head his brown eyes were lively and possessed of a keen intelligence.

'Thanks for coming,' Carrick said. He had asked Terrington to visit him, not at the police station, but at home. He had felt he should at least give the dying man the benefit of the doubt.

'I only turned up because I've a better than average alibi

for that night,' Terrington said and then laughed, setting himself coughing again. 'No, seriously,' he continued when he had recovered. 'I thought you'd enjoy an in-depth conversation about this unspeakable bastard who got himself topped. Although, of course, I'll try to live up to the good old days on the job and avoid personal prejudice.' He smiled fiercely and humourlessly, resembling for a moment some kind of malevolent oriental idol.

Carrick voiced his reaction. 'You must have scared the shit out of suspects.'

'That's as maybe. Gilcrist didn't say that in his bloody film. According to him I beat the living daylights out of people who wouldn't confess to the crimes I had lined up for them.'

'Give me the details – I didn't see the programme.'

'That's a pity. It was an excellent insight into how people can build a reputation on slander.'

'Hang on a minute. I did read about it in the papers. The man was cleared after serving four years on the grounds that he'd been intimidated into making a confession. In that Gilcrist was quite correct.'

'He said the confession was false and in legal terms – we'd been careless with alterations to notebooks – it was. But we simply wrote down what Jones, the suspect, said before he'd called for a brief – he was blabbing with remorse. We'd picked him up at his favourite pub when he was on his sixth pint. Oh, he was guilty all right.' Terrington drew quickly on his cigarette. 'The whole town knew he was guilty. When he got out of prison he had to go and live somewhere else – or there would have been a lynching.'

'Give me some of the background information.'

'The murder victim, little Lisa, was Jones's niece and as you probably know there was a family arrangement that he picked her up from school and took her to her grandma's as her mother worked full time. Her father was any one of the motley bunch of no-gooders the woman had knocked around with since she was fifteen and probably the best thing she'd ever done was not to marry any of them. Someone saw Jones down by the river with Lisa on the afternoon she disappeared. He said initially he'd taken her to see some ducklings and

125

delivered her to her granny's the same as always, only a little later than normal, and that she must have run out of the house when the old lady wasn't watching.'

'Where exactly was she found? The account I read mentioned a derelict building.'

'An old shed in what had been a factory yard to be precise. She'd been raped and strangled not a hundred yards from where the witness had seen them together earlier.'

'What led you to him?'

'There had been whisperings about him for years.'

'Which didn't reach the ears of his family?'

'If they did, no one believed it. You don't, do you? – that your own flesh and blood . . .' He broke off, shaking his head sadly.

'And you didn't beat him up? There were injuries, though, weren't there?'

'He bashed himself on the cell wall when we first brought him in and the strong ale he'd been filling himself up with took full effect. We got the police surgeon to take a look at him but he couldn't swear on oath afterwards that Jones's bloodied nose was self-inflicted. When the case was reopened Jones's brief put all the right words in his mouth and suddenly I was the guilty one.'

Quietly Carrick said, 'You *had* been previously involved with cases where a little haste and impatience had crept in.'

The other shrugged. 'You know more about me than you've let on. Yes, I suppose I made a rod for my own back. But understand one thing – that bastard's guilty. And Gilcrist doubly so for paving the way for him to go free.'

There was a short silence then Carrick said, 'You threatened Gilcrist.'

'Yes, if rushing into his office and calling him a lying so-and-so comes under that heading. I said to him what I'll say to you now: Jones is living somewhere else and he's the sort to do it again. And *that* little girl's death will be Gilcrist's responsibility – her blood will be on his hands.'

'He's dead.'

Terrington did not seem to hear the remark. 'Do you know what he said to me? He said I deserved to be cleaning sewers. If you ask me the man became obsessed with the reputation he'd manufactured for himself – as though he was God.'

'How did Gilcrist get hold of the story?'

'I've been trying to find that out for two years. All I know is that he got the nod, directly or indirectly, from the inside – someone on the job.'

'For money?'

'More likely a grudge. Coppers don't have many friends, do they?'

'Any idea why it took so long for the story to come out?'

'I'm beginning to wonder if someone didn't just trawl through a few files to see where a score might be settled. Perhaps Gilcrist put it about that he was interested in a scandal or two.'

'But why Dalesland? That's a long way from Bath.'

Terrington blew a smoke ring. 'That's for you to find out if you've a mind to. It might be where his snout was.' He grinned. 'There, I nearly called you sir.'

'I shall have to ask you about that alibi.'

'Oh, it's a bloody fantastic one. The DCI's my brother-in-law – a couple of years ago he married my eldest sister. My wife and I were out for a meal with them that night and then they came back to our place. It got so late they ended up staying the night.' He grimaced. 'We get on really well, Derek and I, but it's more than his life is worth to protect me.'

'And you're a sick man.'

'With not much longer to go. That's what they called it – retiring on health grounds. I suppose I should be grateful.'

'I'm sorry.'

'Don't be. Look, if I'd been mad enough to want to top someone I'd have gone for Jones. He's the cause of it all.' He coughed agonisingly as he headed into the cold night air in the direction of his taxi.

Chapter Twelve

Despite Carrick's caution about the way in which Leo Kelso had been eager – given a little encouragement – to incriminate Amanda Gilcrist, Haine sallied forth very early the next morning to talk to the murder victim's wife again. He took with him a newly promoted detective inspector from Bristol by the name of Hobbs who was visiting Bath for the day on a fact-finding mission. Carrick was very glad about this; it left him free to devote his energies to lines of enquiry which, in his view, were more likely to prove fruitful. First of all, though, he had Larne Painswick charged with assaulting Mrs Kelso, after which he was freed on bail.

Carrick knew he was taking a huge risk. But Painswick's account of smashing most of the contents of Rampsons and getting himself into such an emotional state that he threw up in the garden afterwards was in complete accord with Carrick's own summing-up of the man's personality. He did not seem to be the sort who would follow Gilcrist along the riverbank and kill him in cold blood.

Carrick set off for Bristol, praying that Brian Kelso's sudden flight into Egypt was of no significance. No matter, if the finger of suspicion pointed in his direction he could be met at the airport on his return.

Blair Craxton's antique shop was closed but by dint of hammering on the door with a clenched fist until it rattled in its frame Carrick brought Craxton at the run from a curtained-off recess at the rear. He unlocked the door and yanked it open.

'Are you trying to smash the glass or something? I'm

closed, or can't you read?'

Carrick produced his warrant card.

'What do you want? I've been interviewed already.'

Carrick inserted his slim frame into the gap between the door post and the buttons on the irate proprietor's fancy waistcoat and proceeded to wander around the shop.

'D'you care for this sort of thing?' Craxton enquired loftily.

Carrick was looking at a blue and white teapot. 'Yes, I've a few modest pieces at home.'

'What would you say if I told you that was Wedgwood?'

'I'd agree with you – as long as we both knew we were talking about Enoch and not the far more famous Josiah.'

'What about the Tang horse on the shelf on the wall?'

Carrick hardly glanced at it. 'I'd call it an extremely poor reproduction.'

There was a short silence.

'Talking of phoneys . . .' Carrick murmured. He picked up a plate with a delicate floral pattern on it.

'*That* isn't,' Craxton said nervously. 'It's Worcester.'

'Even I can read a backstamp,' Carrick said, carefully replacing it. 'No, I was referring to policemen.'

'Bent coppers? I don't see what that has to do with me.'

'Did Marvin Gilcrist ever discuss his work with you?'

'No. Surely you must have realised that we weren't that close.'

'But when you first met him and his wife and advised them on a few items for sale at auctions all was sweetness and light, wasn't it? You were entertained by them at their house. You must have got to know them both quite well. It was only later when you became very close to Amanda indeed that things got a little awkward. Although I'm not too sure that Gilcrist cared a lot what she did by that time. They were already splitting up on account of his affairs over the years with various women. In short, Amanda had had enough of him.'

'None of this has anything to do with me.'

'Perhaps not,' Carrick agreed. 'But I was talking to Alan Terrington last night.'

'I was wondering where the bent copper came in. People

129

like him must make you feel really angry – bringing the force into disrepute and all that. Still, I understand the poor guy's about to snuff it – chain-smoked all his life apparently.'

'We all have to go sometime,' Carrick said, gazing at a painting of a battle at sea. There was a seemingly impossible amount of rigging raining down on the decks of one of the ships and the number of cannonballs whistling through the air would have filled an arsenal.

'He deserved to be found out. If I sell something as genuine, knowing it to be a fake, I get what's coming to me. So did he.'

'The point is,' Carrick said, 'that the man who exposed him is now dead. Did Gilcrist offer informants money, do you know?'

'I doubt it, I'm sure that sort of thing isn't normal practice.'

'Perhaps Gilcrist got the information about Terrington from someone he knew.'

'Well, don't look at me. I might know a bit about English furniture but not about the ins and outs of criminal cases involving Northern lowlife.'

Carrick had a sudden idea. He took his leave.

Haine fired a broadside as soon as his target came into view. 'James, what the *hell* is all this about? You know the procedures for the handling of evidence as well as I do. And now this damned thing has half the population of Bath's fingerprints on it. Which case does it belong to? Why wasn't it correctly handled? Where's the bag it should have been in?'

The item he was referring to was in a plastic bag now and when it was dropped on Carrick's desk everything already there bounced.

Carrick winced.

'They didn't know what to do with it and there was a party of probationers on a tour so someone ran a few tests on it by way of a demo. I won't have my department brought into disrepute in this fashion, James.'

'I'm sorry, sir,' Carrick said. 'It was given to me by a friend who thought it was probably similar to the thing I was struck with. I must have left it behind when I took the torch in for testing.'

130

All the air seemed to leave Haine's lungs. 'You mean it's just something that a bloke picked up in the garage at home and brought along to show you?'

'Absolutely,' Carrick said. 'You couldn't be more correct.'

The DCI sat down. 'Would you be so kind as to tell me who this friend of yours is?'

'His name's Patrick Gillard.'

'I'm asking because that monkey wrench was found to have traces of human blood on it and a single blond hair trapped in the grease on the adjusting nut. I think we'd better talk to him, don't you?'

Carrick reached for the phone.

By the time Gillard arrived, after a remarkably short period of time, Carrick had given Haine a few details about the man they would be interviewing. It was agreed that the DCI would do most of the talking. Carrick was frankly fascinated by the turn of events and had been careful not to explain the reason for the requested chat to Patrick when they'd talked on the phone.

Haine, who was watching closely for signs of dismay, guilt or apprehension when their visitor caught sight of the piece of ironmongery on Carrick's desk, was forced to admit to himself that all he could detect was extremely reserved glee.

'Ah,' Patrick said when the introductions had been made and he had drawn up a chair in front of them and thus instantly made both policemen feel that they were the ones being interviewed.

'What can you tell us about this?' Haine asked a trifle tetchily.

'It belongs to my father. I asked him about it – my wife and parents arrived back at the rectory late last night. He'd lent it to Graeme Campbell who lives next door.'

'Oh, brother,' Carrick whispered.

Haine shot him an impatient sideways glance. 'Go on,' he said to Gillard.

'There's not much more to tell except that up until my parents went to Devon about ten days ago it had not been returned. I found it in the stable the day before yesterday. I presume that Inspector Carrick has told you why I showed it to him.'

'*Is* this definitely your father's monkey wrench?'

'He tells me there's a letter J scratched on one handle – presumably a previous owner's initial. Dad bought it at a car boot sale.'

They had to peer through the plastic cover but the roughly scratched-on letter was there.

'Is the stable normally kept locked?' Haine wanted to know.

'No, there's nothing of value kept in there.'

'It could have been returned without your father's knowledge.'

'In theory, yes. But a few days before they went away Campbell hailed my father across the village street and said it was all ready to be returned – he had it sitting on the floor of his car at that moment. Dad asked him to hang onto it until they got back and bring it round one evening. I think the idea was that Campbell could stay for supper – Dad knew he was a bit lonely.'

'So this tool was normally kept by your father in his garage?'

'That's right.'

'I accidentally left it behind at the Path. lab,' Carrick said.

Gillard beamed upon him. 'And by the grace of the patron saint of bored lab technicians someone did a few tests? Wonderful. A smear of human blood, perhaps? A couple of hairs? Perhaps I shouldn't ask. Anyway I was coming to see you both this morning in any case. I have a few items highly relevant to the case which ought to be in your hands.' He placed upon the desk something small in a plastic bag, what looked like dusters in another and an audio tape cassette. 'The recording on the tape isn't particularly interesting,' he said, 'and I'm fairly sure it couldn't be used in evidence.'

He pushed the small item in the plastic bag in Carrick's direction. In complete silence Carrick contemplated his skene-dhu.

'It was in the shrubbery just to the right of the entrance to the Crawford Hotel,' Gillard said. 'Which bears out Campbell's story. But I'm not saying another word until you've both listened to the tape.'

'Well, that's it then,' Haine commented when they had

132

heard Joanna's conversation with Fraser Campbell. 'I wish – er – Lieutenant Colonel – that you'd not acted alone in this. I'm afraid, James, that it looks as though . . .' He stumbled to a stop when he observed the impatient fashion in which he was being regarded by the army officer.

'He's *lying*,' Gillard said. 'From where he was standing, or says he was standing, you can't see the main entrance. There's a sodding great oak tree slap bang in the middle of the car park and he'd have had to move quite a distance either side to see what he said he did. If he'd walked to the left he'd have been in the way of cars leaving – to the right and he'd have ended up in the bushes. That makes no sense if he really was standing by his father's car arguing with him. I'm fairly sure he invented the collision with the mystery man to explain away tossing the skene-dhu there after he'd picked it up. He probably cursed his own stupidity later for not waiting until they were well on the road and throwing it out of the car window. Or, of course, he might have had the entire scheme worked out at the time and put the knife there deliberately.'

Nostrils flaring, Haine said, 'You're saying, in effect, that Fraser Campbell lost his temper with his drunken father and hit him with the monkey wrench that –'

Gillard butted in. 'It would be wildly premature to suggest anything like that unless you've evidence in connection with the monkey wrench to support such a theory.'

'There are traces of blood and a single blond hair on it,' Carrick said. 'All three Campbells are fair – although Graeme's hair has quite a bit of grey in it.'

'And then James came upon the scene,' Haine went on scornfully, 'and tried to interfere, whereupon Fraser and his brother set upon him and rigged up the car accident to conceal what had really happened. That's so far-fetched it's –'

'Fraser came home yesterday afternoon and immediately cleaned his father's car,' Patrick said. 'Very thoroughly. The almost empty dustbag from the vacuum cleaner plus a couple of far-from-old polishing cloths are in that other bag in front of you. Very early this morning a taxi collected him and, at a guess, took him to the airport. *Quo Vadis?*'

'Well, I think I'm going along with what Fraser Campbell

133

'Well, I think I'm going along with what Fraser Campbell says,' Haine said, thanking everything holy for being able to remember a little of the Latin he had been taught at school. 'Until something happens to make me change my mind, that is. It's quite possible that his father cut himself when he was doing some job or other with the tool and for one of the hairs from his head to become stuck to grease and muck on the thing isn't impossible either. From personal experience of crawling in attics looking for stop-cocks and so forth I'd say it's one of the most hazardous forms of DIY that an ordinary man can tackle. I must point out that the trace of blood on the thing *is* only a trace. Our hands are tied until someone makes an official complaint or tells us that the man is really missing.'

'Why take the monkey wrench back to the rectory and put it in the stable without saying a word?' Carrick asked no one in particular.

'Because he was unexpectedly called away or decided to go north and pay a surprise visit to his lady friend,' Haine said. 'He might have been shy of telling the rector about her, mightn't he? Especially in view of the fact that she's already married. He took it back early the following morning before he caught his plane and, finding the garage locked, left it in the stable.'

Carrick had the dreadful suspicion that Haine was rapidly losing interest. The man from Bristol, Hobbs, had come out of the blue too. Could it be that . . .?

'Find Graeme Campbell if you've a mind to,' Haine was saying to Gillard. 'But that's *all* I can permit you to do. This time I shall turn a blind eye to the matter of entering private property, arranging to plant recording devices in a private house and –'

'Wasting police time?' Patrick interrupted sweetly.

'The disciplining of my officers is a police matter,' Haine retorted. 'We do not operate under the cloak and dagger rules that you appear to. I have to work with the *facts*. The best way you can help James from now on is to stop interfering.'

Nothing could be read in the bright grey eyes. 'But I *can* find Graeme Campbell?' Gillard asked earnestly.

'If you feel that strongly about it,' Haine told him.

134

'Okay,' the other said laconically and departed, belatedly wishing them good day just before he closed the door.

'You bloody fool,' Carrick said under his breath.

Haine stared at him open-mouthed.

'That man has the kind of mandate which allows him to serve up Graeme Campbell on a plate with an apple in his mouth.'

'Not on my patch he doesn't,' Haine countered.

Carrick walked out.

The big dark blue car was ticking over quietly in the parking space reserved for the Chief Superintendent and as Carrick approached it the front passenger door was pushed open.

'I'm really sorry,' Carrick said, sliding into the seat.

Patrick chuckled. 'I hope that wasn't an apology.'

'Of course it was. He's always like this when he's been anywhere near a police conference. Gets all fired up and we have to put up with a pompous ass for a few days. But this is worse than usual – I think he's reached the stage where he's behaving unprofessionally in his eagerness to get rid of me. We've never seen eye to eye.'

'Just keep that monkey wrench nice and safe somewhere.'

'You aren't really going to look for Graeme Campbell!'

'But naturally. "Old Tenacity" they called me in the army. Besides, I'm superfluous at the rectory now the family's home – early, I might add, as Ingrid has an overwhelming desire to go shopping in Bath. And as there's a little frost hanging over Hinton Littlemoor at the moment . . .'

Carrick raised a questioning eyebrow.

'A small matter of my leaving Joanna at the rectory while I went to the Crawford Hotel last night. She fell asleep on the sofa.'

'And your wife arrived . . .' Carrick whistled softly. 'Would you like me to give her a ring and try to smooth things out?'

'Normally,' Patrick said sadly, 'she's bombproof as far as I'm concerned. But a bad attack of baby blues seems to have struck.'

'I'll phone her,' Carrick promised.

'Take her out for a drink if you like. I'm sure she'll leap at

135

the chance to talk to you as she's researching a new novel and it's to be a whodunnit. Take a big pile of procedures manuals with you and she'll be in her element.'

Not at all sure whether to take this seriously Carrick said, 'I got the impression when I spoke to her at the Framleys' party that she used to work with you.'

'Still does sometimes.' Looking reflective Patrick added, 'Women are wonderful but strange creatures, aren't they? Ingrid is a good shot, can abseil, map-read more effectively than I can and if she really had to, could kill someone. I can't get used to the idea that the same person can go down with post-natal depression.'

'Blokes would have to have babies to find out why,' Carrick observed.

Hobbs was in the canteen, gloomily munching his way through a bacon roll.

'So you're gladdening our hearts for a day,' Carrick said, pausing by his table and eyeing the tailored suit and smooth dark brown hair. The grapevine was not being polite about the newcomer, one of the more outspoken damsels in uniform concluding that he had designer labels on his balls.

For an answer Hobbs pulled out the chair next to him and patted the seat chummily.

'I'm busy,' Carrick said, having already decided to take his coffee back to his office. Haine had gone out, probably in a huff.

The other swallowed his mouthful, grimaced and said, 'I just thought you'd like an update on the attractive widow. *Quite* disappointed you weren't with us.'

Carrick gave him the full benefit of a chilly Nordic stare.

Hobbs stared back. 'I'd really appreciate it if you wouldn't skulk in the wings playing bloody Macbeth.'

A smile tugged at the corners of Carrick's mouth but he slew it at birth.

Hobbs said, 'Did you know that her old man was a serious hoodlum in London until a rival mobster pumped him full of lead one night?'

'Yes. Mick O'Reilly.'

'He used to send her money. Did it for years because

136

Gilcrist was only a struggling assistant producer in those days. The woman's adamant that she didn't know what he did for a living and when he was killed and she found out she sent the equivalent amount of money to charity. They were better off by then, she said. But she couldn't afford to keep up the payments on the big life insurance policy she had for Gilcrist so she jacked it in. The other thing is that Gilcrist had changed his will. It's all going to something along the lines of The Best Boys' and Focus Pullers' Benevolent Association. She said she didn't know.'

Carrick said, 'She told me she didn't know how financial matters stood.'

'Did you believe her?'

'Yes. And it was hardly a motive for murder if she wasn't a beneficiary.'

Hobbs lolled back in his chair. 'How about revenge?'

Carrick responded with another question. 'When did he change the will?'

'Quite a while ago apparently.'

'Then why kill him now? If she did know she's had a while to get over it. Besides which, a divorce settlement would probably have given her a good slice of his assets. Financially speaking, the last thing Amanda Gilcrist needed was a dead husband.'

'I meant revenge for him playing around with the Kelso woman. She's probably still got quite a bit of dosh from O'Reilly stashed away somewhere. She could have hired a hit-man knowing that as she would be financially worse off the Bath plods wouldn't suspect her. End of hubby poking hated rival and she could set up home with Craxton.'

Carrick shrugged and went back to work. He was almost missing Bob Ingrams.

Chapter Thirteen

Marvin Gilcrist was to be buried in the churchyard at Broadstoke; Stoke Ford, the tiny hamlet where he had lived, being in that church's parish. On the morning of the funeral, which his brother in Ireland was unable to attend on account of early lambing, it snowed heavily, huge wet flakes that soon covered everything in a sodden white carpet.

'We'll be lucky if we get out of here again,' Haine muttered, watching cars skidding as they tried to ascend the steep village high street. There had been a couple of minor accidents already.

'We'll just have to call up one of Traffic's Range Rovers,' Carrick said, only half serious.

Haine grunted.

The church was vast for a village of that size, and very cold. The congregation surreptitiously rubbed their hands together and shuffled their feet, their breath forming a faint mist in the nave. The vicar apologised, blaming lack of funds; when everyone shuffled out a brass offertory plate quickly overflowed with notes.

'Well, I wonder when the deceased was *last* in church?' Haine said crisply, adding his own contribution to the pile. 'At his wedding probably, like most people.'

'They were married in a registry office,' Carrick said. 'Amanda had been wed before.'

'No useful leads in that direction?' Haine demanded, turning an accusatory gaze on an old stone font which had dared to get in his way.

'No. Her ex-husband was killed in a car crash some years

138

ago.'

'Pity. You know, I come to funerals hoping to spot an individual looking unduly cheerful or over-smitten by remorse but I've never seen anything like this lot. They all look as guilty as hell. *Everyone* hated his guts. Which doesn't help us at all.'

'The lady talking to Amanda right now is his sister. Perhaps she didn't.'

'How the hell do you know that?' Haine barked.

'She looks like him.'

'Oh – yes – I see what you mean.'

'There's hardly anyone turned up,' Amanda was saying in an anguished whisper to the woman. 'Ah, there you are, Inspector Carrick. This is my sister-in-law Anne Thomas.' She gave Haine a cold look, presumably on account of his recent heavy questioning in the company of Hobbs.

Anne Thomas had her brother's arrogant profile and fair colouring. Brows arched she surveyed them both as though they were skinheads who had just crashed a motorbike through the churchyard wall.

'I wonder you have the gall to show your faces,' she cried, her eyes red from weeping. 'My poor brother . . .' and here she dabbed at her face with a handkerchief, 'was at the *top* of his profession and then along comes some madman and puts a stop to it all. He was just snuffed out like a candle. And what have you done about finding his murderer, may I ask? Nothing, by the look of things. My poor little brother . . .' She flung her arms around Amanda's neck in a fresh paroxysm of tears as Haine and Carrick took the hint and crept away.

The coffin was lowered into the cold, wet earth and the twenty or so people present stood around shivering, the snowflakes going down their necks and ruining their hats and good leather shoes. The man from the BBC's documentary department, an earnest soul wearing heavy-framed spectacles who had read the lesson, was the first to leave, apologising to the widow for not being able to accept her hospitality as he had to rush back to town for an urgent appointment. Others told her they had long journeys to make and the weather was dreadful, wasn't it? Almost all took their leave of Amanda

139

Gilcrist and went away.

'Sorry about Annie's outburst,' she said to Haine and Carrick. She was with Blair Craxton, an arm hooked through one of his. There was no sign of the sister-in-law.

'But she's right really,' Carrick told her.

'Would either of you gentlemen like to come home for a little refreshment?' she asked brightly, her gaze on Carrick.

'No thank you,' Haine said stiffly. 'I've left a colleague in charge and although I've every confidence . . .'

'Hobbs?' Carrick enquired of him.

'Hobbs,' Haine agreed.

'You've left him *in charge*?'

Haine became flustered. 'James, someone has to answer the phone.'

'Isn't that your mobile sticking out of your pocket?'

'I'll see you later,' the DCI said darkly and walked away.

'Oh, dear,' Amanda said. 'I'm sorry if that was my fault.'

'No,' Carrick said. 'My apologies for involving you in our grubby little squabbles. And as much as I'd like to accept your invitation . . .' He threw caution to the winds and gave her a hug. 'I'm sorry.'

'He's in some kind of trouble,' she whispered to Craxton when Carrick had gone. 'A pound to a penny that awful man Haine is going to replace him with a truly dreadful creep he called round with – that Hobbs they were talking about.' She fixed Craxton with a rather wild gaze. 'Really ghastly. If he was a piece of furniture he'd be a whatnot from Woolworths that someone had stuck a Sotheby's lot number ticket on.'

'Sounds quite a guy,' Craxton said.

The snow continued and traffic in and around Bath slithered to an almost complete standstill. Carrick, who had an appointment at the out-patients department at the hospital, drove straight there from the funeral and then, due to the sheer impossibility of further travel, went home. Even that short journey took him an hour.

'You're frozen!' Joanna exclaimed, a hand on each side of his face. 'What did they say at the hospital?'

'This won't hurt a bit,' he replied, warming his hands by the fire.

140

'No, I mean *after* they'd taken the stitches out, silly.'

'They said go home, have a nice cup of tea, then a shower, then ravish the first women to cross your path.'

'The kettle's on,' she said.

Later, the prescription having been fully followed, they had lunch, sitting by the window watching the snow turning everything into a white, silent world.

'I feel guilty about this,' Carrick said. 'I'll have to try to get back to work later.'

'You're really worried about this Hobbs character worming his way in, aren't you?'

He shrugged dismissively. 'I'm not even going to think about it. How come *you* aren't at work?'

'It's very quiet at the moment.'

'Business bad, eh?'

'I don't think it'll survive – unless I move to Bristol or London.'

'What do you really want to do?'

'I'd like my old job back.'

'Then *go* for it.'

'And how many years would it take to get back to CID Sergeant? I might not even be accepted for re-entry. No, dreams don't pay the mortgage.'

He glanced at her quickly. 'I've already asked you to move in with me and you've said no. I understand your wanting to stand on your own two feet but I wish you'd think about it again.'

'What if we break up?'

'Just now you were saying you wanted to work with me again.'

'Not quite. I said I'd like my old job back. Besides, you can work with people without sleeping with them.'

'Point taken.'

'James, I didn't mean it like that.' She rose from the table. 'Oh, I don't know how I meant it. It's just that if things don't improve very quickly I'll have to give Greg his notice and I really can't do without him.'

'You can employ me when Hobbs has taken over my job.'

Joanna rounded on him, thinking he was being facetious, but saw that he was regarding her soberly. 'You *can't* resign!'

'I might have to if this drink and drive thing sticks.'

The exchange left an uncomfortable silence between them. Later, Carrick went outside and was just in time to see a snowplough bury his car under about four feet of snow. He didn't have a shovel and his head was aching so he went back indoors and fell asleep in a chair. When he awoke Joanna had gone home, on foot he realised with a guilty pang when he saw that her car had been buried too. It wasn't far to walk but he rang to make sure she had arrived safely. Then, the removal of the stitches in his head wound having awakened some kind of agony gremlin, he took two painkillers and went to bed.

Hobbs was in his office when he got to work at eight-fifteen the following morning, after three-quarters of an hour's work with a borrowed shovel. 'We thought you'd got lost,' he said with a superior smile.

'Is that the royal plural or did Haine think so too?' Carrick asked, slamming the door.

'We've both been here all night solving your murder case for you,' said Hobbs, gathering an armful of files nothing to do with the Gilcrist case from the shelves and dropping them down on the desk. He looked up and grinned mockingly. 'Just thought I'd see what else you have outstanding.' The grin was wiped off his face when he perceived that he had gone too far and was in acute physical danger. 'You wouldn't dare,' he breathed. 'It'll look really bad for you,' he went on in a panic-stricken whisper. 'After your head injury and all. They'll think you've gone off your rocker.'

'No, they know I'm always like this with stupid shits,' Carrick said, moving a bit closer.

Hobbs' nerve broke and with a bleat of fear he wrenched open the door and bolted.

'Gone to change his trousers, sir?' Woods called across from the desk. He chuckled to himself, but stopped abruptly when he saw that Hobbs had literally run into the DCI and was relating what had happened. 'Bloody little toady . . .'

Carrick had replaced his files and was gazing about his office to see what else had been moved when Haine, followed at a suitably subservient distance by his protégé, erupted through the door.

142

'There have been developments while you were otherwise engaged,' he said loudly. 'Mrs Kelso had an intruder break into her flat last night. We've picked up the man you released – Painswick. She said he's been pestering her at work and over the phone and she's convinced that he broke in in the early hours. He has the flu and that's how she knew – she heard him sneezing.'

'Coughing, sir,' Hobbs corrected obsequiously.

'Coughing, sneezing – what the hell does it matter? James, I think it's only fitting that you ought to go over and apologise, don't you?' Without waiting for a reply he continued. 'I'm convinced now that he killed Marvin Gilcrist. In Painswick's own words, Gilcrist liked to wind people up and that's what he did at that cottage.' He carried on standing there, unshaven, features blurred from lack of sleep, and Carrick had no choice but to leave immediately.

Leo Kelso had a friend with her. Tina worked in the florist's shop downstairs and had a bedsitter on the top floor. It was she who let Carrick in, without speaking once she had asked for his warrant card. The atmosphere in the tiny flat was distinctly unfriendly.

Leo was smoking nervously, her hands unsteady.

'You told Haine he'd been pestering you,' Carrick said.

'Yes.' Her voice was barely audible.

'In what way?'

'What way do you think? Talking to me when I didn't want to talk to him. Phoning me up all the time. Not leaving me alone.'

'Yes, but what did he *say*?'

'Making out he was sorry. Saying he'd make it up to me. He just wouldn't go away.'

'Are you hurt?'

'I tripped over the coffee table.'

Carrick indicated the one that stood between them. 'This one?'

She nodded.

'Can you tell me about it?'

'I've already told that other smartarse.'

'Hobbs?'

'I think that's what he said his name was.'

143

'So Detective Chief Inspector Haine wasn't here?'

'No. Does it matter?' she asked dully.

'Only to me. Please try and tell me what happened.'

She drew deeply on her cigarette and blew a cloud of smoke towards the ceiling. 'I feel like a punchbag must do after a workout session. D'you know what that's like?'

Like being in a car which has gone through a hedge ... 'Yes,' Carrick said.

Tina could hardly believe it when he took one of Leo's hands and the two sat for what seemed a long time, gazing at one another. He was actually quite a dish, Tina thought, with his blue eyes with sort of chips of ice in them. He came from the other end of the universe to that slimy poser, Hobbs.

'I heard a noise,' Leo said. 'I didn't know what time it was because my alarm clock's broken but it must have been between two and two-thirty. The noise came from the kitchen. I was sleeping in here on that sofa you're sitting on – my bedroom's freezing cold when there's an east wind blowing and I can't afford to have the heating going all night. I got up, thinking that the neighbour's cat had come in. She does sometimes, poor thing, as the miserable old cow chucks her out at night. Then I realised that it was a man.'

'You leave a window open then?'

'Yes, just a few inches. Amber's not very big and while I don't actually encourage her I can't bear to think of her outside in this weather. I'm stupid, I suppose, because that's how *he* must have got in.'

'And you immediately knew it was Painswick?'

'No, of course not. But he'd been pleading with me to see him and saying he'd come round and camp on my doorstep until I let him in. So when I heard him cough I just knew it was him. I was very frightened. I didn't know what he might do, not after the way he grabbed me in the park. I got out of bed thinking I'd go up to Tina and ring the police. Only I forgot I wasn't in my bedroom and fell over that table.'

'Hang on,' Carrick requested. 'Why not phone from here?'

'There wasn't time, was there? He was in the kitchen, he was seconds away from me.'

'Are you *that* scared of Painswick?'

She shrugged angrily. 'I thought I knew him really well.

144

Now I simply can't fathom how his mind works. One minute he's in tears on the phone saying he wants to apologise and the next –'

'Is that what he's been saying?'

'Since he's been off work with the flu, yes.' She searched his face for a few moments and then shouted, 'Well, don't just sit there looking at me like that! It was him, I tell you!'

Impassively, Carrick asked, 'What happened after you tripped over the table?'

'Nothing for however long it took me to pick myself up. I'd hit my head on something and went all dizzy. I panicked then as I had an idea he was right in the room with me. I just screamed and ran down the hall and onto the stairs. Then I rushed up to Tina. We didn't dare come back down here until the police arrived and by then he'd gone. But not before he'd turned this room upside down.'

Carrick gazed around. 'But you've put everything back now. Pity.'

'Hobbs said we could when he'd had a good look round.'

'Was anything broken?'

'No, but all my work stuff – notes and so forth that I keep at home – was pulled out of that cupboard over there. I've only just finished putting it all back together. He'd chucked all the books off those shelves too.'

'And the pictures off the wall,' Tina added, almost enthusiastically. '*And* he'd thrown all the sofa cushions and your blankets on the floor.'

'But at no time did you actually see the intruder?' Carrick said.

'I *heard* him,' Leo insisted. 'It was Larne, I tell you. He'd told me he'd smashed up Marvin's cottage and now he's done the same to me because I won't have anything more to do with him.'

Carrick sighed. 'Has it never occurred to you that this man's madly in love with you?'

'He has a funny way of showing it,' she retorted.

'Suppose it wasn't Painswick last night.'

'But I *heard* him –'

'Mrs Kelso, approximately two thousand people in Somerset and Avon have the flu right now.'

145

She bit her lip, lowering her gaze.

'Revenge is a terrible thing,' Carrick whispered. 'I suggest to you that you had no idea who it was and made up your mind to drop Painswick in it afterwards.'

'Have you arrested him?' she countered furiously.

'Not personally.'

'But you have taken him in. Well, see what *he* has to say. *I'm* not saying another word.'

Neither was the suspect. He had his head pillowed on his arms on the table in number two interview room, and was shivering gently. Carrick observed this state of affairs and the look on Hobbs' face, then went and found a first aid box.

'He has a temperature of a hundred and two,' Carrick reported to Haine when he had run him to earth in the gents endeavouring to have a shave using cheap soap and a borrowed razor.

'What do you want me to do, James?' asked the DCI grimly. 'Release him into your custody?'

'If I request the police surgeon to attend he'll tell you he's too ill to be interviewed further. And being as the man was hauled out of bed in the first place and is swearing on everything holy that he hadn't left it since yesterday afternoon . . .'

'The man is a *murder* suspect! Have you read the case-notes lately? Half a thumbprint at the cottage turned out to be his.'

'Then post someone outside his front door. He's too ill to stay here.'

Haine had just nicked his face and was in no mood to be sympathetic. 'I've overlooked your insubordination so far because I appreciate you've been under a lot of strain. Kindly don't tell me how to do my job.'

'Then make a decision,' Carrick told him. 'Either throw me to the wolves and forget everything I've ever achieved here – in which case I'll probably go outside and ram Hobbs' teeth down his throat – or go along with what I'm doing. There's no middle course.'

The blood trickling unheeded down his chin, Haine stared in amazement. 'You're prepared to put your entire career on the line over this?'

146

'I'm half hoping you'll turn me down,' Carrick said through his teeth. 'You see, all Hobbs is after is to prove me wrong. There was no scene-of-crime team work done at Mrs Kelso's flat, no fingerprints, no photographs, no nothing. By the time I got there everything had been put back in place. Now you're telling me Painswick's in the frame for murder, too. What are you grooming Hobbs for, Chief Constable?'

The DCI was busy dealing with the spots of blood down the front of yesterday's shirt. When he realised that dabbing it was only making things worse, he decided to undertake damage control of a different sort.

'Very well. For the time being I'm prepared to see things your way. Hobbs, I'm forced to admit, hasn't repaid the trust I've put in him. But don't disappoint me, James. As you well know, there's a lot at stake.'

Which was all fairly meaningless, of course. It still meant Haine could, if Carrick failed, apportion all the blame to him. And after the Burns Night fiasco ... In Haine's opinion, Carrick was still up to his neck in trouble.

Chapter Fourteen

The snow had not amounted to much farther north – a mere half-inch of slush on the pavements that was congealing rapidly to ice as the night grew colder. The roads, salted, were awash with dirty water that formed into sullen grey lakes when it wasn't being dashed away by the tyres of vehicles. Pedestrians picked their way carefully through these hazards, coat collars turned up against a biting east wind from the moors.

Carrick, who had been in the town of Wemdale for only two hours, shivered. Living in the south made you soft.

Although he had never visited this part of the north-east before there was an air of gritty cheerfulness, almost, but not quite, concealing the quiet desperation that he recognised from visits to Glasgow as a boy. All was very different in that Scottish city now, but that desolation survived here. At least there were no drunks in the gutter – the sight of these had been quite an unnerving experience for a ten-year-old. On the other hand, nor was there the amazing architecture; his mother had taken him to see just about every Glasgow building designed by Charles Rennie Mackintosh. Perhaps that was what was missing: a sense of design. Wemdale was featureless, its old streets demolished to make way for shopping malls and underpasses. The heart had been ripped out of it.

Despite adopting a general tone of non-cooperation, Leonora Kelso had sorted through all the paperwork that had been found scattered over the floors and furniture at Rampsons. She was even able to read Gilcrist's handwriting.

Some of the pages of his copious notes had been numbered and these she had quickly reassembled into what turned out to be the research into his impending production about British immigration policies. Another sheaf of paperwork had been identified as public reaction – letters mostly – which he had received after the showing of the programme about the Jones case. Gilcrist, Leo had said, had had no inclination to file anything on a computer.

'Why?' Carrick had asked her.

'He had a thing about hackers,' she had replied, holding out a single sheet of paper. 'Someone once told him that a clever hacker could break into any system.'

'What's that?'

'An oddment. It doesn't seem to marry up with anything else. The paper's different too – the rubbishy stuff we keep for rough work.'

Carrick had taken it from her and glanced through it. 'There's a name here – or at least what appears to be a nickname: Smiler. Does that mean anything to you?'

'No.'

'Are you quite sure about that?' he had persisted.

'Absolutely.'

Smiler.

The police central computer, which had millions of facts on file, listed eleven criminals who were using, or had been known to use, the name. But of course Carrick had no way of knowing whether it had been a private code name known to Gilcrist and the person involved alone, or even a real surname. There was every chance that this person had no criminal record.

Of the eleven Smilers on record three were in prison, another, in his eighties, was in an old people's home, two were deceased and the remaining five were presumed to be still at large. Of these five two were of no fixed address but had last been seen in London; one, a burglar, was rumoured to be dead, the second specialised in stealing cars. Another, 'Smiler Joe' was heavily involved in gang warfare, protection rackets and associated crime in Southampton. 'Mr Smiler' on the other hand, whose real name was Frank Norris, dealt exclusively in drugs and the murder of rival dealers in the

149

north of England. 'The Smiler' had terrorised parts of West Sussex for several months, raping seven women in their homes. He had never been caught but the attacks had suddenly ceased following the death of a local lorry driver who had been found in an exhaust-filled car at a lonely beauty spot. Lack of any real connection between the events meant that the cases remained on file.

Carrick had decided to look for 'Mr Smiler'.

'I don't care what you do,' Haine had said, 'as long as you don't go upsetting the Dalesland force. They have had quite enough flak about Terrington as it is. You're not even to cross the threshold of any of their nicks – and that's an order!'

Fortunately, most of the information written on the sheet of A4 paper was printed so it was not necessary to struggle to decipher Gilcrist's handwriting. There were dates that went back several years, sets of initials that might be short for people or places and other words – 'uncle', 'aunt' and 'nephew' – that Carrick thought might refer to different sums of money. Was it, in fact, a record of payments by Gilcrist to an informant?

The initials were interesting and it wasn't until Carrick had translated 'WS' into 'White Swan' and 'GM' into 'Green Man' that he realised that 'M of G' was that old stalwart the Marquis of Granby. Pubs, then.

The north of England was a big place and Norris, Mr Smiler, had been known to operate from York, Newcastle upon Tyne, Bradford and Carlisle. Of late, since 1990 that was, he had been lying low. This was not to say that crime figures for drugs dealing or murder had fallen, far from it. It was simply that Norris was more adept at covering his tracks these days. He was keeping a lower profile, working from somewhere smaller. Like Wemdale.

Carrick had not mentioned to Haine that he had visited Amanda Gilcrist to ask her, belatedly, about the silver-coloured torch. It had not been the real reason for his visit and, as he had expected, she told him she had never seen it before. He had gone on to ask her a few questions about Blair Craxton and she had answered them readily for they seemed innocent enough.

Crossing the road on foot Carrick approached the first

driver in a taxi rank and soon established that indeed there were pubs in Wemdale that went by the names the initials had suggested to him.

'How about "BA"?' he asked, having explained that he was engaged on a car club's treasure hunt.

'Battersby Arms,' said the man unhesitatingly. 'Brown's Yard, Judd Street. Dodgy place though, guv. I hope you aren't going to take any real ladies in there.'

'Not a chance,' Carrick said ruefully and the man guffawed.

Returning to his car Carrick drove the short distance to a phone box he had noticed earlier and made a call. After leaving a very carefully worded message with the duty sergeant, he went on a short tour of the town and then parked his car at one end of Judd Street and walked. His walk took him right past Wemdale's main police station, down a narrow passageway between a Chinese restaurant and a dry cleaner's and into a dimly lit square.

Brown's Yard had probably at one time been used for stabling horses and there were buildings that might have been wagon sheds. (He found out later that the entire site had been a brewery in Victorian times and that the pub, the Battersby Arms, had originally been the brew house, selling ale made on the premises.) These were now in use as lock-up garages with a cut-price tyreshop – 'The Cheapest Remoulds in the North!' – in one corner.

The whole place stank; a kind of inglorious combination of tomcats, stale beer, urinals and last week's fish and chips. Carrick, who never ceased to be amazed by the sordid conditions that some members of his own sex were prepared to drink in, walked through the door. Too right, he thought, it *was* worse than anything he had encountered in Bristol.

It was not so much the dirt and the noise – rap at a million decibels – or the fact that the air was so thick with cigarette smoke that passive smoking was probably far more dangerous than a high-tar one of your own, that made the place so repellent but the graffiti on the walls, all obscene.

The bartender, a pale individual, started when Carrick spoke to him as though he was not used to being addressed. Perhaps it was because Carrick had had to shout to make himself heard. Watching everyone, when he had settled himself into a vacant corner, he soon realised that there was a kind of sign language in operation, backed up by lip reading. An alcove became free and he moved into it. It was quieter.

He sat there for an hour, occasionally sipping his drink (a half of lager), impassive as a cat watching for voles on a river bank. Then, when another fifteen minutes had gone by, a burly man in his twenties came through the crush, gazed about and then came over to Carrick's table.

'Tell me why you tolerate a place like this,' Carrick said.

'Because it's only five hundred yards from the nick,' was the reply.

Carrick placed a five pound note on the table. 'D'you mind getting your own poison?'

'What will you have?'

'I'm okay.'

'I understand you're a friend of Blair Craxton's,' said the man when he returned.

'That wasn't what I said. I said I knew him. And all I knew about you until I arrived was that your name's Phil. Thanks to Sergeant Adams on the desk I now know you're Detective Constable Phil Deakin.'

'So?'

'I'm afraid I didn't tell him the whole story. But I'm damned if I'm going to wave my warrant card around in here so you'll just have to believe me when I say I'm DI James Carrick, Avon and Somerset Police. This is, I must add, an unofficial visit.'

Deakin had sat bolt upright, spilling some of his beer.

'Does the name Marvin Gilcrist mean anything to you?'

'No!'

'So you're not his snout. What a shame.'

The other buried his head in his hands, his fingers taut in his thick curly hair. 'Oh *Christ*,' Carrick heard him mutter.

'So we're not going to be able to sort out this can of worms, otherwise known as Wemdale nick,' Carrick continued. 'But while you're here perhaps you can tell me how I can contact a bloke who calls himself Mr Smiler.'

Deakin raised his head and stared at him. 'You can't, sir.

152

You *mustn't*.'

'You started all this,' Carrick pointed out in conversational tones. 'And all good things come to an end.'

'If you think it's been *good* –'

'Were you offered money?'

'No!'

'Unless of course friend Blair – army days, was it? – pocketed any inducements and just left you with your feeling of satisfaction that Terrington was being exposed at last.'

'I didn't want any money,' Deakin mumbled. 'Blair said it was my duty.'

'And now there's the business of Mr Smiler, the little scandal that Gilcrist sat on for quite a while. Only now he's dead and all I have to go on is a single sheet of paper, a piece of evidence that his killer left behind.'

Deakin moaned softly.

Carrick leaned over and spoke very quietly. 'It's finished, laddie. And although you're in big trouble and you'll probably be out of a job for the simple reason that when there's a pile of shit a film producer isn't the first person you tell, if you help me you'll come out better than most. If only you'd gone about this the right way.'

'Gone through the proper channels?' Deakin asked. 'Is that what I should have done, sir?' The tone was bitter and sarcastic.

'Like asking your DCI's advice, for example?'

Deakin was actually on his feet and turning to flee when Carrick caught him by one arm.

'So he's in on it too? Sit down.'

Slowly, the other complied.

'Just fancy,' Carrick said. 'This is the sort of pub where if I clipped your jaw no one would bat an eyelid. Perhaps we need a few like it in Bath after all. Now, if I give you the phone number of a pal of mine in Complaints, will you give him a ring? Just say you've been talking to me and I advised it. I realise that another force is involved here, but we'll worry about the liaison bit afterwards.'

Deakin nodded. 'Okay.'

'So which of these dubious characters do I ask to take me to their leader?' Carrick enquired, eyeing the gathering.

'He's retired,' Deakin said, a ghost of a smile on his lips. 'A very respectable man these days, is Mr Norris. He employs other people to do his dirty work for him now.'

'Where can I find him?'

'I couldn't tell you.'

'Why don't you ask the boss?'

The full enormity of the question hit Deakin. 'Sir, that's *dangerous*. I can't just knock on his door.'

'It would be an interesting way to get at the truth and I could do with a few short cuts right now. But I might have to rely on you to rescue me.'

'But you know as well as I do that I can't –'

'Use your initiative. It shouldn't be too difficult for you and a chum to follow me for a while. Tell the boss everything but that, and about the phone call to Complaints. I'll be in the Marquis of Granby drinking orange juice.'

Unorthodox, reckless and downright crazy, Carrick reflected on the way out after they had talked further. He was not absolutely sure he could trust Deakin to do as instructed, mainly because the constable was scared silly.

It was to be hoped that Haine would have his wits about him.

Carrick stayed in the Marquis of Granby for two hours and no one approached him, not even Deakin. The establishment was a vast improvement on the previous one and it was easy to while away the time by having something to eat. People came and went and soon it was almost closing time. The landlord had actually called time when a man wearing a silver-grey raincoat strode into the bar and halted, raking the assembly with a grim gaze. It came to rest upon Carrick.

'I believe you want to talk to me,' he said when he had walked over to where Carrick was seated.

'You're not Frank Norris,' Carrick said.

'No.'

'That's a shame. I could do with having a chat with him – even though he would deny he had any friends in Wemdale nick.'

The man leaned both muscular arms on the table and spoke softly. 'I should be very careful if I were you. I'm still senior

154

to you. Shall we go where we can talk in private?'

'My car will do – it's just round the corner.' Under the man's contemptuous gaze he drained his glass of orange juice.

'As you wish.'

'I like to know who I'm talking to,' Carrick said when they were seated in the car.

'My name's Derek Rogers.'

'Of course, you're Alan Terrington's brother-in-law and his boss. His *former* boss, that is. Tell me, what else had Marvin Gilcrist discovered about your little empire?'

'That's the whole point. Nothing.'

'So the connection with Norris is purely imagination on my part?'

'Precisely.'

'In that case why was Gilcrist's cottage retreat turned over and a bunch of notes stolen? We found a single page that his killer had overlooked, a copy of which I have in my possession, which I believe refers to meetings Gilcrist had with an inside informant over a period of months. The venues of the meetings with him are also listed: pubs in this town. The information was in connection with what I'll call irregularities that you condoned or ignored. A couple of days ago someone broke into a flat in Bath where a researcher employed by Gilcrist lives. I think whoever did it was looking for the missing page. It clearly mentions a Mr Smiler.'

'May I see it?' Rogers asked urbanely.

'Certainly. Be assured though that the original is safely locked away.' He switched on the interior light so that Rogers could see to read.

'Oh, by the way,' Rogers said when he had donned half-moon spectacles, 'Deakin didn't make that phone call you suggested – he came to see me *first*.' He read in silence and then folded the piece of paper neatly and returned it. 'Interesting. But it's history. Finished.'

'Nothing's finished until I find Gilcrist's killer.'

'There's no reason why you should look in Wemdale.' He smiled sympathetically. 'Inspector Carrick, I took the liberty of getting in touch with your Chief Inspector Haine. You don't appear to have his full support in this particular line of enquiry.'

In the dim light Carrick watched Rogers closely. He was a powerfully built man, probably in his fifties, his hair the right shade of silver-grey to tone with his overcoat, hands well manicured, the flash of gold rings on his fingers.

'I believe you,' Carrick sid. 'It's the only thing you've said so far that I *do* believe.'

Rogers frowned. 'It was a good ploy,' he resumed, 'to give Deakin Haine's phone number so he would tell your boss everything. I take it you *don't* have a friend in Complaints?'

'No.'

'This little escapade of yours wasn't very well thought out, was it?'

Carrick was still holding the piece of paper. Planting the ghost of a kiss upon it he said, 'I'm still working on it. And something seems to tell me that these details aren't about meetings where information was given to Gilcrist but the information itself. Does this refer to the dates you met Norris, when he handed you your reward for services rendered? That's a *very* nice Rolex you're wearing.'

'What you're insinuating is utterly preposterous.'

'It would have been naive of me to expect you to agree with every word. But I was really expecting Norris to turn up.'

'This visit is unofficial, I understand,' Rogers said, opening the car door. 'Keep it like that and you'll get no trouble from me. I haven't even clapped eyes on you.'

'You're involved,' Carrick told him. 'You're Terrington's alibi.'

The car rocked as the door slammed hard and Rogers strode away. Carrick was gazing after him when a girl emerged from the shadow of a doorway and opened it again.

'No thanks,' Carrick said.

'We could be really friendly,' she said, sliding in. She took his left hand and placed it on her breast.

'You've picked the wrong guy. I'm a –'

With her free hand she operated a pepper spray in his face.

Blinded, choking, his eyes, mouth and nose seemingly on fire, Carrick was hauled from the car. He fell and scrabbled frantically at the filthy slush, burying his face in a handful as he rolled on the pavement, spitting it into the face of the man who yanked him to his feet. There was a short journey into what he guessed was a side alley and then they really set to work.

The name of the game soon became obvious. Every time they knocked him down, he groped for melted snow and immersed his face in it. Then, when he could see, he started to fight back. It was hopeless, of course, but the certainty that he had broken someone's nose made it almost worthwhile. They were careful, though, only rendering him semi-conscious so that when they wrenched his mouth open and forced the neck of a bottle between his teeth, he did not choke. What he did not swallow was afterwards poured over him as he lay gasping on the ground.

In the thirty seconds or so when he was left to his own devices Carrick forced two fingers down his throat and tried to vomit. He had parted company with his supper when he was kicked as punishment, carried and tossed into the back of a van. Jolted, soaked and slithering from one side of the vehicle to the other as it was driven at speed around the streets, he did not totally succeed in his objective until he was being frog-marched into Wemdale's main police station. The duty sergeant glared at him. He'd had quite enough of drunks for one night.

Chapter Fifteen

Joanna had undertaken the task of trying to trace the man Fraser Campbell had said Carrick had collided with outside the Crawford Hotel. After spending all morning on the phone to both taxi firms and minicab drivers, she had a list of twenty-three names, employees with whom she had not spoken directly. Two were immediately discounted as they were women.

'That's the easy bit,' Joanna said to herself. 'All I have to do now is find them.'

After visiting every taxi rank in the city and spending more time on the phone she had only three potential names left on her list. Otherwise, she had drawn a complete blank. None of the men she had asked had gone headlong into a guest leaving the hotel. So perhaps it hadn't been a taxi driver – or, as Patrick was convinced, hadn't happened at all. Joanna then rang the Crawford Hotel and asked the Functions Manager the name of the agency which had supplied emergency staffing that night. Patrick had suggested she try tracing the barman. A few minutes later she had a new list of seven names, and no, the agency had no idea how each person had been deployed. Another call to Grayson did not help in that direction as he had been too rushed off his feet to remember the names of the helpers.

'But surely the name of the man serving in the Appin Lounge is written down somewhere.'

'No, I'm afraid we just gave the agency their fee. Horribly impersonal, I'm all too aware. I usually get to know people a bit better but that night . . .' He sighed with feeling.

158

'Seven more blokes then,' Joanna said when she had rung off. At least the agency, when she had explained, had given her their names and addresses.

She struck lucky straight away.

'That was Gavin,' said the man at the top of her list, Dave Stringer.

'Gavin Fuller?'

'That's him. He's my mate so that's how I know what he was doing that night.'

'Do you mind describing him? Only I wasn't there, you see. This is for a friend of mine.'

'He's about five feet nine, dark hair and gold-rimmed glasses. Hey, he's not in trouble, is he?'

'No, it's my friend who's in trouble.'

'You might have a problem getting hold of him if you need to talk. He's gone home – to his parents' place, that is. They live somewhere in Dorset. Sorry, but I don't know exactly where.'

'Never mind,' Joanna said. 'It's only one of the largest counties in England.'

'You could ring his girlfriend. I'll give you the number.' When he had done so he said, 'Gavin had a great time that night. He was telling me about it. He's writing this crime story – dead keen.' He chuckled at the pun. 'Sorry. He wants to be a crime writer. He was telling me how he'd been talking to a real live police inspector, asked him if he'd read his manuscript and tell him if he'd got the police procedures bits right.'

'Did he say what time he spoke to him?'

'Oh, when it was all over. He could hardly talk to him while things were hopping. I think he took the bull by the horns as it were and rang up to his room.'

Because Carrick's wallet and warrant card had been stolen, the duty sergeant at Wemdale police station had no choice but to ring Haine to check the identity of the latest drunk. Carrick was permitted to clean himself as best he could and was then shown into an interview room where he waited for a very long time.

It was now nine-thirty in the morning and Carrick had no

recollection of what had happened after he had been dumped unceremoniously in a cell, in the company of several others. He had, he supposed, passed out. Right now, though, he felt surprisingly clear-headed.

It was plain to him now that two groups of men had been involved; the second of which had been police acting on information received. They had not *rescued* him, but were merely obeying orders to pick up someone who was drunk and disorderly. Carrick knew where that information had come from.

And he himself was right up to his neck in what Joanna always called 'the brown stuff' . . .

Rogers put in an appearance at nine forty-five.

'Unfortunately I wasn't around when you were brought in,' he began. 'Otherwise I would have been able to smooth things over and Haine need not have been made aware of –'

'Kindly spare me the bullshit,' Carrick said. 'You had me set up.'

'Well, if you persist in behaving like a character in a pulp fiction novel what do you expect? Now we're going to let you go. I'm afraid I don't know where your personal possessions are and your car seems to have been stolen but I'm sure you'll manage.'

'I'd like to make a phone call.'

'Be my guest. Use the one in my office two doors down. I'll come with you if you don't mind. Just the one call, Inspector.'

There was no reply at Joanna's flat, nor at the office, and Carrick found himself listening to the answerphone. As Rogers was standing close by – ready, Carrick felt, to snatch the phone away once he had spoken – he left no message but dialled the only other number he could think of, the one Patrick had given him, scrawled on a scrap of paper in his pocket.

'Hello,' said a woman's voice. In the background a baby was crying.

'Is Patrick there?' Carrick asked.

'No, I *think* he's in Scotland. Who is that, please?'

'James Carrick.'

'Oh, hi! This is Ingrid. We met at Eric Framley's do. Can

I help in any way?'

'No, not really. But, look I'm sorry to be a pest but I can't get hold of Joanna. You know the girl who –'

'Yes! I must admit it was a bit of a surprise finding her like that but I know now that she was –'

Rogers was moving in. 'Sorry to interrupt,' Carrick said desperately. 'Ingrid, please could you tell her that I'm at Wemdale nick and I've no –' The handset was removed from his grasp and slammed down.

'Now get out,' Rogers said.

They showed Carrick out the back way and he followed his nose for a little while, too stunned by what had happened to think straight, his previous clear-headedness dissipated.

'The phone rang,' he muttered, heading into an alley. He stopped. 'Yes, I remember now. The bloody phone rang.'

Why should he think of this now? It was as if the murk in his mind was throwing out snippets of totally useless information, continuing to play a cruel joke on him. Better to ignore all that and concentrate on the present situation, having no choice but to be the prey in Rogers' game of cat and mouse. In his mind's eye, he was reading the headlines in the newspapers: AVON POLICE IN BOOZING COP SHOCK.

Or even: DISGRACED COP FOUND DEAD.

He was not to know that, just then, a rectory in north Somerset was resounding to cries of, 'Where the *hell's* Wemdale?'

It was madness to be walking along back alleys. Especially as someone seemed to be following him. Carrick turned sharp right and then right again and was rewarded by the sight of traffic through a narrow gap in the buildings. What he had first thought were echoes of his own footsteps were still somewhere to the rear, but closer now.

His warrant card, wallet, and all it contained, might be missing but he still had in his possession his watch, Swiss army knife and one of the ten pound notes he always kept folded in his inside jacket pocket for emergencies. On the down side he was filthy, disgustingly so, unshaven and had a split lip and a large bruise on the left side of his jaw. The

161

pepper spray had left his eyes sore and bloodshot. He felt as though he was on one of those initiative tests at Hendon Police College. But all he had to do, surely, was have something to eat and make several phone calls. *After* he had lost whoever was tailing him.

The road he came to traversed part of the town that even the small-minded planners seemed to have abandoned. It was a dreary dual carriageway with barriers on either side to prevent people committing suicide by trying to cross; an unending stream of heavy lorries and cars thundered along it. Carrick turned left and walked for some distance before he realised that he was heading away from the town centre. What had been derelict warehouses on either side of the road gave way to open spaces piled with heaps of rubble, broken pallets and rubbish. The only standing building in sight was the offices of what looked like a long-demolished brick-works.

He turned round and came face to face with two men who had been silently walking some ten yards behind him. They stopped. The one on the right had a swollen eye.

'Fancy a bit more than?' Carrick yelled above the roar of the traffic.

They both performed a defensive shimmy when he ran at them, exchanging glances as some kind of strategy was decided upon. As it was they were too long in their delibera-tions, possibly because previous targets had been slower on their feet. The one with the damaged eye got another fist in it and his friend, still undecided, yielded utterly after being kicked in the stomach and chopped across the back of the neck as he folded neatly in the centre. The drivers of the passing cars, blind to what was happening at the side of the road, continued on their journeys.

Carrick carried on running and did not slow down until he had reached where he had emerged from the alley. He went on past the opening and had not gone more than a hundred yards when he saw a phone box. It was on the other side of the road. He broke into a run again, mostly to keep warm, the half-melted snow seeping through the soles of his shoes. Quite soon he came to a dirty-looking café.

'And what's happened to you?' shrieked a grey-faced

woman behind the counter.

'Mugged,' Carrick said, slapping down his ten pound note.

She eyes him dubiously. 'How come they didn't get that then?'

He was in no mood for questions. 'Because in this Godforsaken dump I always carry cash stuffed up my arse. How about some breakfast?'

The woman picked up the note by one edge and held it up to the light. 'We charge four pounds fifty for breakfast.'

'I'll have the change and the typhoid jab right now if you don't mind.'

They stared at one another and Carrick won.

There were no other customers and he had the choice of ten greasy tables. He sat at one right in a corner, near the end of the counter, so as to have an easy escape route through the kitchen if necessary.

The food, when it came, was remarkably good, so good in fact that Carrick was pretty sure it had been cooked by someone else. The pot of coffee was more than drinkable too and he had two rounds of toast and marmalade to finish with.

The chef put in an appearance. 'Someone after you, mate?' asked this giant of a man with a cauliflower ear.

'Bacon and eggs like that had to come from a royal naval galley,' Carrick said. 'Yes. What made you leave London?'

He jerked his head towards the woman. 'Is it the cops or what?'

'Both.'

'You got a real problem then.'

'May I use your phone?'

The bell on the door that opened into the street jangled and three men walked in. They came in Carrick's direction.

'Go out the back,' said the chef.

Carrick went, collecting a frying pan as he ran through the kitchen and using it just outside the back door to topple someone who wasn't prepared, just at that moment, for the action to start.

There was a car parked in the rear yard and when the driver saw Carrick he leapt out. 'Oi!' he shouted.

Carrick skipped nimbly around the vehicle and took to the alleys again. As he turned a corner he heard the man shout once more but he wasn't going to stop to listen.

It was then that the past twelve hours finally took their toll. He became disorientated, wanting to head back into the centre of Wemdale but continually finding himself going in the wrong direction. He wandered hopelessly in interconnecting lanes between old buildings that all looked the same. When he turned corners, when he looked round, they were still there.

He knew he had no chance. He might as well sit down and wait until they caught up with him. But they seemed content to drive him into more and more unfamiliar territory until he was totally lost. He had lost all sense of time. Life became a surreal nightmare where dark doorways yawned; and the lanes were inhabited by whispering voices that seemed to pursue him. So how much of what followed was dream, and what was reality, he was never sure.

Shockingly, and seemingly all at once, night had fallen and he was standing in front of a building that he thought he had seen before. The door had at one time been boarded up but the wood that had been used was now rotten and sagging. He wrenched it aside and went in.

'This is where I told them to bring you,' said a man's voice in the dark.

Beneath the building was a cellar that had originally been the boilerhouse, the old boiler still in situ. They took Carrick down there, his hands tied behind his back, and, by the light of a torch, showed him the rusting cavern within.

Someone lit a cigarette and by the sudden flare of light Carrick saw that there were three of them. But he could not see their faces.

'Haine doesn't believe you,' the hoarse voice continued. 'He *apologised* to Rogers when he spoke to him over the phone, apologised for what you've stirred up since you arrived. He even told him about the report he's written for the chief super about you driving while over the limit – whatever *that* was about. If you give me your word that you'll go back to Bath, resign and keep your mouth closed, that boiler there won't be your coffin.'

Carrick, who had not made it easy for himself, fighting them off until they had clubbed him down, did not respond

164

until someone nudged him to remind him that a reply was expected. 'I didn't mention it when we spoke,' he said, 'but where did you get that torch?'

'Rot in hell, you bastard,' said the man as Carrick was bundled inside the boiler.

He could hear Terrington coughing even after they'd jammed shut the door.

'I mean, God above, we paid enough for the place,' Gavin Fuller's mother was saying. 'And now it looks as though it's going to end up in the sea. The coastal path fell in the sea last year so the council bought some land from the owners of the golf course to make another one and, you've guessed it, a fortnight later it was halfway down the cliff.'

The afternoon sun was gleaming fitfully over Lyme Bay, creating a pale path of light on the calm sea. Up here, on the clifftop at Charmouth, the development of luxury houses – nicknamed 'Hollywood' by the residents of the village – was sheltered from the raw north wind. It rarely snowed in this tiny corner of Dorset.

Joanna had had no problem in finding where Fuller was staying with his parents as his girlfriend, due to arrive for the weekend in a couple of days' time, had given her the address. And as Gavin would be away from his flat in Bristol for a week she had been forced to go in search of him.

'More tea?' enquired Mrs Fuller.

'No thanks.' She had been plied with tea, home-made cakes and ice cream gateau.

'Well, he's only down on the beach looking for fossils so you could always go and find him, dear. You won't miss him if you walk towards Lyme Regis, he's wearing a red anorak and a blue and white striped woolly hat. Do watch the cliffs though – they're really dangerous after all that rain.'

Joanna was not really dressed for plodding across stones and shingle but as the tide was going out Gavin might be away for several hours. He was, according to an obviously doting mother, hooked on fossils.

There were an amazing number of people on the beach armed with fossil hammers, picks, shovels and other implements. Most of them were engaged in whacking at the small round stones and boulders exposed by the retreating tide. Others, perhaps hazarding their safety, delved carefully at places where the soft muddy deposits at the base of the cliffs had newly fallen away. No one in sight was wearing a red anorak.

It was not easy walking as the shingle banks merged into areas where large stones, like stepping stones without flat tops, protruded above the surface of pools that were gardens of seaweed. Joanna floundered through these somehow, getting her feet very wet, and then, thankfully, reached firm sand. Despite her squelchy feet it was a pleasant way to spend a winter's day. It brought back memories of childhood holidays by the sea; sandcastles, picnics, hunting for crabs . . .

In this golden reverie she walked right past Gavin Fuller, who had removed his anorak and neatly folded it over his rucksack while he dug at a rock almost buried by a mud flow. But, turning, she did notice his woolly hat and went back.

'It's an ammonite,' he said excitedly when she got close. '*Parkinsonia parkinsoni* if I'm not mistaken.' He thrust a spade at her. 'Here. Please get rid of the mud before it covers it completely.' And with that he launched himself at the rock, virtually embracing it.

The mud was moving, washed down from above by a small stream that ran down the beach and into the sea. As it flowed over the rock they were struggling to extract the patterns on it were revealed. Eventually it came out with a huge rush and they both fell over in the mud as a fossil measuring some twenty inches across rolled onto the shingle.

'You are here at a glorious moment,' Fuller said poetically, showing her the spirally coiled shell of the long-extinct sea creature. 'It's only right that if and when I sell this I give you a share.'

'How much is it worth?' Joanna asked.

He was thin and studious-looking with rather a pointed nose. When he stood on one leg for a moment, he looked like a heron. 'It's a really good specimen. In the right place and at the right time . . . I suppose a couple of hundred.'

'I'll settle for you telling me what you said to James Carrick on Burns Night that sent him running out of the

Crawford Hotel.'

He tore his gaze from the fossil and looked at her vaguely. '*Said* to him? Nothing.'

'But didn't you phone him in his room about a crime story you're writing?'

'Yes, but I didn't say anything that would have made him go anywhere.'

Joanna took him by one elbow and made him sit down. 'Look, Gavin, this is *very*, *very* important. After Inspector Carrick left the bar you rang him in his room. Is that right?'

'Yes, I did. There was no one on reception but I looked in the book and got his room number.'

'You spoke to him and told him about your book?'

'Yes, but – who are you? Have I been reported to the agency? I didn't think I was doing anything wrong –'

'Sorry,' Joanna said and gave him her name, telling him she was investigating something that had occurred later that night.

'Oh, I see,' Fuller said, relieved. 'Yes, I told him about it and asked if he'd read it when I'd finished. He said he would.'

'Then what?'

'I thanked him and rang off.'

'That was all?' Joanna cried.

'No, hang on, let me finish. I went back in the bar and started to clear up. The three men who had been sitting by the bar for ages had gone and there was only a couple left sitting in the corner. Then Inspector Carrick came in looking for me and said if I liked he could arrange for me to visit a police station if I wanted to get the background info. I joked and said I'd do it on my own if he liked, rob a bank or something. He laughed, told me to give him a ring and said goodnight. He went back into the lobby and as he did the people who'd been in the corner left. The man called to the inspector and as I went back to work I saw them talking by the desk. Don't ask me what it was all about.'

'Did you see Carrick go outside?'

'No.'

'Do you know who the people were who spoke to him?'

'The bloke was wearing a kilt so they must have been to the do. I don't remember anyone addressing them by name.'

'Which corner were they sitting in?'

'The one diagonally across the room from the bar.'

'So anyone standing near the table where the Campbells were sitting and facing the bar wouldn't necessarily have been able to see them.'

'No. I think I know what you're driving at. There's a big plant in a pot there too.'

'Yes, so there is,' Joanna murmured. 'Thank you, you've been a great help. I don't suppose you can remember what the tartan of the man's kilt was like?'

'Yes, I noticed it as a matter of fact because it was the same as the stuff draped all over the bar. No, not the bar, the entrance lobby. Sort of purple and green.'

'Crawford tartan?'

'No idea. But it would figure, wouldn't it?'

Joanna eyed the fossil. 'How are you going to get that thing back home?'

Gavin eyed it too. 'Carry it. I can't leave it here.'

It weighed at least half a hundredweight and they lugged it between them. But at least Mrs Fuller washed and ironed all of Joanna's clothes. In fact, such was the Fullers' hospitality she ended up staying the night.

Shuffling about in his cast-iron tomb Carrick had succeeded in finding a piece of metal. With it, his hands still fastened behind him, he banged on the casing, hour after hour.

Chapter Sixteen

The moment Haine had been dreading had arrived. That a superintendent from the Complaints and Disciplines department should arrive at Manvers Street to see him personally was carrying things a little too far, he thought. Rogers must have really taken it badly. Nevertheless he had every intention of biting the bullet manfully, even if it did mean admitting that Carrick was beyond his control. There was sufficient time for him to ask for coffee to be brought – 'in proper cups, for God's sake' – and then his visitor was shown in. His name, Haine had learned, was Sutherland.

'This is Inspector Hobbs, sir,' Haine said. 'He's from Bristol but I asked him to stay on to take over Carrick's duties.'

Sutherland was tall, dark, ugly and had eyes like a hungry alligator. When he spoke his voice had the merest lilt to it that Haine, who prided himself on identifying accents, could not place. He was too overwrought just then to associate names with places.

'I don't think we need Inspector Hobbs,' Sutherland said quietly and coldly.

Hobbs went.

Sutherland sat in the chair provided, opened his document case on his lap and withdrew from it a fat file plus two sheets of paper stapled together.

'May I?' he asked, indicating one corner of Haine's desk.

'Please do, sir,' Haine said, hurriedly clearing a space.

The superintendent held up the sheets of paper by one corner and laid them down again. 'This is your report on

Carrick's accident. Did you ever wonder if there was a connection?'

'With what, sir?'

'Gilcrist's murder.'

'Not for a moment. Gilcrist was killed the following night.'

'Yes, I suppose it is a little fanciful of me to ask myself if someone really dedicated in his mission to murder a film director would put out of action the CID officer likely to be ordered to track him down. Have you got any further in finding out what happened?'

'Those are the facts, sir. As far as I'm concerned the matter's closed, or at least awaiting the Chief Superintendent's decision.'

'Yes. He gave this to me as he hoped there might be a connection. Pity. Never mind. Perhaps you'd give me a little background information. Why did Carrick go to Wemdale?'

'I believe that when he and Mrs Kelso – she was one of Gilcrist's researchers – sorted through the paperwork found at the cottage they came upon what they regarded as an oddment with what the inspector guessed were names and dates and so forth. So he –'

'What names?'

'Just one in full–er, Smiler. The others were initials.'

The predatory eyes gleamed. 'May I see it?'

'Of course, sir.'

He rummaged around and eventually found it at the bottom of his in-tray, where he had buried it after Carrick gave it to him.

Sutherland perused it for a few moments. Then he said, 'You don't seem to attach much importance to this.'

'No, I don't. I've arrested a man in connection with Gilcrist's death – Larne Painswick. Gilcrist assaulted Mrs Kelso one night when she called at the cottage where Gilcrist worked at weekends and Painswick, who was close to her at one time, admits that he went there on the night that Gilcrist was killed and smashed up the place. We found a thumbprint of his there. He was witnessed making a nuisance of himself to the woman afterwards when she refused to have anything more to do with him and since then, after Carrick released him for lack of evidence, he broke into her flat in an effort to

170

talk to her. Or so it appears.'

'Has he admitted breaking into her flat?'

'Denies it utterly.'

'You don't think the intruder could have been after *this*?' Sutherland said, flicking the sheet of paper with a fingernail.

'No, but presumably Inspector Carrick did.'

Sutherland put the paper aside, and then took it up again. 'May I keep this?'

'It's of no use to me.'

'And did you decide that before or after Carrick got himself arrested for being drunk and disorderly?'

'Before, sir.' The full implication of what was being asked struck Haine. 'I must protest. You're making it sound as though –'

Sutherland cut in with, 'Have you discussed *any* of this with your superiors?'

'No, I thought I was perfectly capable of –'

'But you aren't,' the other rapped out. 'This piece of paper should have immediately been investigated with the utmost priority. Hadn't it occurred to you that Dalesland Complaints became involved as soon as Gilcrist made that film about Terrington and the Jones case? Now that the man's been murdered on our patch *I'm* involved.'

'But –'

'What on earth do you imagine they've been doing all this time? You know as well as I do that if you have one maggot in the apple there are bound to be more. There *had* to be or Gilcrist wouldn't have got the information in the first place. We know who his source is. Have you any idea why Carrick went to *Wemdale*? This Smiler character operates all over the north, as I'm sure you're aware.'

'I'd have to find the case file,' Haine said humbly.

This was duly done and placed in Sutherland's impatiently waiting hands. 'Good,' he said after reading for a while, drinking his coffee. 'Evidently Carrick discovered from Mrs Gilcrist that her friend Craxton had a policeman friend by the name of Phil who had stayed with the Gilcrists one weekend. Carrick took a wild guess and it paid off.' He glanced up. 'Constable Philip Deakin. He was Gilcrist's source. Carrick was seen talking to him in a pub the day before yesterday.'

Haine was experiencing a dreadful sinking feeling. 'So who was *his* source about the one you call Smiler?'

'I'm glad you put that in the past tense. He was found in the river Wem some months back. He fed Deakin details of other irregularities.' Slapping his hand down on the file on his lap, making Haine jump, Sutherland said, 'Chief Inspector, I'm appalled by the way you let your subordinate walk right into what amounts to a lion's den without any backup.'

'There has been,' Haine began in strangled tones, 'a clash of personalities over this matter and –'

'No doubt,' Sutherland interrupted dryly. 'The important thing is, has he contacted you?'

'No, not since I spoke to Rogers.'

'Well, it was a good bit of damage limitation on your part to apologise to Rogers. It might make him relax a bit and not suspect that we're on to him.'

'What!' Haine yelped.

'We have his phone tapped,' Sutherland explained. Realising the true state of Haine's ignorance, he went on, 'Man, he gave Terrington his alibi. He was seen approaching Carrick in another Wemdale pub, and they went off and talked in Carrick's car. Presumably as a result of that conversation he had him beaten up and a quantity of vodka poured down his throat. Good God, you don't think I'd be sitting here on account of a minor car accident and a clash of personalities, do you?'

'Rogers is under investigation?' Haine said slowly and saw Sutherland nod.

'Proving his involvement with Frank Norris – he's the one who calls himself Mr Smiler – is very difficult. Gilcrist seems to have had the details though. You'll appreciate that I became really worried at Carrick's arrival on the scene when I tell you that a carefully orchestrated drugs bust has been organised which we don't want ruined. In the past, you see, Rogers has given Norris advance notice. *This* time a recording was made of the phone call when he warned him. When they shift the stuff the day after tomorrow there'll be a reception committee.'

'So you've been liaising with Dalesland Complaints Department over this, sir.'

'Which you would have been told about if you'd carried out proper procedure. Now I have to give you the really bad news. After Carrick left Wemdale's HQ they lost him.'

'Is he in any danger?' Haine whispered.

'Definitely. They almost rescued him in a café but he misunderstood their intentions because just then a few thugs rolled up.'

Haine was thinking about early retirement. 'God above, what a mess.'

'I'm hoping that it hasn't done too much damage to the operation. If Carrick just stuck to his need to find Gilcrist's killer they might not get nervous about the rest, but I think he must have rumbled Rogers – the bastard set him up for a bad beating.'

'Is there a man inside?'

'Working in the canteen as a washer-up.' He smiled grimly. 'Carrick's quite a lad, isn't he? He threw up all the booze they'd forced down him in the main lobby area and when he was blood-tested was rated as practically sober.' After a short silence he said, 'So what do we do now? Ask MI5 to find him?'

This sarcasm was not appreciated. After Sutherland left, Haine grabbed the phone.

'No, I'm sorry, Chief Inspector,' said a pleasant female voice, 'but my son's not here. I understand he's in Scotland. Ingrid's not here either so I have Justin and little Victoria all to myself. Patrick has a phone in his car, though – can I give you the number?'

Any kind of organised search for Carrick was bound to fail. No one was more aware of this than Patrick Gillard, who had driven non-stop from north Ayrshire. When he arrived at Wemdale he checked into the best hotel in the area, where he had arranged to meet his wife. She was most put out when he refused to let her take any further part in the proceedings.

'I've come all this way,' she protested. She had contacted him as soon as she received Carrick's call.

Patrick was throwing a most disreputable array of clothing from a suitcase onto the immaculate bedcover. He gazed at her and grinned. 'How the hell d'you think Carrick'll feel when he realises he's been rescued by a nursing mother?'

Ingrid flashed him an indignant look and he tried to mollify her.

'He'll need a lot of tender loving care – you're really good at that.'

'If you find him. I wish you'd come when I first called you.'

'I didn't know he was actually missing until Haine got hold of me on the way here. Besides, I couldn't just drop what I was doing.'

'Poor James,' she said softly.

'Yes, he's got himself into a nasty situation all right, but the fewer folk there are making waves in his direction the better. I don't know what gives in this shitty-looking town and I don't think Haine told me half of it, but the fact that he rang me at all shows the extent to which things have gone wrong.'

'I really don't know where you're going to start looking for him.'

'Lateral thinking,' he said. Then he quickly changed his clothes, kissed his wife and went out.

Patrick's theory was brilliant in its simplicity and was based on the assumption that if Carrick had been set upon by various villains he would not have gone down without a fight. Therefore if one combed the town for pubs with a bad reputation and sought out customers with missing teeth and black eyes ... Aware that time was short, he asked a policeman and made his way to the worst hostelry of all.

The Battersby Arms had only just opened so it was a little early to encounter his quarry. Gillard slouched at one end of the bar, making a small whisky go a long way, pushing right to the back of his mind the thought that Carrick was probably dead.

At eight thirty-five, when both bars had filled with people as whole and healthy as might be expected in such a deprived district, the door opened and in walked a strapped-up broken nose, a closed eye and a fat lip close on his heels. After buying a round of drinks, all three seated themselves in a close huddle.

Patrick drifted over, picked up a spare chair, sat on it and blew a plume of cigar smoke into the tripod they had made with their upper torsos. Predictably, they drew back quickly and glowered at him. Hostility wavered when, under their noses, two hundred pounds in fivers were counted out slowly onto the tabletop.

'Where,' said Patrick, 'is he?'

Many hours had passed before Carrick thought of trying to kick his way out. He had eventually abandoned his tapping with the piece of metal – no one after all, could hear his pitiful SOS. He slept for a while. When he opened his eyes he could see daylight, a fact that made him forget he hurt all over. Spitting out the cinders that were in his mouth he gazed about his prison.

The light was coming from around the circular door, which appeared to be buckled, and through several holes in the metal above his head. In places the rusting iron was so thin it looked like a colander, especially where the stove pipe was riveted on. There was no way out there, though; it had to be the door. He started kicking with both feet together.

Ten minutes later, after many rests and after he had had to wriggle back into position several times – the forcefulness of the action had the effect of gradually shoving him head first into the far end – one of the hinges gave way. This was not what he had expected but wonderful anyway. He carried on kicking, concentrating on the area where he judged the other hinge to be.

An hour later he could do no more.

He had considered leaning his back against the door and bracing his feet against the flanges fixed to the sides, but the boiler was too small for him to be able to turn round. In the faint light he tried to see if there was a sharp edge on which he could rub the rope that bound his hands. The flanges themselves seemed promising but that meant curling up into a ball and almost standing on his head in order to get his wrists high enough. 'You were always a fit lad, Jimmy,' he told himself.

There were a few heart-stopping moments when he nearly became jammed, rolled up like a hedgehog while endeavouring to carry out this manoeuvre. After persevering for as

175

long as he could he decided to abandon the attempt. If he was going to have to die let it be sunny-side up, not in a position that could be described as ludicrous.

He slumped back onto his right side. 'Oh, dear God,' he prayed, 'send one of them back to shoot me.' This did not seem the right sort of prayer; his grandfather, an Elder of the Kirk, must be spinning in his grave. So he prayed for Joanna instead.

Would he go mad before he died?

To stop himself thinking about it he kicked at the door, with rapidly dwindling energy, until he fainted from the pain in his feet and legs. When he came round all was dark again.

That they were real voices and not his mind playing tricks with him took a while to penetrate. At least, it seemed a long time but it was in fact only a matter of seconds – almost as soon as he heard them there was a loud clang from the door end of the boiler and a bright light shone into his eyes.

''Tis your good self,' Patrick's voice said. 'Please excuse me for just one moment.'

There was a grunt and a scuffling sound, following by a thump as though someone had dropped a sack of coal.

'I'm back,' Patrick breathed into the metal cylinder. 'Can you get yourself out? I fear these chaps might have –'

They had. When Carrick had wormed his way out he saw by the light of the powerful flash lamp propped on a table that it was two against one. A third had already been taken care of.

Swearing with frustration, Carrick cast about for something with which to cut his bonds. It was an awful shock to him to discover that he could hardly walk. To his ashamed relief he could only be an enthusiastic audience to Gillard making short work of his attackers by utilising quite the filthiest fighting tactics Carrick had ever witnessed.

'I can't understand it,' he admitted weakly afterwards, unable to move his arms even though the rope had been severed. 'You say you dance, and I've seen you do this, and yet . . .' Perhaps one ought not to mention the disability.

'And when I want to swim I tie the lid of the laundry basket to the stump of my right leg and do fifteen knots,' Patrick said and they both giggled like schoolboys.

The daylight Carrick had seen earlier had come through an open doorway at the top of the short flight of steps. When Carrick found that he was, to his embarrassment, not capable of mounting them, he was taken in a swift fireman's lift. Then life became very vague for a while.

'James. James!' The utterance of his name was followed by a not ungentle slap on the cheek.

'What?' Carrick mumbled.

'We're in the underground car park at the hotel. You can't go in wearing those clothes.'

Carrick groaned and prepared to go back to sleep.

'So I want you to get out of the car, strip down to your pants and put on this tracksuit.'

Everyone obeyed that voice.

The unbelievably chilly air wafting down the entrance ramp woke him like a cold shower. Large, comforting, barred gates were closed across the ramp; the car park was a private one, for hotel guests only. He got changed.

'What did Haine tell you?' he asked, teeth chattering, as he stumbled after Patrick towards the lift.

'Not any more than he had to. But I did make him admit that someone from your Complaints Department had been to see him. That's what makes me think that some kind of bust's in the offing. So tonight we keep our heads down and clear out first thing in the morning. I'll ring Haine though, so whoever's looking for you can be called off.'

'I might have hit him over the head with a frying pan . . .'

Patrick hooted with laughter. If Haine had been in the army he would have found himself digging latrine ditches in Bosnia.

This was not the right moment for Patrick to impart his findings farther north. He waited until Carrick had bathed, eaten and slept the rest of the night away. For the sake of security breakfast was taken the next morning in their rooms: Carrick in an adjoining single that formed, with his and Ingrid's double, what the hotel described as a 'family suite'.

'I've something to tell you,' Patrick said when his guest had eaten an enormous and reviving breakfast. 'I don't really know whether it's good news or bad, as far as you're concerned.'

'Say away,' Carrick requested.

'I've found Graeme Campbell.'

'Alive and well?' Carrick asked steadily.

'Yes. His lady love has left her husband and is renting a cottage near Largs in north Ayrshire. He's with her – I saw him there yesterday morning.'

The utter silence that followed this remark was broken by a knock at the door.

Chapter Seventeen

Carrick, his companions deploying themselves suitably, obeyed Patrick's silent instructions and stood well away from the door as Patrick opened it. A charged few seconds passed until Superintendent Sutherland identified himself.

'I see I should have rung from reception,' he observed. 'No, don't apologise, Carrick. Haine told me of the nature of your rescuer.' He surveyed Patrick with a smile. 'I hope this isn't official as far as you're concerned.'

'No, I'm giving my wife a weekend break in sunny Wemdale,' Patrick answered. 'And I don't want any of this – my involvement, that is – to go public.'

'I understand that.'

'Shall we go next door?' Patrick suggested. 'I'll ring for coffee.'

'Is the victim mobile?' Sutherland asked, looking in Carrick's direction.

'In a manner of speaking. But I don't really think we want him to crawl,' Patrick murmured. And he and Sutherland provided the necessary support for the short journey.

'I never thought I'd have an arm around a super's neck, sir,' Carrick said when he had been lowered into a chair.

Patrick answered the unasked question. 'He was inside a stationary version of Thomas the Tank Engine in the basement of a building that looked as though it had been part of a brickworks. Finding him was no problem after I'd chewed my fingernails to the bone waiting for the pubs to open. I simply looked for yobs who'd recently been on the receiving end of physical violence and put quite a lot of money on the table.'

'I owe you for that,' Carrick said.

'God, no. I took it off the bastard after I'd made sure he wouldn't follow us. Part of the deal was that he'd accompany me on his own. That his two partners in crime decided to break the deal was his funeral – and theirs.'

'They surely got the number of your car though,' Sutherland said.

'No. We'd gone to the brickworks site in a taxi. Ingrid tailed it at a safe distance in my BMW. I'd taken the precaution of muddying up the number plates.'

Sutherland turned to Carrick. 'I told the people up here that I'd carry on handling Somerset and Avon's side of things. Do you feel well enough to give me a full account of what happened to you?'

He did, just. It took a good twenty minutes. 'It was Terrington, sir,' he finished by saying. 'He murdered Marvin Gilcrist and I'm not going back to Bath without him.'

'He won't come to trial,' Sutherland observed. 'He has only a month, at the outside, to live.'

'I don't care if he chokes it in the cells. Gilcrist had a lot of info on something which implicated Rogers right up to his neck. Why Terrington acted as hit man I don't know either. Perhaps Rogers has promised to help Terrington's wife financially when he's dead. Or perhaps a dying man just wanted revenge. I'm not at all sure how they got to hear of what Gilcrist was planning. It's possible that Deakin's snout – and I'm assuming that there was one, and whoever it was was inside Norris's empire – made money in all sorts of directions.'

'I can tell you about him,' Sutherland said. 'We'll refer to him as Jed. The *late* Jed, I should say. He was found in the river in what one must regard as suspicious circumstances a while back and I *think* his death was as a result of having grassed on someone else who's now in prison. Jed was one of those people who seems to have had a grudge against everybody. How Deakin managed to cultivate him, God only knows, but Jed hated Rogers so perhaps he'd been Rogers' snout at one time and it stemmed from that. Anyway, it seems that he was keen to let Deakin have everything he knew about

180

Norris's dealings with Rogers. None of this will come right out into the open until there have been arrests. So I'm afraid, Carrick, that *you* can't have Terrington until *we* have Rogers. We simply can't risk letting the cat out of the bag. It might already be well and truly out, of course, now that Rogers knows you're free – and I can't believe that one of those thugs hasn't passed the word around.'

Patrick said, 'They were still tied up and gagged when I checked first thing this morning. So I bought a good padlock for the door just in case someone wandered in and found them.' He looked quite unabashed as three pairs of eyes stared at him. 'I had every intention of mentioning it this morning, I assure you. It was just a matter of finding a copper that one could – well – rely on.' He smiled disarmingly. 'Would you like the key?'

While Sutherland was making a phone call, Patrick asked Carrick, 'What led you to Deakin?'

'Blair Craxton, Amanda Gilcrist's lover. When I spoke to him he seemed to know an awful lot about Terrington. So I asked her if she'd met any friends of Craxton's. She said a bloke called Phil who was in the police had spent the weekend with them. He didn't confirm it but I think they were pals in the army.'

'It doesn't sound as though she knew what Gilcrist was up to.'

'No, I'm fairly sure she didn't.'

'And when Rogers found out that Gilcrist was about to expose him he decided to shut him up.'

'For all I know he asked Terrington merely to go and get hold of the evidence. Murder might not have been part of the game. But Gilcrist's killer was well motivated, judging by the frenzy of the attack – I've just remembered something. Terrington had me chucked in the boiler after I'd asked him where he'd got his torch from. He said –'

'What?'

'It doesn't matter,' Carrick whispered.

After making several more phone calls Sutherland told Carrick that he was to stay out of sight at the hotel until he received further orders.

'That's it,' Carrick said when Superintendent Sutherland

181

had gone. 'Haine must have taken over. I might as well resign now and save a lot of hassle.'

Ingrid had kept very quiet up until now. 'If I was your Chief Constable I'd make sure *you* got Haine's job.' She shot to her feet. 'Well, I suppose I'd better get back to Bath. I can't really expect your mother to look after the children single-handed any longer, Patrick. Perhaps you'd be kind enough to take me to the station.' The phone rang and she answered it. 'Joanna!' she announced.

'I'm afraid it was a waste of time,' Carrick said when he had listened to the account of the fossil hunt. 'Patrick found Graeme Campbell living with his lady friend in Scotland.'

'Before I say anything else, have you remembered any more?'

'I'd remembered the phone ringing and now you've told me it was Fuller I've a vague recollection of talking to him. But I've no memory of coming back down into the lobby. Nor of anyone buttonholing me – not even a man wearing a Crawford tartan kilt. It doesn't matter now anyway.'

'And if I told you that I asked to see the guest list, and there was only one Mr and Mrs Crawford present that night, and I've just returned from talking to them . . .'

Such was the urgency of her voice that Carrick lost patience. 'What, for God's sake?'

'The Campbells had been having some kind of argument. They were speaking quietly and Mr and Mrs Crawford couldn't really hear what was being said. They got the impression that the Campbells had forgotten all about their presence. But after you left it all flared up, mostly between Fraser and Bruce.'

'Didn't Fuller hear all this?'

'Apparently in the course of clearing up he went down to the cellar for a few minutes. I've just rung him to check that. When he returned the Campbells had gone. That was when he rang you about his book. Meanwhile the Crawfords were agonising over whether they should say something to a member of staff about what they had heard. When you reappeared they told you.'

'Told me what?'

'Well, most of the argument was conducted in such broad

182

Scots that they couldn't make head nor tail of what was being said. But it ended by Fraser threatening his brother. Threatening to *kill* him. Where *is* Bruce?'

'I think I know who can find out,' Carrick said and rang off, promising to keep in touch.

'Officially, he's on leave,' Patrick reported after making a couple of calls. 'His regiment isn't expecting him back for another eight days.'

'This is still clutching at straws,' Carrick said. 'We Scots say all kinds of things when we've had a few drams. We tend to lapse into the vernacular.'

'That's it then,' Ingrid said. 'End of assignment. I should have stayed put and gone shopping in Sainsbury's instead.' She began to throw things into a suitcase.

'One can hardly go and rake Campbell's love-nest with gunfire,' Patrick pointed out, possibly unwisely.

His spouse was waspishly telling him that Bruce's whereabouts could be further investigated at no particular inconvenience to anyone when Carrick made his way back to his own room. He had no wish to become involved in a marital spat; he was too tired. Perhaps he ought to take himself off to the Outer Hebrides and carve porridge spurtles for a living.

'Are you all right, James?' Patrick called.

'No, I'm about to lapse into the vernacular,' Carrick replied. 'Awa an bile yer heids!' He slammed the interconnecting door. Ten seconds later he opened it again. They were still staring in his direction. 'My apologies,' he said.

As Carrick had predicted, what triumphs there were to be gleaned from the Gilcrist case did not come in his direction. Not that he was avid for praise, but he had hoped for a neat and tidy conclusion.

The raid that Sutherland had spoken of was successful. Drugs with a street value of hundreds of thousands of pounds were discovered in a garage rented by Frank Norris, where they had been moved following Rogers' tip-off. Norris himself was arrested by the drug squad and personnel from the Complaints and Discipline Department moved swiftly into the police station at Wemdale and instigated a full investigation. Rogers, Deakin and a uniformed sergeant were suspended awaiting enquiries.

On the morning after the raid Alan Terrington was rushed into hospital after suffering a sudden massive haemorrhage. Haine, who had travelled up with Hobbs to Wemdale, had no choice but to kick his heels and wait. A few days later, when Terrington's condition had improved a little, he was permitted to sit at his bedside for a few minutes, under strict instructions from the medical staff not to ask any questions. They need not have worried. Terrington didn't get the chance to say a word. He died that night.

The DCI didn't get much further when he obtained a search warrant for Terrington's home. His wife, obviously distraught, insisted that he had never discussed his work with her and she had never asked. When questioned about his red torch she did admit that it was not the original rechargeable one they had possessed, the first having broken when it had been clipped back incorrectly into its wall bracket and fallen on the floor. Alan, she thought, had used an old silver-coloured one and, then a couple of weeks ago, had acquired this replacement. There was nothing Haine could do to prove that such a mass-produced item had once belonged to Marvin Gilcrist, especially as later forensic tests revealed that only Terrington's and his wife's prints were on it.

The only other point of interest at Terrington's house was in the garden – a small green incinerator used for burning leaves and other garden rubbish. At the bottom of it were the charred remains of what had once been a sheaf of paperwork, now black and sodden after heavy rain. Terrington's wife said she had no idea what he could have been burning.

Rogers, meanwhile, was denying that he had been involved in Gilcrist's murder, that he had given Terrington a false alibi and that Gilcrist had obtained incriminating information about him. He admitted talking to Carrick in the Battersby Arms but was emphatic that he had had nothing to do with the subsequent attack on him. On his involvement with Norris he refused to comment.

The questioning went on, and would continue to do so, for several weeks. Carrick himself would have to give evidence. Meanwhile he was ordered to return to Bath and did so, driven by his somewhat illustrious minder. He did not know quite what to say to Gillard. How do you thank someone for saving your life? Or admit what you'd rather be doing right now?

He decided to tell the truth.

'I'm not surprised,' Patrick said. 'If I was in your shoes I'd want to go and get plastered too. But promise me one thing – if you decide to go ahead give me a bell first. Never get drunk alone.'

Carrick smiled. 'Thanks. Are you going home soon?'

'Tomorrow, according to my nearest and dearest.'

'Sorry that I didn't quite manage to cheer her up.'

'Oh, you did. By staying in one piece.'

The big car purred away.

The heating seemed to have been turned off in his flat and Joanna was out. Not that he had expected her to come home early from work just to welcome him . . .

Never get drunk alone.

If this no doubt worthwhile advice was to be followed to the letter he would have to go somewhere else. But first of all he rang the garage to confirm that the car he had rented from them had not yet been found. His wallet and warrant card had not been recovered either. All three were probably at the bottom of the black expanse of water known as Wemdale Lake.

He went somewhere else.

'Come in,' Amanda Gilcrist said. 'I've just found a bottle of Chardonnay at the back of the fridge.'

In that case there was no point in asking the taxi driver to wait.

'I've had a big bust-up with Blair,' she said when she had seated him by the open fire in the living room. 'He had to go and help the police with their enquiries and when he came back he told me why.' Carrick noticed that she was a little flushed – the wine had not been her first drink that afternoon. Perhaps that was why she was being so forthcoming. 'The little shit took a pile of money off Marvin for some information about Terrington that a policeman friend – I told you about him – sniffed out. Blair came straight out with it, as bold as brass – said he didn't want anything to come between

185

us. I told him that the front door would do for a start.'

'I thought you might like to know how things are progressing.' And Carrick told her almost everything, omitting only the name of the man who had found him and the impending court case involving Wemdale CID.

'Terrington?' she said softly when he had finished. 'I tried to keep an open mind about Marvin's so-called scoops but when I saw the film I thought he looked a bit shifty. And he had you banged up in an old boiler ...' She sighed and reached for the wine bottle. 'Marvin must have been quite obsessed about the whole thing – I've never known him offer money for information before.'

'There's no *proof* Terrington killed your husband,' Carrick said, holding out his glass for a refill. 'And now he's dead we might never know.'

'How did he know about the cottage? You don't think Blair –'

'I shouldn't imagine that Craxton ever met Terrington. But Terrington was an ex-cop. He was patient and knew all the dodges.'

'So why not just pinch the paperwork and go home? Why kill Marvin?'

'Perhaps Terrington thought the cottage was unoccupied. It must have been quite a shock to him to find Marvin there, and the place already turned over. Anyway, at some point the two men set off back to the pub. And then, when they were on the riverbank, he killed him. Not leaving so much as a fingerprint – an ex-cop would remember to wear gloves.'

'And he did it as a favour to some bloke who you're not prepared to tell me about.'

'I can't. There's a big investigation going on – it's *sub judice.*'

'You know, even after all the misery Marvin caused me I can't help feeling sad. Even when he wasn't really speaking to me he quite often brought me a bunch of flowers when he came home. He might have forgotten my birthday, but once or twice a week there'd be a big bunch of flowers. They were usually a bit wilted, dropping their petals – I think he got his secretary to buy them at lunchtime and they stayed on his desk all afternoon.' She brightened. 'I'm glad it wasn't

Larne, though. Who killed him, I mean. That Kelso woman isn't worth going to prison for.'

Carrick had not mentioned the more sordid details of Gilcrist's relationship with Leonora. He had decided some things were best left unsaid.

'This has been hell for you, hasn't it?' Amanda said into the quietness.

'Yes,' Carrick said simply.

'You look as though you've been done over by a mob.'

'I was.' He hadn't told her much about that either.

'I wish I could make it up to you.'

Carrick kept quite still as she crossed the room and sat alongside him.

'But I know how strict you lot are about gifts and things like that,' Amanda went on, 'and I'm sure a man like you has a wonderful woman in his life whom he wouldn't dream of being unfaithful to, so there's not a lot I can do.'

'Right now,' Carrick said, 'I doubt if I could participate in what's on your mind.'

Her knowing gaze drifted over him. She chuckled. 'Would you like to participate in a little supper instead?'

He declined, gracefully, without offending her. When he got back to his flat Joanna was there with a man in overalls who turned out to be a central heating engineer.

'The boiler had packed in,' she explained. 'Only a thermostat, though. But, tonight,' she added, 'you're coming home with me.'

'Warmer there,' Carrick said, kissing her cheek. '*Much* warmer.'

It was another damp and dreary morning in Fenwick, Strathclyde. The digger driver swore softly under his breath as his JCB approached the trench he had dug over a week earlier. Since then it had rained so hard and so incessantly that further work had been impossible until that day. The trench was being readied to receive drainage pipes; anticipating the rain, the digger driver had dug a narrow channel at the lower end, so excess water could escape into a nearby stream. But inexplicably, it now appeared to be full of water.

Someone had filled it in again.

They had filled it, or at least part of it, with apparently anything that had come to hand. Incredulously, he jumped down from the cab to have a closer look and surveyed a jumble of bricks and blocks – these having originally been stacked nearby, ready to construct a culvert beneath the access road – plastic sacks, stones and rubble from a demolished wall, all of it partly covered by a thin layer of waterlogged soil.

Not quite covering a shoe, however.

It was a man's shoe. The digger driver recognised it as the kind of footwear worn with Highland dress for evening. He got into the trench and looked closely at it, the water lapping precariously near to the top of his boots.

There was a sock in the shoe. And the sock was covering a foot.

Chapter Eighteen

Bruce Campbell was identified from his kilt, made for him by John McNultie of Glasgow. This well-established firm of kiltmakers always embroidered the order number inside the waistband of their garments, the details of which were recorded in a large black book that dated back to 1890. Campbell had given his address as that of his regiment, stationed at Dreghorn Barracks, Edinburgh, and it was there that CID officers from Strathclyde Police continued their enquiries. Information gleaned from this source – the address of his father, listed as next of kin, and his known whereabouts on January 25th, this detail furnished by a friend of Campbell's – resulted in a phone call to Chief Inspector Haine at three o'clock in the afternoon on the day the body was discovered.

Haine was delighted to be of assistance. He assured them that preliminary investigations had already been made due to a strange occurrence that night that had involved one of his own men. In fact the Bath police already had the murder weapon in their possession. To which the bewildered officer in Strathclyde commented that he had not yet described the manner of death. Haine, smiling like a cat that had been at the cream, then asked if perchance, the deceased had been killed by a blow to the head from some kind of heavy metal object? Yes, the murder weapon, a monkey wrench with a trace of human blood and a single human hair on it, was definitely in his possession. Perhaps his colleagues north of the border would like to bring a specimen of Campbell's hair when they came down to further their enquiries?

189

'Get Carrick,' he ordered briskly when he had slapped the phone back on its rest.

Hobbs, who had entered Haine's office carrying an armful of paperwork thirty seconds previously, chortled. 'Don't tell me his fairy tale's come true after all!'

Haine still felt weak at the knees after hearing some home truths from higher authority earlier that afternoon. 'Just *get* him, and stop being so bloody clever!'

'I'm here,' Carrick said, framed in the doorway, which had just been left open.

'You can go now, Crispin,' Haine said heavily.

'*Crispin*?' Carrick drawled softly. 'Was that after the saint?'

Hobbs stalked away and Haine went straight in at the deep end. 'I want you to contact Gillard and find out if he had any success in tracing Graeme Campbell.'

'Yes, he did. Campbell's with his woman friend at a cottage in Ayrshire.'

'Have you got the address?'

'No, but – sir, d'you mind telling me what's going on?'

There was a short but agonising silence.

'James . . . I – er – I'm afraid you were right. But it's Bruce Campbell who's been murdered. And – um – I owe you an apology.'

Carrick was feeling magnanimous. 'That's all right, sir. Where was his body found?'

'Near a place called Fenwick. Know it?'

'I've heard of it. It's not far from Kilmarnock.'

Haine swept all the files that Hobbs had placed on his desk into a battered cardboard box which served as an overspill in-tray. 'Let's be sure of one thing, though – we keep at least two steps ahead of Strathclyde Police all the way.'

Carrick knew exactly where his loyalties lay. He said, 'You'll need to talk to Joanna too.'

Patrick Gillard was in London, but once he heard the news, he had no intention of staying there. Insisting that a murder enquiry took priority over the more mundane business of national security, he promised to be with them as soon as possible. He had travelled to London from Devon by train but

190

would commandeer transport.

'Does the MoD have car pools or that kind of thing?' Haine asked dubiously when he learned of this arrangement. 'I'd much rather he'd tell us what he knows over the phone – it might be tomorrow before he gets here.'

In fact Patrick was shown into Haine's office just over an hour after Haine voiced these misgivings, an army helicopter having touched down briefly on the nearby sports ground. And it soon became apparent that he had not gone to all that trouble simply to furnish them with an address.

Amongst what one gathered was a hastily grabbed collection of possessions – briefcase, overcoat, binoculars, which he had cradled in his arms during the ten-minute walk from the sports field and now allowed to descend into a heap upon the floor – was a gun harness. He saw their gaze fasten upon it. 'Don't worry. The important bit's locked in there.' And he indicated the briefcase with his forefinger.

The DCI cleared his throat but Gillard spoke first.

'It's quite simple,' he began. 'I traced Graeme Campbell's old address through Fraser. There were no clues to go on so I presented myself at Strathclyde Police's HQ at Pitt Street, Glasgow. Carrying an MI5 ID card works wonders sometimes. It had already occurred to me that Fraser Campbell was exactly the kind of man to drive like a maniac and this proved to be correct. Luckily his driving offences took place while he was still living at home so I was able to get the address. So I went to Newton Mearns and engaged his one-time neighbours in conversation. You'll both appreciate, I'm sure, that I was only interested in finding the father, not Fraser. I was not trying to do your jobs for you, only achieve what I had been asked to do.'

Haine squirmed in his chair.

'One of the ex-neighbours had known the Campbells very well and she and her husband tried to comfort Campbell when his wife died. The lady-friend, one Molly Wilson, used to be Campbell's secretary and, according to my informant, their friendship blossomed when Campbell was on his own. Molly's husband works on North Sea oil-rigs. When Campbell moved south Mrs Wilson bought a house in Aberdeen. She has money, apparently, and the previous

191

arrangement was that her husband only came occasionally to where they were living in Glasgow and the rest of the time stayed with someone he knew in Aberdeen. One gets the impression the marriage wasn't too healthy. Perhaps Molly moved north when Campbell closed the Scottish end of his business down in an effort to save her marriage. Anyway, the Wilsons have now broken up for good and Molly is renting a cottage in Largs until she's made up her mind what to do.'

'Did Campbell himself tell the neighbour all this?' Carrick asked.

'Yes, he still keeps in touch with them apparently. He hadn't let on that he was staying with Molly, though, and she only had the address because he'd phoned her a while back and asked her to post Molly copies of the local newspapers as she was thinking of moving back into the Glasgow area.'

'I'm surprised this neighbour gave Molly's address to a total stranger,' Haine commented.

Patrick smiled. 'I didn't even ask for it. I'd just said I was passing and as my father and Campbell knew one another . . . I didn't mention that they lived next door to each other in Hinton Littlemoor. It's strange how much people give away without meaning to. She'd already said that the cottage was on the outskirts of Largs and mentioned that Campbell had told her Molly had had bother with snow and icy roads. Good views were mentioned. And a farm next door that sold fresh produce. Now, Largs is a resort on the Clyde coast and –'

'Doon tha watter,' Carrick said. 'Sorry, do go on.'

'Yes, of course, at one time a favourite holiday destination for Glaswegians. So a cottage likely to be troubled by snow and ice has to be set high in the hills that surround the town. It took me a couple of days to track down the right farm because there were several that fitted the bill. Only one had a cottage next door with extensive views over the Clyde estuary. I parked the car and treated myself to a spot of hillwalking and birdwatching but didn't see him that day. He emerged, briefly, on the following afternoon to take a small dog for a walk. The weather was pretty bad.'

Carrick had built up a vivid picture in his mind of a man with an artificial leg circumnavigating peat hags, granite and streams in driving rain for hours at a time. 'Was the woman there?'

'Yes, she'd been going in and out to fetch shopping and so forth. She drives a pale blue Mini. He didn't go with her on any occasion that I witnessed. And then of course I was called to Wemdale.'

Haine said, 'There was really no need, Lieutenant-Colonel, for you to come in person.'

'Fraser,' Gillard said.

'Fraser?' Haine echoed. 'I'm sure he'll be answering questions very shortly.'

'You have to catch him first. Don't forget there's only one person who witnessed what happened in that car park. Fraser knows it too and I'm sure that he knows because of Joanna's efforts to question him. At my request. I was an utter fool.'

'I'm sure you need not worry,' Haine said. 'And I'm sure he doesn't represent a danger to –'

'He might,' Patrick interrupted. 'The lady who lived next door to the Campbells never liked Fraser. He'd injured her cat by taking a pot-shot at it with an air rifle. When he was older there was trouble with cars: careless driving, drinking and driving and ultimately, driving whilst disqualified. He's still interested in shooting but has transferred his sights to stags. Not that that endears him to the woman I was talking to. Graeme told her that Fraser is a crack shot.'

'But surely he's not going to come gunning for James!' Haine protested.

Patrick shrugged. 'Probably not. But for the sake of my own conscience I'd be grateful if you'd allow me to give him a little advice on personal protection.'

'For a moment I thought you were going to offer to be his bodyguard.'

Patrick glanced in the direction of his briefcase. 'A hand gun is no protection against a hunting rifle. I must remind you that he's probably tried to silence the witness once already.'

Haine picked up the phone. 'I'll get on to Strathclyde Police and see if they've arrested him yet.'

Carrick was beginning to feel slightly naked. And when Haine – after establishing that Fraser Campbell was neither at his home address nor at work – had been called from the room on other business, he said, 'I've a feeling you have something up your sleeve.'

Soberly, Patrick said, 'An entire murder inquiry rests on you getting your memory back.'

'No one, I can assure you, is more aware of that than I.'

'I wasn't reminding you, just stating a fact. With a bit of luck we can persuade Haine to stage a reconstruction.'

'With me centre-stage? No thanks.'

He was quite unprepared for the vehemence of Gillard's reaction.

'We're a good team, aren't we? A Scotsman with cold feet, an Englishman with a wooden leg and a has-been with no brain.'

'My sergeant's from Bognor Regis and has mumps,' Carrick said, straight-faced.

Gillard laughed and relaxed.

'I've a better idea,' Carrick said. 'In a couple of days' time it's the Annual General Meeting of the Caledonian Society. We have the meeting and then there's a small private dinner for the committee and their ladies. It's held at the Crawford Hotel. Perhaps my memory will be jogged if I attend – I can wangle you an invitation as my guest.'

'With the proviso that we push for a proper police reconstruction if it fails to do the trick?'

'All right. If you wish. But there's no guarantee that that'll work either.'

'Is it black tie?'

'Definitely.'

Patrick sighed. 'I'll be the only one in trousers, no doubt.'

'There's no reason why you shouldn't wear the kilt if you want to.'

Gillard stuck his right leg out in front of him and regarded it thoughtfully. 'I've my own knee so I shouldn't send people away screaming in terror. With long socks . . .' He grinned. 'Which tartans are Sassenachs allowed to wear?'

'Basically anything you like. But traditionally people with no clan connections wear Jacobite, which is orange and green, or Caledonia, mostly red, or green Hunting Stewart. I'd choose the latter if I were you, it's by far the most attractive. I'll organise it for you, if you like.'

'Thanks. But I'll bring my own knife.'

When told by the Strathclyde Police that his youngest son was dead Graeme Campbell collapsed. The officers, taking no chances, called a doctor who diagnosed a mild heart attack and Campbell was admitted to hospital in Greenock. When he had recovered sufficiently to be questioned he remained adamant that both his sons had seen him off at the airport on the morning following the Burns Supper. They had teased him, he recalled a little tearfully, as he had had a bad hangover. Bruce had flown down from Edinburgh and planned to take a flight back later that morning. Fraser, who had driven, intended to have a couple more days in the south. He had spoken to neither of his sons since.

When asked about his lack of luggage – Haine and his northern colleagues were working together by now, whether Haine liked it or not – he told them that he had crammed a few things into his briefcase, which was quite roomy, as he intended to buy new clothes in Glasgow. Why? Well, there had been no time to pack properly that morning. He himself had had to travel in the clothes he'd slept in.

Campbell admitted that the evening at the Crawford Hotel had not been a success and that Fraser and Bruce had quarrelled. Asked to elaborate, he said that the brothers had been quarrelling for almost as long as he could remember. Mostly, it was Fraser's fault and the problem was worse now his elder son tended to drink too much. Pressed on this, Campbell admitted that Bruce had always been his favourite. Fraser, he hated to say, could be difficult.

There was no reason that he knew of, Campbell said, for Bruce to be anywhere near Fenwick. Had his car been found? Perhaps someone had stopped him on the road, attacked and killed him then stolen the car.

When told that the car was still parked where Bruce normally left it in Edinburgh, Campbell shook his head sadly. Yes, he vaguely remembered Fraser talking to James Carrick at the hotel, but he couldn't remember what, if anything, happened in the car park afterwards. Regrettably, he had had too much to drink himself that night and events were little more than a blur.

195

At this point Campbell was reminded by a crusty sergeant from Pollockshields that the police had the murder weapon, a monkey wrench. Had he told either Fraser or Bruce that it belonged to the Reverend John Gillard? Campbell thought not and when asked if he himself had returned the tool said he could not remember.

Nursing staff then intervened and put a stop to questioning until the patient was stronger.

When Haine was told the outcome of the interview his heart sank. Everything pointed towards Graeme Campbell having been present when his son was killed. So why would the news of his death have come as such a terrible shock? A shock so severe that it had precipitated a heart attack? Unless, of course, it was the *discovery* of the body which had come as such an unwelcome surprise ... But a good defence barrister would make mincemeat of the police evidence. So what if Bruce had been killed with a wrench belonging to his father's next-door neighbour? The killer could have stolen it from either the Campbells or the Gillards – maybe in an attempt to implicate Fraser – and then replaced it. A gullible jury could even be convinced that Carrick himself had attacked the man – particularly in view of Carrick's newfound friendship with the rector's son.

Haine felt sure that Graeme was lying to protect his son. But it was the word of a hitherto unimpeachable, respectable gentleman against that of the police – and he knew on whose side the jury were likely to come down. His only comforting thought was that Fraser, in the tradition of the guilty, seemed to have gone to ground. Would he surface when news of Bruce's death was made public?

During the next couple of days there were no further developments. Statements had been taken from Gavin Fuller, the barman, Joanna Mackenzie and the Crawfords, plus all other guests at the hotel on Burns Night. And Patrick Gillard, of course. Haine, shuffling papers around on his desk in an agony of indecision, realised that he had no choice but to agree to the army officer's somewhat startling proposals.

The first thing Gillard insisted upon was a news black-out on Bruce's death. And a 24-hour police guard was put on Graeme Campbell.

196

Carrick was about to go home on the night of the AGM when he was told that Larne Painswick wanted to talk to him. Painswick was still in the reception area, the entire building seemingly throbbing with activity, when Carrick came upon him.

'There's nowhere private where we can talk,' Carrick said. 'I'm afraid even my office has been taken over. And I'm sorry I can only give you five minutes as –'

'It's quite okay,' Painswick interrupted. 'I only came round to give you a tape that Amanda let me have. It's one of Marvin's.' He took a cassette from his pocket and placed it on the counter. 'I took the tapes in the spirit that she gave them to me – as a peace offering. Marvin liked heavy rock, Mahler and Wagner, and Amanda knew I was keen on the latter two so she asked me if I wanted them. This is a home recording of a concert from the radio, one I'd missed. I think you should listen to it.'

Carrick was baffled. 'How does listening to Wagner help my murder investigation?'

'I don't mean you should listen to the *music*. Gilcrist had recorded over his own voice – the music finishes halfway through the second side. It sounds as if he was making verbal notes. He mentions Terrington – "that little runt", he calls him. And he talks quite a bit about another bloke – someone called Rogers. I just thought it might be important, so . . .'

'It must be Christmas all over again,' Carrick murmured. 'Many thanks.'

'I came to thank you too,' Painswick said awkwardly. 'I've been such a damned fool.'

'Aren't we all at some time or other?' Carrick said, clapping him on the shoulder.

Listening to the tape, at home, he was almost late for the meeting.

Chapter Nineteen

'I'm told,' Patrick said, 'that my Great-great-great uncle Bertram fought alongside General Gordon at Khartoum. His sword is hanging on the wall at the rectory. And that is apparently the closest that any of my ancestors got to the Scots as a nation.'

A chuckle rippled around the long dining table. The meal, a very good one, was over and the diners were relaxing with coffee and liqueurs. It was not customary for there to be an official after-dinner speaker but Gillard had been eased into the role by the president of the society who had instinctively sniffed out a good raconteur.

'So I regard it as a great honour to be permitted to join you tonight,' he went on, 'and I'm deeply admiring your efforts to keep your faces straight in view of the fact that I'm wearing your national dress.'

He related a few highly amusing anecdotes concerning Scots he had served with, then fluently toasted them all in Gaelic, to thunderous applause.

'Did I get it right?' he asked Carrick when he sat down.

'Word perfect. It was just as well I warned you that Hamish has a habit of asking guests to sing for their supper.' He saluted the man he was referring to, sitting at the head of the table, who smiled broadly and waved back. 'The next time he bounces a guest of mine into it I shall coach them to call him a silly old bugger in Gaelic. That would really bring the house down.'

'Phew,' Patrick said, wiping imaginary sweat off his forehead. 'Saved from being spitted by that claymore on the wall over there.'

It had been decided to make a proper occasion of the evening, and as a nanny had arrived in the Gillard household Ingrid had travelled up from Devon and was at this moment keeping Joanna company in the Appin Lounge. Patrick had voiced his feeling of guilt at depriving the latter of a formal dinner, guests being limited on this occasion to one per member, but Carrick had informed him that she found such Scottish revels slightly tedious. Both ladies had wined and dined in convivial fashion in the restaurant.

Privately, Carrick had abandoned the idea of using the evening to cudgel his brain into remembering what had happened on Burns Night. He had decided to relax and enjoy himself instead – there had been far too much of cudgels and boots recently. So when he and Patrick swung out of the room and headed for the Appin Lounge he was in ebullient mood. He did not notice that Patrick's manner was watchful to the point of extreme vigilance, nor that the hotel appeared to have a few more staff that night than seemed strictly necessary.

Joanna had noticed, though. Having observed Gavin Fuller serving behind the bar, and the Crawfords seated in the corner by the window, she knew that an effort was being made to reconstruct the night when, almost certainly, Bruce Campbell had been murdered. She had no idea to what extent Patrick was responsible for all this and no intention of asking.

Carrick and Gillard made a good pair, she thought as she saw them approach: both accustomed to give and receive orders, to operating within a fairly strict set of rules. Of the two Patrick seemed the more volatile; James, unusually for a Scot, was better at pouring oil on troubled waters.

'Has James always been in the police?' Ingrid asked.

'No, he trained as a physical education teacher, but it wasn't exciting enough,' Joanna replied. 'So he joined the Met. He lived in London in those days.'

'I can't believe how quickly he's recovered from what he suffered at Wemdale.'

'How about Patrick? Did he go straight into the army from school?'

'No,' Ingrid said with a grin, 'he joined the police. It wasn't exciting enough.'

'My ears are burning,' Patrick said, pulling up a chair.

'It's the whisky you've been drinking,' said his spouse briskly. She moved her evening bag off a chair so Carrick could sit down. 'I see the button's been sewn back on your jacket. You were lucky the fabric didn't get torn.'

Carrick sat down. Soon he was tapping a foot in time to the Scottish dance music that was being relayed, quietly, over the hotel's speaker system.

'Is that a reel?' Ingrid asked.

'Yes, it's the Reel of the Fifty-first Division,' Carrick said. 'It was created by men who were prisoners of war.'

They were sitting at the table nearest to the large stone fireplace. By the bar another was occupied by three men who appeared to have every intention of drinking the night away. Other than the fact that all three were fair-haired and wearing kilts of the same tartan there was no similarity between them.

A little later Patrick looked at his watch. 'It's eleven-thirty already,' he said and made a bad job of concealing a yawn. 'You know, I think I'm going to turn in.' All four of them had arranged to stay the night at the hotel.

'Early to rise, I hope,' Carrick said. 'Shall we meet at the pool? I'm all agog to see this fifteen knots with the help of the lid from the laundry basket.'

'Damn!' Patrick said, looking aghast. 'I didn't bring it.'

'I think I'll go up too,' Ingrid said and they both said good night and left.

Joanna could not believe it. She had assumed that Patrick had intended to take James through the Burns Night evening once more, prompting his memory in the fashion that had proved partially successful on the previous occasion.

'Something the matter?' Carrick asked.

Some sixth sense prompted Joanna not to share her thoughts. 'No. I just thought it was a little early for the evening to end.'

The phone on the bar rang a couple of minutes later and Gavin answered it. 'Miss Mackenzie,' he called, holding the receiver aloft.

'Joanna,' said Patrick's voice, 'make an excuse and leave

him. Say you have to make an urgent, work-related call. Leave the room, cross the lobby and then go through the door by the desk marked Staff Only. Got it?'

'It was Greg,' she said, going back to the table. 'He's in a phone box and has no more change. Sorry, but I'll have to ring him.'

'It's a bit late for the poor devil to be working, isn't it?'

'One of those surveillance jobs,' she explained. 'Shan't be a mo.'

Left on his own, Carrick's attention was held by the three men who were getting steadily more noisy, arguing amongst themselves. He decided to go into the other bar and rose to his feet. He noticed the Crawfords sitting in their corner; they waved to him. He changed his mind. Better wait for Joanna in the lobby, otherwise she would not know where he had gone.

'Care for a dram, Inspector?' said one of the men, the one leaning on the bar.

'No thanks,' Carrick said. How the hell did the man know who he was?

Another, facing Carrick, seemed too drunk to know what was going on; the third turned to give him a sulky scowl.

'Where I come from it's not considered polite to refuse,' said the man who had first spoken.

'No offence intended,' Carrick said. 'But I'm with a young lady.'

'Bring her along,' the other said with a smirk. 'We all like young ladies, don't we, lads?'

Carrick controlled his anger. 'Nevertheless, I'm afraid I can't,' he said, and made a quick getaway.

The Crawfords left right behind him. They looked a timid duo, the kind of people who would double-lock their doors at night and tend to regard everyone with suspicion.

'About that time I spoke to you last,' Mr Crawford said, catching Carrick by the elbow. 'You know – about the row when we were afraid something dreadful might happen?'

'Have you remembered anything else?' Carrick asked.

'No, not really. We stayed the night on that occasion so we didn't see what went on.'

'We've parked the car in that little side bit,' Mrs Crawford said nervously. 'I thought it would be safer from any car thieves or vandals tucked away out of sight like that. Don't you think so, Inspector?'

'It's better to leave your car where *everyone* can see it,' Carrick pointed out. 'But as a matter of fact the window over there overlooks that part of the car park.' He went over to it and twitched aside the curtain. 'There you are. I remember I looked out when you told me about –' His body became rigid. 'Good God,' he whispered.

The first time he had looked out like this he had seen his own car and a black one, the latter with the boot lid raised and three men drunkenly struggling. Now there was just Gillard's – they had arrived together – but otherwise all was as before. What was happening before his eyes now was just as unbelievable as it had been then. Only this time Patrick was the one being attacked. He was on the ground, a couple of dark figures drawing back their feet to kick him.

Outside – Carrick was hardly aware of having run into the open – there was an eerie stillness. From the spot where he had momentarily paused, not a soul could be seen. He ran another few yards and then stopped dead.

No. He *didn't* believe it. Surely he couldn't have been set up as the bait in a mantrap, alone and unarmed in the centre of a huge, lighted arena. It was the stuff of which nightmares are made.

Not quite unarmed, however.

Not quite alone.

Fraser Campbell had been sitting in his car for about ten minutes, biting his nails, waiting, quite unaware of any drama taking place in another part of the car park. When he saw Carrick approach his first instinct was to drive away. Then he changed his mind and got out of the car.

'Dad said you were in hospital with a blood clot on the brain,' he said.

'No, it's your father who's in hospital,' Carrick told him.

'He asked me to meet him here to discuss the future.'

'To give you money, you mean?'

'You don't know anything about our private business matters.'

'Perhaps you shouldn't have had a row with him within

earshot of your cleaning lady.'

'That old bitch,' Fraser said viciously. 'So I suppose it's a trick and my bastard of a father's set me up.' He smiled humourlessly. 'But I was forgetting. You've lost your memory.'

'No, I've remembered quite clearly now,' Carrick said. 'And you're under arrest.'

Fraser shook his head. 'You seem to be on your own, Inspector.'

'Go on, run,' Carrick whispered. 'Give me the pleasure of bringing you down.'

'My car's right here,' Fraser said, smiling still.

Carrick drew his skene-dhu. 'Then let's get *really* personal. You dishonoured this blade by laying hands on it and according to ancient Scottish tradition – you might think it a little quaint – that can only be righted by dipping it in your blood.'

'*Quaint!*' Fraser shouted. 'I call that downright barbaric!'

'Oh, I'll settle for taking you into custody,' Carrick replied calmly.

'I should have stuck it in your guts instead of sending you down that hill in your car. Go to hell!' He made a leap for the car door, distracting Carrick's attention, then snatched for the hand gun that was in his pocket.

What followed was not particularly quaint; but then, neither was it barbaric. And if Fraser's hand was cut quite badly after a rapid kick to the wrist made him drop the gun, then it was his own fault for making a grab for the skene-dhu.

Gillard stood quietly watching as the police – including the two constables in mufti who had never thought they would actually be asked even to pretend to beat someone up – emerged from the shadows.

'It was no use trying to recreate what had happened that night right down to the last detail,' Patrick said later at the short debriefing. 'All I wanted to do was to make James relive the same *emotions*. So, courtesy of three young men from the Bristol Old Vic who acted in similar fashion to the way the Campbells had done, and several members of the Territorial Support Group who turned their hands to a bit of hotel work

203

in case Fraser tried to enter the building, the thing was achieved. Not forgetting, of course, the Crawfords and the proprietors of the hotel. And, lest you think I placed anyone in danger, security measures were *very* tight.'

'It was really down to the Crawfords,' Carrick said. 'Talking to them made me remember I'd looked through the window on Burns Night.'

The entire hotel car park had been ringed with police, some of them armed. Every vantage point had been carefully checked to make sure that Fraser had not suspected a trap and arrived early armed with a rifle.

'So he wasn't expecting James to be here,' Joanna said.

'No, of course not,' Patrick replied. 'As far as he was concerned James was at death's door, due to complications to his head injury.'

Carrick said, 'He came carrying a gun, however. Thank God the Strathclyde team managed to convince Graeme that the best place for Fraser was in prison.' He looked at Patrick. 'And I remained in ignorance of the whole plan.'

'Well, it was only set up this morning,' Patrick said. 'We managed to persuade Graeme Campbell to ring his son – as we suspected, he knew all along where Fraser was holed up. Graeme was instructed to say that he was coming back South immediately and wanted to meet Fraser somewhere private. Maybe Fraser intended simply to threaten his father, to ensure his silence. It's pretty obvious that Graeme went in fear of his eldest son. Or – who knows? – Fraser may have wanted to shut him up for good. He probably thought that if no one else knew Graeme had returned home, he could do what was necessary, drive the body back to Scotland and dump the dead man somewhere very remote indeed. Then, if Bruce's body was discovered, and Graeme had disappeared, everyone would assume that it was just another family tragedy. An enraged father, a wayward son, an argument that went too far . . . Such things have been known to happen.'

'So why did Fraser kill Bruce?' Joanna asked.

'I imagine the whisky played a large part in everything that took place that night. Fraser was desperate for funds and he knew that in the event of his father's death he would be wealthy. We might never know what really happened;

Fraser's temper might have snapped out in the car park and he picked up the monkey wrench. It would seem from what the Crawfords overheard that Bruce had been baiting him all evening. Perhaps Fraser went for his father when he refused to get in the car and Bruce intervened – one can hardly imagine him standing idly by – and was struck instead.'

Carrick said, 'It was impossible for me to tell exactly what was going on from a quick glance out of the window. I just registered that a fight had started.'

'What happened when you got to them?' Patrick wanted to know.

'Bruce was flat on his back on the ground with Graeme standing over him sobbing in a state of complete shock. Fraser came at me like a wild animal but he wasn't holding the monkey wrench then. It must have been Graeme who hit me with it from behind.'

'*Graeme?*' Joanna breathed.

'He probably didn't know what he was doing. Or, instinctively, he was trying to save their skins. Desperate people are capable of almost anything.'

'Graeme told Strathclyde police that he's been frantic since that evening,' Patrick said. 'Unable to confide in anyone, even his Molly Wilson. I think he was relieved to tell the truth about Fraser, to get it all off his chest. And, of course, when he was told about the discovery of Bruce's body he knew he was finished – hence the heart attack.'

'And now he's lost both sons,' Carrick said wearily. 'Now, perhaps you'll excuse me.'

'You're going to work. To interview Fraser,' Joanna said.

'It's my job,' was the simple reply.

Haine and Hobbs were still in the building when Carrick arrived. They observed his rather splendid attire, avoided one another's gaze and said nothing.

When Bob Ingrams presented himself for duty about ten days later there was a slight hesitation on his part before he knocked on the office door of his immediate superior.

'You look as though you've lost weight,' were Carrick's first words to him.

'I didn't really feel like eating, guv,' Ingrams mumbled

205

sheepishly. 'And the doc said I ought to lose a couple of stone anyway. So the missus took that to heart and I've been having a lot of salads and stuff like that . . .'

'Life's a real cow sometimes,' Carrick said. 'Still, cheer up, you look a lot better for it. Take a seat.'

'Someone said you've sorted the Gilcrist case,' Ingrams said when he had lowered himself carefully into a chair. In truth he had been quite ill and was still feeling weak.

'Yes, Rogers decided to cough. He's given Complaints everything apparently: how he gave Norris info about other drugs dealers so Norris could remove the competition, how he tipped him off about raids that the Dalesland Drugs Squad were about to carry out. There doesn't seem to have been a real fortune in backhanders involved and it appears there was actually a system whereby Norris gave Rogers the nod about various Persons Wanted. He slipped him the name of a man involved in a murder case once, according to Rogers.'

'Then Gilcrist came along and spoilt everything.'

'It couldn't possibly have lasted. A snout by the name of Jed – who had once been handled by Rogers himself – was taken over by Philip Deakin, a chum of Blair Craxton. Deakin was having his ears filled with this amazing stuff about Rogers and Norris – he already knew about Terrington, of course. With Craxton acting as middle-man he gave Gilcrist the information on Terrington first. The rest followed.'

'And Terrington shut Gilcrist up.'

'Rogers insists that there was never any question of murder. Anyway, according to Rogers Terrington agreed to break into Gilcrist's cottage to have a snoop around. Rogers assumed – rightly as it turned out – that as Gilcrist's means of getting information was dodgy to say the least he'd be keeping anything secret or of a sensitive nature at the cottage rather than at the office. So Terrington was instructed to go there first. Presumably it didn't occur to him that it would be occupied at the weekend. Gilcrist was probably in a bit of a state – he'd just endured a confrontation with Larne Painswick, who saw himself as Leonora Kelso's avenging knight. To complicate matters as far as we were concerned, Painswick had also smashed up the cottage and chucked papers everywhere. Anyway, Gilcrist was probably more in need of a drink than he'd ever been in his life and he decided to go to the pub, not caring a toss whether Terrington was there or not. Terrington might even have offered a truce and asked to go with him. And, on the riverbank, alone with the man he hated most in the world, he took his chance. Gilcrist was more than a little shaken after his encounter with Painswick and had already been drinking that evening. He ended up dead. Terrington's torch was broken in the struggle and he took Gilcrist's to find his way back to the cottage. Before he did that he removed Gilcrist's wallet from his pocket and stole the money it contained to make it look as though Gilcrist had been mugged. Back at the cottage he must have rummaged among the mess that Painswick had made and grabbed what he could find. We found the remains of a sheaf of papers in Terrington's garden incinerator. But Rogers must have known Terrington had missed a vital piece of evidence – the sheet of paper that linked him with Norris. So, as Leonora Kelso had worked most closely with Gilcrist, Terrington turned her place over too.'

'And Terrington confessed to all this, guv?'

'No, he died before he could be interviewed. But he had Gilcrist's torch in his possession, and his wife admitted after he died that he had been away from home that weekend.'

'I can't help thinking that Gilcrist deserved what he got.'

'He wasn't just the hard-nosed, ruthless journalist. Larne Painswick gave me a tape of Gilcrist's – it records his thoughts about Terrington and Rogers. There's real indignation, real anger. There's no doubt that he knew exposing police corruption would advance his career but I think he felt that, morally, he was doing the right thing. He certainly despised the people he exposed.'

'Despised himself, too.'

Carrick surveyed him thoughtfully. 'Yes, you're right. Otherwise why would he drink so heavily? That's perceptive of you, Bob.'

'And the other business, sir?' Ingrams ventured, pleasurably awash in this milk of human kindness.

Carrick took down a file from the shelf and placed it before him. 'There. Have a good read.'

'So you're not in trouble like and . . .'

Carrick shook his head. 'No, not at all. It wasn't the wild drink that knocked me out that night.'

'I'm really pleased about that,' said Ingrams, meaning it.

Chapter Twenty

James Carrick lay flat on his back on the smooth grass, hands cupped around his eyes as he watched a pair of buzzards circling high overhead. Faintly, their mewing calls could be heard above the burbling murmur of the moorland river – little bigger than a stream in these midsummer months – which ran through the garden. Although it was only ten-thirty in the morning the sun was hot; as he had been up very late the night before there was the distinct desire to doze off. A small but persistent hazard prevented this, however, and it was only a matter of time before it prevailed.

Sure enough, moments later, he was deluged with water from a toy-sized watering can and there was nothing for it but to roll onto all fours and turn into the snarling jungle creature that the situation demanded. Justin, shrieking with glorious dread, made his getaway. Until the next time.

The tors of Dartmoor, hazy in the heat, lay to the east, the cross on the top of Widgery Tor just visible in the shimmering air.

'Fallen in the river?' Patrick asked, entering the garden through a narrow gateway.

'No, just a passing shower,' Carrick replied, pulling a face at Justin who was peeping at him round one corner of the barn that faced the cottage.

'Which can be particularly dangerous at this time of the year,' Patrick commented, eyeing his son meaningfully. 'Sorry I was delayed and didn't get here until so late last night – sometimes I have to go and show my face at meetings at very unsociable hours.'

Carrick and Joanna had accepted with alacrity the invitation to spend a weekend at the Gillard's cottage. A small celebratory dinner was planned for that night, stemming from a meeting that Carrick himself had attended.

'So Haine's off to HQ to help implement the Sheehy report, eh?'

'Yes. He's gone – went last week. I understand that Hobbs is going with him as his errand boy.'

'I don't think we ever met,' Patrick said.

'Thank Heaven for that!'

'You didn't get a bad result at the Campbell's trial. A pity, though, that they saw fit to reduce the charge against Fraser to manslaughter.'

'I had expected it. But don't forget the GBH charge for his little caper with me. By the time he comes to court again, on the fraud and embezzlement charges in Scotland, he'll end up in prison for a very long time. That was why he was so desperate for money. He'd pocketed deposits and other funds at the estate agency where he worked and they were on to him. You were right when you said it was the whisky that drove Fraser's brain that night. He just snapped. He actually already had the monkey wrench in his hand – he'd picked it up from the floor of the car to chuck it out of the way before his father got in the back. Graeme staggered into him – or so Fraser said, and he lashed out with it. It only met air, as he was staggering drunk too, but it infuriated Bruce who punched him in the face. We know what happened next.'

'But he might have belted the old man, too, if you hadn't rolled up. Then, presumably, Fraser threw the monkey wrench down, Graeme grabbed hold of it and hit you from behind.'

'He just panicked.'

'You almost have to admire how they tried to cover up what they'd done though.'

'Yes, they piled Bruce and me into their car and then drove to the top of Wood Lane. Then Fraser went back to fetch my car – I'd absent-mindedly picked up my keys from the bedside table in the bedroom when Gavin Fuller rang me to talk about crime fiction and was still holding them when I

210

went back downstairs – got me into the driver's seat and sent the car rolling down the hill.'

'Then they took Bruce's body home. Lord, one can imagine the state they were in.'

'But they seem to have kept their heads. After Graeme insisted that Fraser sneak back your father's monkey wrench they sat the rest of the night out and then Fraser took his father to the airport. If he'd packed a case properly instead of just cramming a few things into his briefcase it wouldn't have aroused suspicion. Graeme, in the cold light of morning, just wanted to run and hide. So he did.'

'While Fraser drove the body up to Scotland and buried it at the roadworks. After that he went skiing. I suppose they hoped that if and when it was found everyone would think that Bruce had met his death north of the border. And they kept their fingers crossed that you hadn't lived to tell the tale. No, they should have got more than ten years and four years respectively, even though Graeme did turn Queen's evidence to help catch Fraser.'

'I'm content,' Carrick said, turning to face the sun so that the warmth would dry his shirt.

'If anyone deserves promotion you do, James.'

Carrick was being stalked again. 'I propose we apprehend the miscreant and demonstrate the long arm of the law.'

'Good idea. You catch him and I'll get the real watering can ready.'

Joanna was watching from an open window upstairs, leaning on the ledge, enjoying the sunshine. How sad, she mused, that in the aftermath of the murder investigations no one seemed to have spared a thought for the young man who was now dead. On the last evening of his life Bruce Campbell had played the pipes to honour a poet. She hoped someone would play the pipes for him.

A tear trickled down her cheek and she brushed it away. Tears for an unknown soldier . . .

Below her, James came through the gate at a run, saw Justin and set off again in his direction, glanced up, saw her and stopped again. For a few seconds they gazed at one another in silence.

211

'Are you coming out to play?' he asked with a boyish grin on his face.

'Yes,' she said, and went down.

2/98